DANCER
An Extraordinary Life

Best Regards
Alan Meade

ALAN MEADE

alanmeadebooks.com

FERNE PRESS

Summary: A mentally handicapped man communicates profound wisdom to those around him.

Library of Congress Cataloging-in-Publication Data
Meade, Alan
Dancer / Alan Meade – First Edition
ISBN: 978-1-933916-12-5
1. Mentally handicapped 2. Michigan – Upper Peninsula 3. Michigan – Lower Peninsula 4. Ohio 5. Mental institutions – Athens State Hospital 6. Mental institutions – Ypsilanti State Hospital 7. Ann Arbor – University of Michigan 8. World War II – conscientious objector 9: Vietnam War
I. Meade, Alan II. Title
Library of Congress Control Number: 2007934883

A portion of the proceeds of the
book will benefit Special Olympics

FERNE PRESS

Ferne Press is an imprint of Nelson Publishing & Marketing
366 Welch Road, Northville, MI 48167
www.nelsonpublishingandmarketing.com
(248) 735-0418

To Liz
Endless sunny skies and good fishing, see ya when we get there.

Preface

It's true. Many of us never comprehend that the stuff of life isn't possessions.

Dancer's understanding of this is instinctive. Too bad he keeps such wisdom, like everything else, quietly to himself.

Dancer lives in an uncluttered world, favoring blue work pants and blue work shirts. Equally as accepting of green or gray, he mixes colors indiscriminately. Squeaky clean in person and clothing, Dancer's sense of proper is tempered by the pure joy of a free spirit. His kitchen shelf holds an extra pair of heavy white cotton laces, boots won't work without laces, and a pad of plain paper with two or three pencils, necessary tools to capture the image of a doe with a fawn curled at its feet or the bent branch of a cedar tree. Erasers on Dancer's pencils never last as long as leads; drawings require many changes.

Besides the beauty of an old wooden bowl of pine cones or an empty peanut butter jar holding fresh wildflowers, his few possessions speak of purposefulness and simplicity, each an unwavering characteristic of its owner. The rest of us look around the rooms of our lives and count things, all the clocks and dishes and furniture and little glass vases, the material stuff easily accumulated over years and decades. Fixating on the tangibles surrounding our daily lives, we infuse them with meaning beyond their worth. With absolute predictability, sentimental baggage, kept because grandma so-and-so or great aunt whoever's sister-in-law bought it way back when, moves from generation to generation, handed down, saved, cherished, or stored in one more step of a continuous process.

When lives end we hold funerals and break-bulk, divvying up collections. Wanted or not, material possessions float downstream in every family's unfinished history. In mindless conformity we hold on to *things*, the perceived stuff of life. Doing so, we miss out on true possessions, the intangible, very human memories and ideals and values we need to cherish.

If we're lucky, a central being comes along whose life emphatically shapes ours. If we're lucky, a life around us carries with it simple, priceless, unforgettable ideals not limited in value like hand-me-down stuff. This person's guidance, even if by unspoken example, makes it impossible not to recognize those values. If we're lucky, we always remember and treasure what that person gave us and gave our family. The true stuff of life, the loving memories of the interesting people who provide the measures of integrity we strive to emulate, stays with us forever. We know to cherish those possessions, those memories, if we're lucky.

More than lucky, my family was blessed with Dancer, the oddly young-looking, white-haired man who turned to me seeking approval. Watching him delicately remove the lid and shake the old green copper can, sprinkling my father's ashes across the soft leaves of the rain-dampened low ferns along the footpath, underscored the importance of his place in our lives. Dancer, content and uncomplicated, a shaper of lives, moved rhythmically in his efforts, a last dance with my father.

The occasion inspired formality and finality. Yet, somewhere, Dad sat, relaxed, smiling down, relishing the full circle of life's meaning, his many tasks accomplished. The CO, one of World War II's conscientious objectors, his convictions steadfastly maintained, could now rest. He lived in peace, making the next step in the progression of eternity perfectly logical. Chiseling his name and the dates of his birth and death on a tombstone seemed inadequate, too confining for his brand of spirit. Identifying his final destination required more space and less precision. His marker surrounds him in the land and the sky of the beautiful place on the shore of Lake Huron he loved so much.

Dad found courage beyond killing in a war without weapons. His enemies, prejudice and inhumanity, lay vanquished, conquered by a lifetime spent caring for those God made different. His friend, Dancer, will visit the CO every morning and every afternoon. Love has a way of overlooking differences.

One

The evening Tommy Higgins stumbled up Miss Flossie Duncan's front steps, a passing thunderstorm wet the yard and left the air clean and fresh and unseasonably cool. If only it had cooled the young man's rage and washed the meanness of liquor from his distorted vision of justice.

Miss Flossie gripped the front door tightly, holding it ajar barring his entrance, attempting to calm him. "You'll just have to understand. Things are different now, Tommy. She's going to help me move to Michigan. You need to give her time to get used to not having her son, her constant companion, with her. Give her time and let her decide what she wants for her future."

No logic or reasoning could reach Tommy Higgins, but his clenched right fist could reach Miss Flossie. "Old woman, you tellin' me I gotta let her decide? I'll show ya'll who does the decidin.'"

Struck from above, the rail-thin old spinster recoiled, falling backwards into the front hallway. Tommy Higgins pushed at the door, lunging to step over her prone body, paying no attention to the urgency of the male voice approaching rapidly behind him. Turning, the drunken young man stood braced half in and half out of the door

1

as a black wooden policeman's baton rapped his left temple with exactly the correct force and direction.

A large hand clutched Tommy Higgins's shirt, dragging him out onto the porch, moving him around and setting him abruptly on his backside. Mr. Stimson stepped over Higgins, bending to attend to Miss Flossie. Helping her to sit up, he leaned her against the doorframe, examining her forehead. The young mother Miss Flossie's actions protected screamed. Looking through the door's beveled glass, she'd seen the knife in Tommy Higgins's hand. Her warning saved Mr. Stimson and doomed Tommy.

As Mr. Stimson ducked, spinning away from the knife, he raised the baton in a reflexive response, striking out in an instant using all the strength of his muscled forearm. His swing exploded in speed without regard to force. With a sickening crunch, the baton connected with his attacker's temple, a blow every policeman is trained to deliver. The baton's second whack, striking the exact spot as the first but with much greater velocity, went far beyond a policeman's intent to stun. Tommy Higgins died instantly, all the violence and meanness his life promised ended forever in a half second's shattering crack of wood on bone.

Later, talking with a Cincinnati policeman old enough to remember him from his days on the force, Mr. Stimson found out Tommy Higgins hadn't returned to his job on the barges that week. Instead, in a simmering rage, he attempted to drown the perceived humiliation he endured on the trip to the asylum in Athens, Ohio.

The mind-numbing effects of great quantities of whiskey worked well until the binge ended. Then things went terribly wrong. His bravado spiraled out of control, fueled by long, drunken, slurred conversations with his rowdy friends. Pent-up resentment returned in the guise of anger. He sought vengeance and wanted his wife back with him where she belonged. She couldn't just up and leave him–who did she think she was, treating him like that?

His death marked the end of a decline some called predictable, having begun when they arrived in Cincinnati. To pay their rent, put food on the table, and leave enough for his habits and excesses, Tommy Higgins worked long hours on the river barges plying the Ohio River. Instead of coming home at day's end, he lingered in old taverns drinking and playing cards, carousing with rough-and-tumble friends. The city bustled with excitement and provided ample opportunities for Tommy Higgins to do what he did best.

Soon a son was born to the young couple. By the time their boy was five years old, Tommy Higgins's quest, seeking bottom-of-the-bottle answers, escalated into a daily ritual obscuring life's realities. He'd given up. Not wanting to come home, he never brought anyone there, and rarely took his wife and child anywhere. People stared. He couldn't stand their scrutiny. Who where they to judge? They stared and turned away, whispering quiet remarks, shaking their heads in knowing pity. The boy wasn't right; he wasn't all there, as people said. The hours he managed to spend with his young wife and their little boy brought anguish and ever-escalating complexities.

The child could hear, startling at even small new noises, and he watched and listened to people. He stared back at those observing him, mimicking their concentration, returning it with his gentle, unblinking gaze. Birds and dogs and cats and squirrels, any creature he saw, received his full, transfixed attention. Strangely, many of them gravitated closer and closer, unafraid of the boy, drawn by the irresistible pull of his rapt attention on their movements and sounds. A life-long affinity, a mutual attraction with nature's smaller constituency, began before he was old enough to go to school; a privilege the boy would never enjoy.

Unable to communicate with his son, barred from the fatherly satisfaction of even playing normal games with him, disappointment bred anger and emotions exploded. The boy gazed off at nothing. Playing catch meant letting the ball rolled to him bump his knees, spinning harmlessly away. Reacting violently, Tommy Higgins pulled further and further away from his beautiful young wife as if he thought she blamed the boy's deficiencies on him, but she never did, not once. She carried the guilt herself, holding her sorrow in, secreted beneath a veil of silence, blaming herself and her sins for life's punishments and her little boy's limitations, his blank expression and lack of responsiveness.

His son's disabilities beyond his comprehension, any kind of understanding or acceptance beyond his capabilities, Tommy Higgins's temper flared, cresting in shouted obscenities and threats echoing beyond their windows over the little neighborhood market. His anger, vile fruit ripened on the vine of frustration, shook their tiny world perched on the steep hillside of Cincinnati's winding river valley. Many evenings culminated in his explosive exit from their third-floor walk-up, the sound of his heavy boots pounding, racing past the rounded edges of the steep flights of worn stairs, diminishing until the door slammed far below, punctuating his departure in its wooden crash. Her husband went out, finding solace in cheap whiskey, returning in the middle of the night to take out his frustration and undefined recriminations on his wife with his fists, forcing her into a bed where violence and degradation long ago replaced what he knew as love.

Born in 1930 on the cusp of the decade, too many months before the first anniversary of their marriage, his mother named her baby boy Thomas, Jr. She called him Tommy, hoping her husband's pride in having a new son, a namesake, would deflect questions about such a good-sized baby being born so early. Her husband's normal attitudes eventually dispelled her concerns. Tommy Higgins lived his life day to day with only a limited consciousness of weeks passing. Counting months, or even spelling their names correctly, held no priority.

In all the long hours, the mornings and afternoons spent playing alone with the boy as he grew to be two and three and four, she called him Daniel, the middle name she picked. It was her way of maintaining a connection in time to embrace a day of love. The name dulled those difficult years, bringing soothing, better memories. Her husband accepted it, ignoring the fact the middle name Daniel didn't match anyone in his or her family. Saying it was Biblical, she was sure he remained oblivious to its source; he would kill her in one of his rages if he ever figured it out.

She long ago accepted the reality her son would not repeat his secret name to her husband. Although able to make sounds and show emotions like disappointment and fear and delight, words stayed beyond his grasp. When Tommy Higgins struck his mother, the boy's fear was visible. Only two or three times, in drunken tantrums, had he actually slapped the boy. Strangely, when he did, the little boy, Tommy Daniel Higgins, never cried. Instead he stared at the incensed Tommy Higgins with a delicate, transparent, tearless hurt in his eyes. For the boy, the fear was there, but it was mixed with forgiveness or, at the least, acceptance. But, then again, how much can a five-year-old boy who can't talk or play ball or do what children who are all there can do, really feel? For his mother, concern for her child's safety increased with her husband's brutality. Eventually his attacks must reach beyond her, harming her defenseless son–although without a defense for herself, she could act, moving her son beyond his reach.

*   *   *   *   *

It wasn't as if living in the city of Cincinnati or having a mentally deficient son caused Tommy Higgins to start drinking. As long as she'd known him back in their West Virginia village, Tommy excelled at drunkenness. Displaying great determination at an early age, Tommy Higgins perfected drunk and mean as life skills, practicing them nightly. Staggering and cursing came easily, great doses of alcohol fueling a disposition intent on achieving new heights of pure nastiness. His binges stretched to days, required little encouragement to initiate, and ended only when his funds ran out.

Like his daddy before him, Tommy Higgins approached life looking for a fight and taking what he could grab. The next generation in a long line of legendary drinkers, he lived up to the Higgins family tradition, keeping a firm grip on the neck of a whiskey bottle. Neighbors hoped for the best but expected the worse, past history giving credibility to easy and obvious predictions.

Her pregnancy undeniable, the choice agonizing, doing what life forced her to, she sought him out and accepted his advances along with his faults, living with both. He provided two necessities: an immediate solution and a way out.

Enduring disgust and repulsion, she gave herself to him, every calloused touch another penance for her condition. To have her, he readily agreed to her demand to move west. Later, walking by his side, she fought to avoid flinching, not pulling away from his rough hugs, ignoring his coarse manners, over-protectiveness, and jealousy as he paraded her, his new acquisition, through the village. Tolerating his crudeness, she clung to him, her ticket out and sole means to flee the West Virginia roots that now promised the immediate wrath of her parents. The imminent visible advancement of her pregnancy guaranteed their reaction. In Ellenboro, wedding vows and maternity required a very specific sequence.

Tangible tension gripped the wedding party in the parlor of the justice of the peace's home as the civil ceremony joined her and Tommy Higgins, the groom sober and nervous. Her mother cried while her father scowled. The newlyweds rarely spoke on the long trip west across southern Ohio to Cincinnati.

Away from their West Virginia valley, memories of years growing up in its confines lost meaning, relegated to a long blur of undefined boredom, a small life among the small lives of the residents of the little village of ramshackle houses clinging to weed-covered slopes. From skinny, awkward, tomboy beginnings, nature intervened in her teens, changing everything. More beautiful meant more unique, the little girl too soon a woman, an object of curiosity, not belonging, a perfect rose in a garden annually promising only weeds and drought. Shocking everyone, her sudden marriage to Tommy Higgins provided the distance she sought, separating her from her childhood home and the nosy opinions of the curious.

Only one person in the first seventeen years of her life was truly missed, leaving an empty place in her heart called love. Keeping their mutual secret, shielding her secret love from criticism and reprisals, she simultaneously protected his mother from the indignation and ridicule unavoidable with its disclosure. Their act of love, albeit a naive love, came in a sudden mistake of passion as youth and the intensity of attraction mingled with circumstance to overcome reason. The images were permanent–the two of them, afraid, out of breath from running, holding hands and laughing, standing in puddles of rainwater dripping off their bodies onto the worn linoleum of the old screened porch, mixed with memories of the storm's wild displays of lightning and the wind and the pouring rain turning afternoon to night. Each stayed, an indelible scene in her thoughts; but mostly there was Daniel.

She could still see the sagging daybed in the front room with its patchwork quilt, the makeshift blanket they hid beneath shivering from cold and wet and feeling the nervous excitement change to an unknown, unstoppable trembling. The sounds of the storm, the smooth touch of her hand on his chest as warm embraces replaced wet clothes. His small, almost feminine hand, hesitant, first cupping her breast then moving, questioning, delicately exploring. Returning to those moments of love in her mind, she curled up in his arms again; nothing could deny her those precious memories.

Only fifteen years old, a boy with thin arms and soft hands and features not yet hardened by maturity, he possessed the same deep, questioning intelligence she loved about his mother. Chance put them in the daybed in his front room together after running home in the unrelenting downpour, afraid of the thunder, unafraid of being together. Realizing no one would be coming up the street in the violent storm or in the door until the storm abated, they were alone in a private world. Proximity, touch, electric wonder, and the magic of budding sexuality all intertwined, allowing a forbidden act to occur. What happened between them started without intent and ended with neither inhibition nor regret.

His mother, widowed by World War I, was more than her teacher at school; theirs was a very special relationship. After school, the girl often sat in her cluttered classroom, entranced as Daniel's mother spun stories of great authors and how they became writers, speculating on what they would do growing up in a tiny town in the quiet valleys of West Virginia. Daniel sat there too, listening, knowing his mother's stories, waiting patiently to walk home at the end of a long day. On several occasions she walked home with both of them, staying for a simple dinner, or walked home with Daniel by himself while his mother went to the store or stopped at the church.

The day of storms and flash flooding changed their lives and the innocence of all of their relationships. Going back to the way things were before became impossible, prevented forever by muddy waters coursing down the hillsides, chewing away the edges of single-lane dirt roads, toppling rusty mailboxes, carrying away small trees and shrubs, and sweeping away childhood. Years later, that afternoon existed in her daydreams and she wondered if it was God's playfulness or a vengeful Nature or vice versa combining the day's circumstances. The day put two cold, frightened, rain-soaked adolescents in a time and a place and an embrace which grew into something more. Her beauty and blossoming maturity unbalanced the equation of the physical reaction he couldn't control as adult urges crept past the surface of a boy's longing. She dreamt of him often; Daniel, her life's secret.

* * * * *

Miss Flossie Duncan lived on the top of the hill above their apartment on the curving street rimming the river valley. She met Miss Flossie one beautiful afternoon when exploring with Tommy Daniel. They stood at her wrought-iron front gate, each holding its glossy black vertical bars, staring in awe at the height of the beautiful Victorian home.

An almost shrill voice, stretched by the distance from the street to the porch, called out to them, "Did you see the sign?"

She responded awkwardly, startled by the question but recognizing the age of the voice asking it. "No, ma'am. What sign is that?"

"Why this sign, honey, it says, 'Domestic help wanted.'"

A long silence widened the distance between them until the high-pitched voice called out again. "Bring that beautiful little boy up here and talk to me, I'm too old to be shouting across the yard."

That afternoon, and their introduction to Miss Flossie, marked a change, a crossroads bringing friendship, hope, and a warm place in a cold world. Miss Flossie, a fragile and ageless spinster who inherited her older sister's home, bent down, reaching out to take Tommy Daniel's small hand in hers. He immediately reached out in response to her gesture and a true companion was gained. In the months to come they spent countless hours together, neither speaking; Tommy from his inability to do so and Miss Flossie from a deep, loving spirit that neither questioned his silence nor demanded conversation. Being there was enough. She would be there for both of them when it mattered the most.

The big Victorian house meant nothing. Not property and not wealth; none of that could replace her sister. The beautiful house overlooking the Ohio River's wide valley only contained her sister's belongings, artifacts of a life without the breath and song and warmth of the living. Feeling lost, she banged and bounced around inside its huge rooms and long hallways, tiny below its high ceilings, longing for the sound of voices, wondering why she went on surviving, purposeless, all the voices of her life silenced.

In her opinion, talking to herself seemed perfectly normal and not a bit eccentric; never married, no children, and living alone at her age allowed such idiosyncrasies.

"Talking to yourself is natural," she expounded, "even good company, you just have to avoid the appearance of arguing a point and losing."

The girl and her little boy brought life back into the empty house. Before their presence, only footsteps echoed down the hallways. Voices didn't break the silence as the boy was mute and the girl insisted on working so hard; time for conversation remained elusive. Spring moved toward summer. Passing weeks gave the threesome the opportunities needed to cement new relationships. The girl worked diligently and Tommy Daniel never strayed more than an arm's reach from his new friend, Miss Flossie. No longer talking to herself, Flossie talked and read to the little boy whenever they weren't dedicating their time together to quiet reflection. She showed him drawings in the books she read, explaining every detail while the child's eyes alternated between the page and her wrinkled face. Tracing the shapes in the drawings, his tiny fingertip became a brush or pencil or stick of charcoal, moving with amazing control.

Walking about the yard hand in hand with her charge, she described the fragile, delicate flowers and the massive, towering trees, stopping to listen whenever a bird's song broadcast its melody. The boy mimicked her upward gaze, often pointing at the source. Their conversations, although one-sided, replaced the silence of their first weeks together.

Arriving with the bright, revealing sunlight of morning on her face, the young mother's frequent bruises and occasional scrapes caught Flossie's attention, yet the girl refused to respond to the old woman's attempts at concerned questioning, turning away to hide tear-dampened eyes. Fidgeting and sometimes openly worrisome on many mornings, the boy held his mother's hand tightly as they came rapidly up the sidewalk. They walked side by side so closely together their combined shadow assumed the loping canter of a four-legged creature; neither free of what threatened both.

When the boy appeared visibly upset and shaken, Flossie watched the girl calm her son by kneeling down in front of him, holding his tiny hands in hers, rubbing her thumbs over the backs of his hands, and staring directly into his eyes. She smiled and rocked slowly back and forth. In practiced ritual, a dance to the music of a mother's love, she leaned forward and kissed his cheek. She then rested her head gently on the boy's shoulder and whispered his name in his ear. Within moments the boy visibly relaxed, his face losing its tension, his little body beginning to sway, gently copying, side to side in an exact reflection of his mother's movements.

Miss Flossie watched, heartbroken, concerned for mother and

child, wishing she could break through the barriers of acquaintance defining their new relationship to help them both, knowing she must do something.

Later in the day Flossie joined the dance. A large dog pacing back and forth, head down, beyond the thick hedge row separating the yards, frightened the boy. Dogs never responded as this one did. Outstretched in curiosity, his tiny arm hesitated in midair, met only with piercing, dark eyes and curled black lips. The boy looked about, near panic. He wavered on the sheer edge of flight or fight, too para- lyzed to flee and, by nature's design, a gentle soul, incapable of any violent action even in self-defense. The old woman waved her skinny arms about, shushing the dog away, and, grimacing slightly from the pain in her knees, knelt on the grass in front of the boy, grasping his hands in hers. Limited by the stiffness of age, she tilted from side to side searching for a long-forgotten tempo. The boy immediately sensed and copied her actions, beginning to move gently back and forth, rocking on little feet with the smooth fluidity childhood pos- sesses so cavalierly and age dissolves, creating enough motion for both of them. Tommy Daniel's world now held two dance partners.

Checking on them, the little boy's mother happened to see the last moments of the confrontation from an upstairs window, pausing to watch Miss Flossie comfort her son. Knowing what could have hap- pened, she said a prayer of thankfulness for Tommy Daniel's safety and the old woman's love. For months she'd thought of finding work, but knew she never could without someone to watch over her son. By whatever miracle, each side of the equation of her wish came true.

After dinner, as she and the boy now often stayed to prepare and share an evening meal with Miss Flossie, the three sat in the painted summer chairs on the huge front porch.

"I can't stay here much longer. I suppose you can understand that, can't you?" the old woman said.

Tears welled in the young mother's eyes for the second time that day.

"I love having you and Tommy Daniel here, you know that, but

I'm getting too old not to be near family. I've spent my whole life taking care of family, now I may need one of them to take care of me. First it was my parents, I was the baby and the duty fell to me, then it was my sister's husband, she wasn't up to the task, and, finally, with him gone, it was her."

Tommy Daniel and his mother sat spellbound, the young woman listening, the little boy sensing through his mother's changing expression the loss of the comfort and safety Miss Flossie provided.

"I ended up alone," the spinster said. "Maybe it was God's will. I might not have been meant to have a family of my own. Now I'm alone."

She concentrated on her next words, aware of their importance.

"There are worse things than being alone, honey. I've seen that several times over the years–yet it's one of the hardest things for a woman to admit. I've watched you work around this house for weeks, you just keep polishing and scrubbing and cleaning, never giving up. You've worked so hard and so long you must know that you've done your best and there isn't anything else you can do to make it any cleaner; marriages can be like that too."

The young mother, clinging to her son and each word, held her breath knowing the old woman meant more but was caught up in finding the exact way to express her thoughts.

"The man you're married to, no matter how hard you try to do everything to make things better, you can't, it's impossible. He isn't right for you. I can see it. Everyone can see it. You've done your best. The way he treats you isn't going to get better, it'll only get worse. And he isn't right for this boy and you know it. Whiskey is a curse and a killer, darlin'. I've seen it bring down good men who can't understand its powers, let alone weak men who think it's their friend."

Miss Flossie paused, studying the yard as the sun fell in the evening sky casting the long shadow of the house across the shrubs and flowers and trees, reaching to the street. "There comes a time when a person has to stop what they're doing and admit the fix they're in. That time's come for me. I can't go on forever here. I need to be close to my nieces in case the same fate befalls me that took my sister; I've got one big problem: I'm old. And the time's come for you to admit the fix you're in except you've got two big problems you're not facing up to."

The girl started to object, but Miss Flossie raised an arthritic finger, silencing her. "Your man's trouble, honey, he'll go on hurting you and he'll hurt your boy before he's done. Besides, one day he's going to quit coming home. Then you'll be on your own with no one good or bad to help you get by. And as much as you love this little boy, there is going to come a day when you can't help him, just like the day came when my sister and I couldn't help Herbert."

Hearing this, the young woman began to cry softly, pulling her son closer, her tears acknowledging what she already knew in her heart but didn't want to hear.

"When I came here it was to help my sister care for her husband Herbert. He was such a wonderful man it just broke your heart to see him fall to pieces, unable to think straight or care for himself, but still gentle. My sister couldn't stand it. She'd always relied on him to care for her—there wasn't the substance in her to make a go of it the other way around. I did the best I could to help, but before it was over caring for him was too much for me or her or the two of us. We did what we had to do and it was the right thing. We took him to a place where he could get the care he needed. He lived for two more years and it was better for him and her. Then, and maybe the loss of her rock was too much for her, she just withered and died. I could see it happening. I could take care of her here, but there was nothing I could do to slow down the deterioration or stop it."

Looking for answers beyond the story, Tommy Daniel's mother asked, "Who took care of your sister's husband?"

"It's a place over near where he came from, a beautiful place south of Lancaster, Ohio, where his family owned a lot of land. Now there's a story. Herbert ended up being smarter than all his brothers when it came to the land down Stump Hollow Road."

"Where?" the girl asked, her brow wrinkling up, perplexed at the sudden turn in Miss Flossie's dialogue.

"Oh, honey, I did admire Herbert. He was quiet and smart and he studied his county maps for hours on end and listened when the politicians talked, searching out the future from among their nonsense, bragging words, and campaign promises. He saw it coming and it made him rich. That's how they ended up here in Cincinnati with him owning three businesses."

Relieved by the conversation's gossipy tone and its diversion from the sadness of her situation, the girl relaxed.

"You see, he had a voice in what acreage of the family's land he wanted when it was divided among him and his brothers. He picked the winding ridges and hillsides that followed the Hocking River north and south, not the best farm land, the flat open expanses of land away from the river his brothers coveted. They thought he was being dumb and they snickered and said, 'Yessiree, Herbert, you take all those hillsides.'

"The smartest one of those brothers, Herbert saw the future coming. When the railroad came, he owned all the land they needed to run their tracks along the river, avoiding expensive bridge crossings. His land became many times more valuable than those tillable acres his brothers owned. That's how he got started and he bought and sold businesses there in Lancaster until he outgrew the place, coming to Cincinnati. Funny how things end up–recognition as the best farmer wasn't for him, never was. He made bigger plans then worked hard to achieve his goals. But most important of all, he planned for the future. Now I'm trying my best to honor his memory by planning for my future and yours and this beautiful little boy's. Herbert was right about so many things.

"Now there was a good man, honey. He never drank liquor and he treated my sister like a queen. Damn shame they were childless because I think he would have been a wonderful father. Money, turns out that's all he left to this world. Left it to my sister first and she left it to me and it doesn't do a thing for me now; can't keep me from gettin' older."

*   *   *   *   *

Two days later, three of them and the little boy sat at Miss Flossie's kitchen table after the dinner dishes were cleared. In silent concentration, Flossie Duncan watched the girl's face during the initial minutes as she listened to Mr. Stimson, a family friend who had worked for Herbert.

First impressions can be powerful. Mr. Stimson's countenance, the strength of his features, vary in direct relationship to the situation, his audience, and the comfortable smile that comes and goes, softening otherwise severe lines and crevices. On this occasion he radiated charm and gentle caring, a kind father advising one of the world's daughters.

Physically, nature and time worked together, chiseling his long face into a series of angles supported by webs of fine creases. He wore his thinning gray hair long and combed straight back. A massive chin held a cleft rivaling the sculpted busts of the heroes of ancient Greece.

Whether the little boy's mother recognized the brute strength Mr. Stimson's height, wide frame, and muscled forearms represented or not, she appeared at ease with his soft-spoken explanation of his past and his years of respect for Herbert. Years earlier, when Mr. Stimson was in his twenties, he proudly wore the uniform of a Cincinnati police officer, expecting to continue in that role. At thirty-two, however, that career ended with an injury. No details were offered, only a shrug and a matter-of-fact explanation that any tall, lame policeman lacking the ability to outrun crooks, chasing them down alleys or over fences, found himself out of work. Mr. Stimson then worked for Herbert in one of his businesses. Thankful for the opportunity given him, he became very loyal to the employer who eventually became his friend. Miss Flossie chimed in, pointing out the respect was mutual since Mr. Stimson proved himself both dedicated and hard working, enabling Herbert's brick and building supply company to grow and prosper.

Gaining her confidence, Mr. Stimson helped push the girl's ultimate decision over center, giving her strength to stand up to the reality of her situation.

"You know Miss Flossie is right, don't you?" his deep voice intoned, each word enunciated precisely, underscoring his seriousness. "These may be the most difficult decisions you ever make. You need to stand up and recognize how you can best provide a future for yourself and your son."

"This place in Athens, do you really think it's the right place for Tommy Daniel?"

"They cared for Herbert, making him comfortable and keeping him safe when he couldn't care for himself. I know your son is young and unique, and, because of that, the care he needs is going to be different than what Herbert required, but they have doctors who will do the best they can to care for him. The place is famous for the care they provide for people who need special help and attention, has been ever since it opened about ten years after the Civil War."

"But he's just a little boy."

"It seems strange, I know, but he won't stay a little boy. He'll grow and mature physically even if his speech and other abilities don't change. I have two boys and a daughter. It was amazing; they grew up so fast I couldn't believe it. My girl's married now–who knows, I may end up a grandfather soon."

"You're convinced Tommy Daniel would be happy there?"

"Yes, I am. And there's another side to this we really haven't talked about. Miss Flossie thinks the world of you, says you're a smart, hardworking young woman who deserves a life of her own. No matter how much you love your son, your life isn't your own if you devote your whole existence to caring for him while ignoring your own happiness. And someday he might not be as easy to care for as he is now. In the end you'll both lose, each missing out on the chances for happiness you might have found. It's not easy, but sometimes real love forces a person to make tough decisions that consider everyone's welfare and everyone's future." He reached across to pat her hand, reassuring her.

"But my husband, Tommy, may say I can't do this, he may just refuse."

"It's not his decision, it's yours. I know how he treats you. Miss Flossie told me all about it. That's not how a husband acts and certainly not how a father acts. Don't worry about anything he says. I may have a little talk with him about how to treat a lady–it sounds like no one ever explained that to him."

"Oh, please don't. He can be mean when he's angry."

Mr. Stimson laughed, turning to look at Miss Flossie. "I think we can reach an understanding."

"Mr. Stimson can be very persuasive, I'm sure," Miss Flossie said. "And he's volunteered to come with us and drive the Buick. Do you know how to drive an automobile, dear?"

"No, I don't, but my father taught me how to operate his orchard tractor."

"Driving a Buick can't be any more difficult than a tractor. My sister taught me how. That was a sight to see, the two of us going up and down these hills–took a while for me to sort out those pedals. Clutch for this, shift gears for that hill, push down the brake to slow down or stop; we probably scared the neighbors until I got the hang of it."

"Well, it's settled then," Mr. Stimson said. "We'll all go and I'll teach you how to drive Miss Flossie's Buick. Or I may sit in back watching her teach you, I think I'd enjoy that."

*   *   *   *   *

Tommy Higgins studied the passing countryside. His deliberate gaze helped him avoid eye contact with Mr. Stimson, although where each sat made Tommy's preoccupation unnecessary. Mr. Stimson, busy and happy driving the black '36 Buick Sixty Series, his long arms encircling the giant steering wheel, sat several feet removed from Tommy. The young man leaned against the armrest of the right rear seat feigning disinterest but not succeeding.

Whatever words passed between them before leaving Cincinnati hung in the air unrepeated but not forgotten by Mr. Higgins. The silence proved intimidation is rooted in an established sense of dominant force or the implied threat of force. It created a new level of respect required for all interactions with Miss Flossie and the young mother and her son. Drawing a line in the sand, Mr. Stimson stood on one side, arms folded across his chest, ready to enforce his expectations.

The boy held onto the dashboard in front of his mother, watching the road, bouncing and swaying with every motion of the elegant Buick. A well-meaning God created excitement for little boys or little boys for excitement. Either way, the match made in heaven existed, as true and right as Santa and reindeer on Christmas Eve. Miles rolled by easily. The huge straight-eight motor beneath the long pancake hood hummed contentedly, pulling the car effortlessly over the crests of hills. It never bogged down or hesitated, if not knowing its destination, at least unconcerned with any terrain in between. Twin spare tire covers, one in each front fender, pointed the way east.

At day's end, with the trip across Ohio completed and Cincinnati lost in the distance in the rearview mirror, they spent the night in a red-brick, two-story rooming house in Lancaster, prepared for the final hour's trip in the morning. Negating the need for three rooms, the boy and his mother slept in a room with Miss Flossie while Tommy Higgins bunked with Mr. Stimson. Change spun around them, palpable in each look exchanged. Sober, but wishing he weren't, Mr. Higgins remained respectful and silent.

The next morning Tommy Daniel Higgins, holding his mother's hand, walked through the two heavy front doors of the Athens Asylum for the Insane. The little boy's mother, although repulsed by the name of the institution, marveled at its size and the kind acceptance given them by the white-coated doctors who interviewed them, asking questions about her son's history.

Miss Flossie and Mr. Stimson waited at the base of the hill on Richland Avenue. Their view north and west toward the city of Athens took in the great sloping, landscaped grounds of the institution with its majestic ponds and picnic areas. Turning back toward the huge, twin square towers at the entrance to the brick building atop the hill, their eyes naturally followed the curve of the sidewalk ascending the hillside. Large, precisely spaced gas lamps paralleled the walk, segmenting the distance. The spinster's thoughts lingered over the last years of her sister's husband's life. She said a silent prayer for Herbert, knowing his months inside one of the wings of the tall four-story red-brick facility smoothed his way to a better place. Her faith told her he slept in peace, his entrance to heaven assured by kindness, good works, and a lifelong belief in the value of both.

Mr. Stimson's thoughts focused on tomorrows, concerned with what the future held for the young woman. "Miss Flossie, you know her problems aren't over, don't you?"

"She's facing up to that, too. Last night she agreed to move to Michigan with me. She can tell her husband it's to help me get settled or she can tell him goodbye. If it's goodbye, I may be beholden to you to keep an eye on her until she's safely out of Cincinnati."

"My privilege. I'll help you any way I can, Miss Flossie. Whatever you and the girl decide to do, I'll be there to get you moved. We can use a company truck and driver and I'll be glad to go along."

"I knew I could count on you. I don't want to get teary-eyed, but standing here with you, watching you help this young girl, makes me so proud. I know Herbert would be too. If I'd been blessed with a son, I would have wanted him to grow into a man just like you."

Towering over Miss Flossie, Mr. Stimson's arm descended from above her, encircling her shoulders. Giving her a hug, wordlessly acknowledging her comment, the gentle giant looked across the grounds toward Athens, Ohio, humbled by a kind-hearted old woman. They stood together at the base of the hill until the young couple returned, hurrying down the descending crescent of the sidewalk without the boy. Not asking them any questions, the foursome got into the Buick.

For the return trip, Miss Flossie sat in front with Mr. Stimson. In the rear seat, the boy's mother cried softly. Her husband, unemotional or uncaring, returned to his chosen corner, again studying the passing view. Longing for a drink, seeds of revenge germinated in the fertile fields of anger in his thoughts.

Back in Cincinnati, the young woman, her small suitcase in hand, took up residence with Miss Flossie. Tommy Higgins protested, but Mr. Stimson quietly reassured him that everything would be just fine and drove him to his apartment.

Everything was quiet for three days until Tommy Higgins, in a drunken rage, stumbled up Miss Flossie Duncan's front steps, struck the old woman, and made the fatal mistake of pulling a knife on Mr. Stimson.

A month later, Mr. Stimson drove Miss Flossie and the young woman to Michigan in the spinster's Buick. A trusted worker from the brick and building supply company followed with Miss Flossie's furniture covered with tarps on a flatbed truck.

The young woman, now widowed, cried as she watched the hill-sides of the deep river valley disappear behind them, replaced by rolling farmland on the road north toward Dayton. Years of abuse trailed away into her past. As she faced a new future, she thought only of her little boy, wondering about his new life.

Two

The old nurse remembered the day Dancer came to the asylum. She stood hip-shot in the hallway, describing the details of the event to the young attendant.

"Nope, can't say we ever knew it. They said Roosevelt, like the president, but his daddy stopped a couple times, thinking too long spelling it. His momma stood trembling and looking away. We more knew than suspected they lied, giving us a made-up name and runnin' off, happens a lot with the young ones; the parents don't want to be found. We figured the boy's first name was Tommy though, from Thomas like his daddy wrote down. He answered to Tommy or at least looked around when he heard it. Our idea, the name Dancer, some of us here helped with that. Trust me. Watch him for a day or so and he'll live up to the name we gave him." She paused, verifying her memories.

"Dancer, that's his name now. He showed up a few years ago. About '38 I think—a jumpy little kid, eight or nine years old. He was safe here, that's all that mattered. After a while he accepted us, getting comfortable like. Grown some and calm now, you can tell. A name on an old certificate ain't important here. Don't get used much anyhow. This is a 'hey you' kind of place and, with most of 'em, trying to explain something is like throwing feathers upwind. Suspect he'd been scared as a kid and he doesn't have anything to be scared of anymore. I'm proud of being a part of makin' at least that possible for him; little guy's so sweet he deserves to feel safe."

They watched the boy struggle, all elbows and shoulder blades, pushing and pulling the broom with its oversized, rag-wrapped crossbar. The downward force of his efforts ground the red shaved wax crumbs into the hallway's ancient, scarred wood floor.

"He always work so hard?"

"Yup, works like a mule; don't know no better or purely enjoys it. Really can't tell why, he's only said about ten words we understand. He's a head nodder when he's up to listenin' or answerin' back. Think he understands more'n he let's on."

The attendant, a young conscientious objector, or CO as they were called, shrugged wide shoulders. He was enjoying the conversation with the old nurse. As they parted, he nodded "good day," saying a wordless "thank you." His clear, almost feminine eyes, said even more, thanking her for talking at all when so many wouldn't give young men opposed to killing the time of day.

She returned his look minus the nod. Nods and wordless conversation sufficed, meeting the needs of those working here just as they worked for the boy, Dancer. They continued watching his trance-like devotion to moving his broom back and forth. The overworked days of the remaining nurses and attendants allowed almost no opportunities for conversation and precious few real moments of caring for the responsive inhabitants of the huge facility.

The following afternoon the CO saw the old nurse outside the little boy's room. When he walked up behind her, he unintentionally startled her. Acknowledging his presence, she returned to her prior pose leaning against the doorframe, not speaking, observing. The boy stood, silent as always, hands on the sill, gazing out at the countryside. Neither watching nor watched moved until the slight swaying of Dancer's knees, side to side, answered a rhythm only he perceived.

"Bingo," she said under her breath.

The boy's concentration remained steady, focusing on distant horizons untouched by the confinement of his institutional world, unaltered by his movements. Inside his room, distance disappeared, a lost dimension in a world defined in right angles and shiny enamel-painted walls. Enveloped in a melody of silence, Dancer's swaying invited anyone passing to pause, enjoying the warm aura of tranquil acceptance surrounding him, a visible glow of little-boy happiness.

Beyond the rusty, painted iron grillwork in the tall, curved-top window frame, was everything gentle and welcoming that the sterile walls of the interior of the famous old Kirkbride-designed asylum could never offer. The light green paint on the walls mocked the vibrancy of the bucolic landscape outside. Peaked ridges, like random teeth, stretched to the horizon. Dancer danced, softly bending and dipping, moving back and forth, his orchestra the bright afternoon sky.

Without concern for the boy's ability to hear her, the nurse filled in the blanks of the young attendant's unasked questions.

"Boy's right out of these hills, his folks said they hailed from across the state line, somewhere east of Parkersburg; weren't much more talkative than him. His daddy looked wild-eyed mean; probably shoulda turned the key on the man and sent the boy on with his momma. She wouldn't have it though. Kinda desperate-lookin' little gal, can't tell you much about her 'cept I still 'member the hang-dog, beat-on look in her eyes. Not too many years back she'd been pretty–shows up real strong in the boy. Too many bruises though; they can dirty up pretty, leaving sad long after the marks go away."

The CO nodded, absorbed in observing the boy, cataloging his history, learning about the unique inhabitant of the new world where the Civilian Public Service office ordered him to live. Readily accepting the government's orders, he relished his role helping others, respecting his obligation to society in this time of war but bound by his conviction never to kill another human being.

"The big Depression kicked the soul outta a lot of decent folks, probably her too. But, hear me now, any bit of handsome in the boy came from his momma, no doubt about it. Even if the man claimed he was the daddy, seeing them together made you doubt it. Nothin' but back roads in that man. Probably got a temper fit to scare or kill dependin' on the occasion," explained the nurse, whose love for Dancer showed. "There's nothin' in the boy but sweet n' kind."

Turning from the window, Dancer's movement ceased. Big, doe-like eyes caught the conscientious objector and the nurse, alternating between holding each quietly in a soft, unblinking, loving stare of uncomplicated childhood. Unbothered by their scrutiny, the boy smiled. His eyes spoke, replacing words of greeting, neither asking nor offering, windows open on an inner calmness. A serenity that belied wisdom unearned by age or schooling effused the boy's expression. The conscientious objector many disparaged as a "conchie" found himself trapped in unbreakable eye contact, suddenly teetering on role reversal, unsure he was still the examiner.

Contained within Dancer's gaze, a look nourished by innocence, a captivating sense of simplicity emerged, reaching out to the nurse and the young attendant. The boy nodded, an action showing recognition while simultaneously posing unanswered questions about what he actually understood.

In the womb or at birth, perhaps later in a night's high fever, the muse of thoughts waved her wand over Dancer, barring unhindered, thoughtful, spoken expression. The chances that come with the risks of life imposed cognitive disabilities on the boy. He was limited by several encapsulating and incurable, lifelong mental impairments. His hands off the window frame, awkward physical actions, slowed mannerisms, and hesitant steps immediately spoke of inabilities. Without the contact of his hands on the sill, without the imagined reassurance of an unseen partner, the dancing stopped.

Watching him closely, summarizing the child's symptoms, caused the observer to doubt the boy could retain much of anything academic, yet he reflected serenity, calmness below the surface of his slackened facial expression saying it was okay, the loss really didn't matter. What was intelligence anyway? When he chose to study people or animals, the sense of wisdom the boy's eyes projected defied both his countenance and the importance of facts, foretelling a level of caring and common sense, making knowledge of information suddenly trivial.

Can understanding exist without the network of remembered information and facts we call knowledge? You bet. Can someone learn to grow vegetables, wash them, prepare them and blend them, combining the ingredients in homemade soup without knowing water boils at 212 degrees Fahrenheit? Of course; Dancer could and did. Decades later, Dancer's friends would watch him prepare homemade soup and marvel at his skills.

The soup of life simmers and bubbles. The raw vegetables prepared by simple hands soften just as time heals if we let it, making it possible for even the belligerent to reach a level of acceptance of others, for everyone to learn tolerance.

Tastes commingle in a steaming kettle of soup, mixing texture and aroma. Repetition becomes habit which, in turn, mandates a sprinkle of salt without the need to be reminded. Great aromas waft through the air, escaping the surface of the softly simmering broth. The bubbles only mean the soup is very hot.

The liquid's precise degree of temperature causing the popping, steaming, whirling ascent of bubbles is merely a number, a measurement. Soup is soup, sustenance is life, and the pure, motiveless enjoyment of simple things occurs without memorizing lists of facts. It's soup, and, as the CO would learn, often life, and Dancer, and all the different people who live it, can aspire to no more noble a goal than the simplicity of a good homemade soup.

Is it fair to call a person simple like a soup? Like the basic goodness of homemade soup, simplicity requires a lack of complication. On the rare occasion of its application to a person like Dancer, if there could be others like Dancer, simple becomes a compliment. Knowing him brought on a personal redefinition, inspiring the adulation of simple joys while rendering unimportant the clinical classifications of differences in abilities.

Three

A biographer compiles stories and facts, written and told, every detail they can learn from myriad different sources. Short of that level of diligence and unconcerned with too many personal details, my overriding interest rests on telling how Dad and Dancer affected others. Their legacy includes how we all view people with different abilities. Looking back to their early years together, the years Dad and his generation called the war years, much of what I know about the time Dad served as an attendant at the asylum in Athens, Ohio, came indirectly, recounted by my mother. She loved him for the man those years created and the path they caused him to choose.

He spoke to me about those years, but only reluctantly, and then only after I came home from Vietnam. I suppose we discussed World War II as one veteran to another, even if our wars belonged in different eras. Historians see Dad's war as a global epic reshaping world history, ridiculing mine as a political disaster haunting subsequent decades.

Looking back, we did share something. We both served our nation, although only one of us wore a uniform. Talking about our experiences helped us understand that, even if we each served in a different way and for different reasons, neither of us needed to feel ashamed of anything. Each did what he did with a clear conscience. The commitment Dad made, refusing to kill another human being, represented an incredible, life-changing feat of conscience. He lived with the repercussions of his decision all his life. By comparison, I followed orders, not challenging authority; I have to live with the fact that perhaps I subordinated moral principles, refusing to stand up for my individual beliefs.

In the end, a lasting armistice built on mutual respect existed between Dad and me. I learned a great deal about war and life from him, a lifelong pacifist, and I believe he learned a little bit about life the way I viewed it. Dad never judged me for breaking his commandment, knowing I killed enemy soldiers when ordered to do so, just as he never judged and always honored the soldiers of his war although he didn't fight alongside them.

The war years–in a little more than three and a half years, Pearl Harbor to VJ Day, the world changed forever. Hundreds of thousands of Americans fought and lived or died. Of those a merciful God allowed to come home, some, knowing the horrors of war, forgave the conscientious objectors, some, understandably, couldn't. Based on the strength of their faith, a few of those who lost the most, like my mother, learned to forgive before the others. For them the balance of the scales of life leveled, recognizing the magnitude of individual contribution, not differentiating between how people participated. For others, the price paid in lives and carnage defied calculation, blinding them to forgiveness, forever prohibiting empathy.

Reducing war to its lowest common denominator, a single life affected, offers one way to understand how everyone changed. Mom and Dad, two single lives, falling in love and joined in marriage in the aftermath of World War II, both changed. Mom was changed by the death of her only brother in the Battle of the Bulge and Dad from his years as a conscientious objector assigned to work at the Athens Asylum for the Insane. Combining their lives created a synergy of purpose. They each grew stronger, exemplifying the healing that comes from pain and loss.

Dad wove his stories about what he learned from his experiences in Athens, Ohio, from threads spun in part from Dancer's life, retelling anecdotes years later when their lives were tightly entwined. To say he learned from Dancer is both an understatement and a mystery–during those years in Athens, Dancer should have been the student, not the teacher. As decades passed, the depth and substance of the relationship between them became more evident, crediting Dancer as the catalyst even if his contribution probably came from love and not intention. The spark of concern Dancer ignited grew into the primary, sustaining purpose of Dad's existence. Part of the inexplicable nature of Dancer's effects on others has always been how the role of the one needing help, needing to be led, actually provided the clarity that showed others the way, leading them.

Gaining purpose from Dancer, Dad stepped beyond the questioning and wandering so normal to young men in their early twenties. Recognizing a permanent role greater than self or the war or all the unanswered daily variables of life, Dad, with a little help from Dancer, found his direction and moved forward.

Others faced the same issues by ignoring them. Some listened to the advice of parents and family, and, entrapped by their ideas, took the easy, supposedly proven route. Dad could have followed his father's advice, walking down the next generation's path of his father's life in the shoes of a rural Ohio minister, scraping at life's hard edges, living on the generosity of faithful but impoverished parishioners. Reverend Conway never owned a home or land, but accumulated the riches of solid ideals and Christian virtues, sharing them freely.

In Athens, in the midst of the war years, Dancer pointed Dad toward human challenges, eventually stretching the scope of my father's efforts and influence coast to coast and across oceans through the reach of his books. Knowing Dancer all my life, I've come to accept the unexplainable, impossible-to-prove fact that he knew, somehow, in his own unspoken way, that Dad's destiny awaited him. Using the power of a force we're not meant to understand, Dancer directed him toward his life's role.

During those war years Dancer changed too, growing in size and energy and curiosity. A stringy, sapling-thin teenage boy of average height, he held sway over the hallways of the administrative wing of the Athens Asylum for the Insane, darting in and out of its tall arched doorways, going to and fro on imagined and actual errands. The main authority figures in his daily existence—my dad, Paul Conway, Jr., the conscientious objector; and the old nurse, Miss Mattie Bigelow—kept tabs on him.

Each year brought more buildings and places on the grounds within the expanding diameter of Dancer's world and his purposeful endeavors. Still too young and frail to work in the orchards or the piggery or the dairy, the latter being too far removed from the main buildings, delivery boy became Dancer's favorite duty.

Knowing the few remaining doctors, those too old to serve in the military, by their first names, the boy took pride in delivering their messages. Old Doctor Henry might send him to Cottage A–the address marked on the note–following a map with a system of letters invented by the CO and kept on a card in Dancer's pocket so he could show the card to a doctor or nurse or attendant if he became confused. The recipient of Dr. Henry's message might, in turn, send Dancer to the laundry or the kitchen with another note, and so on. The valuable service the boy provided free of charge, although a hug or a smile was appreciated, kept him running throughout the day. Everyone deemed the activity beneficial, and Dancer, as always, radiated happiness whenever busy.

If not so employed, Dancer acted as unofficial greeter for the institution, watching for approaching cars from his perch on the old stone three-step carriage stairs left in place on the front lawn, a relic of the institution's horse-drawn beginnings. The height of the steps gave him a better view of the hillside. When no vehicles approached for long periods, Dancer could be seen at play, walking a tightrope on the edge of the top step, or stretched out in Tom Sawyer repose. Responding to a childhood urge, he was seen leaping off the not-so-precarious two-foot height of the back of the stone steps, arms outstretched, lost in private visions of birds in flight. Then, running around to the front, Dancer ascended them again in his rather unusual stair climbing technique involving a series of bounces, each sideways or backwards, limited by rule or custom to one step at a time.

When official duties interrupted boyhood imagination, Dancer served well, accepting his responsibilities as the institution's Ambassador of Goodwill, First Class. He opened the doors of cars that pulled up under the portico, assisted ladies and old men with luggage and packages, directed visitors to the correct office, and, by all his efforts, gave a lovable, human face to the otherwise formidable and intimidating brick edifice.

The CO's months working long days at the asylum ran together, separated only by weather and season, his arduous, repetitive tasks caring for patients, cleaning rooms, and changing beds, an unending tunnel, constrained within the institution, away from the war-driven turmoil of the outside world. Time spent with Dancer and Miss Mattie broke the monotony, providing relief and a sense of purpose to his toil.

The year 1942 ended and '43 became '44. The name, Athens Asylum for the Insane, changed to Athens State Hospital, a more friendly, less ominous moniker, yet conditions within its walls worsened. Constant shortages of cleaning supplies, clothing, and linens plagued day-to-day operations with needed supplies diverted to the war effort. The number of patients, especially soldiers coming home with shell shock or what later became known as Post-Traumatic Stress Disorder, increased. Staffing at the Athens facility, attendants and nurses and doctors, continued to decline. The few remaining doctors, although working feverishly, were overwhelmed, unable to keep up. As overall conditions deteriorated, tension rose. Then the shooting war in Europe came home.

The huge facility, with five hundred forty-four rooms, held almost two thousand patients. The overcrowding contributed to a changing, angrier environment. Built to house veterans of the Civil War so affected by battle they lost their ability to cope, unable to live in society, Athens understood the lasting reach of war. Patients who fought on Gettysburg's famous battlefields and in the innumerable deadly skirmishes of the War Between the States came there. Many lived out their lives working on the farm and in the orchards atop the ridges in Athens or in its kitchen or laundry. Their minds forever scarred by war but secure within the institution's insulated world, hundreds stayed to rest for eternity beneath a numbered marker in one of its cemeteries. The Spanish-American War and World War I sent emissaries, victims of their savagery. Athens, holding to its long tradition of caring, opened its doors for them. World War II was no different.

The Athens State Hospital of 1944 originally opened seventy years earlier in 1874, patterned almost exactly off the proven layouts of facilities drawn by the renowned institutional architect, Thomas Story Kirkbride. His thinking placed the most violent patients the furthest down the hallway from the administrative offices, which were located at the core intersections of long wings. Exits at the ends of the wings stayed locked.

The most trusted and gentle patients, like Dancer, as well as some staff and many nursing students, were housed immediately next to those central points. Established procedures and rooms separated by distance and iron gates prevented contact between peaceful and violent patients. Very few breaches of security occurred. When the unexpected happened, the combined effort of all staff members came to bear to quell the disturbance.

Several times the CO sprang into action, forcibly subduing a patient, his youth and lanky size enabling him to step in, stopping an altercation already under way and preventing the violence that comes with escalating tempers and additional combatants. One quiet Sunday evening, however, he couldn't get there in time.

A young GI, his shared room midway down the third-floor cor-ridor of the men's wing, had spent an idyllic afternoon visiting with his brother and his brother's family, picnicking on the grounds. The two brothers talked about the war, the unaffected one trying to calm his younger sibling, hoping to convince him to return home to their parents' farm. Somehow the words exchanged soured, turning ugly, good intentions taken as personal insult, the condescension of older toward younger perhaps fueled by years of unspoken rivalry. With friction building to the thunder of inescapable argument, the younger brother exploded, pushing and pummeling the elder. The screams of the brother's wife as she attempted to separate them and protect her children echoed across the grounds. The sole attendant on duty stood across the pond but within earshot. Older than the combined ages of the fighting siblings and hampered by substantial girth, he called loudly up the hill for help then moved at his version of speed to intercede.

At a dead run uphill across the lawn toward the main entrance, dodging Nazi machine-gun nests in the silent rattle of a fusillade of bullets, the GI ran back to the protection of the asylum's red brick walls, fleeing those who couldn't or wouldn't understand. No one took notice of the folded jacket gripped tightly under his arm, his brother's handgun concealed in its pocket. The screams of his dead buddies echoed in his ears, and German 88s shelled their position in the forest. Blood sprayed, limbs were torn, lives lost and wasted, as the young infantryman, rushing in the grip of his own hell, flew up the winding stairways to the third floor, dashing past helpless attendants, terrified nurses . . . and Dancer.

Screaming, threatening to kill them all, the GI forced his three roommates out into the hallway, the handgun cocked and pointed at their heads. Huddled together, the trio moved to the central nurses' station into the waiting arms of two attendants who calmed them, directing them downstairs, going with them to sound the alarm and summon help.

Arriving at the scene, seeing frightened patients peering out doorways, the CO walked slowly and deliberately toward the GI's room, motioning everyone back into the shelter of their rooms. He reassured them, speaking calmly.

Stepping into the room, Paul Conway, Jr., conscientious objector, found himself face to face with the devils of war seething within the mind of a young American destroyed by their flames.

Gripping his captive, holding his brother's gun at the back of the CO's head, the troubled soldier pushed him down the hallway, realizing the gun gave him control and created fear in others. Somewhere in irrationality, a new strategy in his mind moved ahead, guiding his steps, the gun his means of escape, the CO a captured German soldier, his shield and hostage.

Ahead of the shattered combat veteran stood his childhood, his brother's children, and every orphan walking war-torn Germany's tank-rutted roads. A thin, pale, expressionless boy stood ramrod straight at attention, not blocking his way out, but saluting. His small right hand cocked perfectly at his forehead exactly the way the returning soldiers living there instructed him, Dancer waited.

Confused, the GI stopped, returning the military gesture of respect. The CO attempted to signal, to wave Dancer aside. Instead of backing away, the boy continued to approach, staring directly into the young infantryman's eyes.

Until that moment, a single word from Dancer was anyone else's three-minute speech, his vocabulary limited to simple greetings or first names or excited exclamations like "Sunny!" in response to a beautiful day. His gaze fixed on the soldier holding a handgun behind his friend, Dancer said, "No."

Remarkable in its own right, given its meaning, seconds later the boy's concise, measured statement, "Paul . . . good," caused the soldier to pause, lowering his weapon, breaking his trancelike expression.

Dancer held out his hand. Accepted, it was encircled by the fingers of the GI's empty right hand. The conscientious objector, palm upward, asked for and received the weapon. The three of them walked together, step by hesitant step back to reality and the nurses' station, the moment of terror defused by a boy's compassion and unfathomable wisdom. One's supposedly limited mind, reaching out, a child's caring unencumbered by war or life's complexities, soothed the other's delusional thoughts.

Dancer's actions and especially his words were the talk of the staff of Athens State Hospital for weeks. Doctors marveled at his accomplishment and the risk he took to protect his friend, speculating on what motivated him to act. Nurses spoke of the boy's bravery. The soldiers who had taught him to salute repeated their version of the lessons over and over, proud of their contribution.

The light of notoriety shone on Paul Conway in appreciation of his attempt to calm the troubled GI single-handedly, but the center of the story understandably remained Dancer, the little boy saluting a disturbed soldier in order to save his friend. The combined family of staff and patients at the asylum, those aware of and capable of thinking about and discussing the incident, knew there was something very special about the boy living in their midst. Unchanged and oblivious to the acclaim, Dancer was Dancer, happy to run errands and greet visitors, neither seeking nor acknowledging attention.

Beyond the boundaries of Athens State Hospital, the beautiful little city of Athens, Ohio, and the borders of the continental United States, World War II wound to its end. Hitler took his own life in his bunker and Berlin fell. Victory in Europe, VE Day, was followed three months later by VJ Day, Victory over Japan. Accompanying gasps of amazement, civilized nations shuddered at the war's finale as two atomic bombs exploded over Japan. Most were thankful that many tens of thousands of Allied soldiers were saved. An invasion of the Japanese mainland, its citizens ready to slaughter our forces in total, fanatical devotion to their emperor, likely would have killed up to two hundred thousand U.S. troops. Whether secured by bombs or invading forces, the world's anguish needed to end. In free countries history retells the stories of Japanese atrocities, printing their particulars in schoolbooks. Ironically, the truth was withheld from two generations of Japanese citizens until the advent of the internet provided young Japanese scholars with access to the reality of what happened.

In late November 1945, Paul Conway, Jr., one of three thousand conscientious objectors serving as attendants in mental hospitals at the behest of the U.S. government, was released from his duties. Neither an honorable nor a dishonorable discharge but a simple letter, his notice, arrived from the Civilian Public Service office. Studying the letter's matter-of-fact, emotionless paragraphs, Dad suddenly faced a future without defined plans. His work at Athens State Hospital provided him with a purpose and an outlet for his considerable energy–a place and a means to serve, in his own way and without compromising his central principles revering life, during more than three years of war. Now his duty there was completed.

Leaving behind Dancer and Miss Mattie Bigelow and the staff and patients of the asylum in Athens, Ohio proved difficult. Tears and hugs came with goodbyes, yet he sensed that everything he learned there would remain a part of his life, that leaving them was somehow a beginning, not an ending. He couldn't have known how his future would revolve around Dancer. If anyone knew, Dancer did, and, living in his world in his way, he wasn't saying anything. As usual, he held that knowledge or spark of wisdom quietly behind a screen of simplicity and boyish happiness. He withheld it until fate called it forth and Dancer danced his mysterious shuffle, holding someone else's hand, touching that heart and changing that life.

Dad spent Christmas with his parents, helping his father write his holiday sermons, glad to be home. His immediate plans for the new year came in the form of another letter. The Brethren organization that had supplemented his tiny room and board checks from the government with a meager stipend for living expenses was seeking volunteers to go to Germany. Reading their pleas for assistance for the Jewish people, survivors of the death camps in Germany and Poland, Dad felt a renewed call to serve. His response letter to the Brethren was in the mail by the third day.

Four

Truth always resides within the shadow of adage, waiting for the light of understanding. Opposites do attract. Proven again and again, the physical reality is beyond debate. It is conditional, however. For the process to succeed, for the chemistry or magnetism or electric looks across a crowded room to connect opposite personalities, fate must put the potential lovers in close enough proximity for natural selection to take place. Fate did a great job.

With different sponsors and skills, Mom and Dad ventured from hometowns in Michigan and Ohio to postwar Germany. Arriving within a month of each other in early '46, less than a year after the end of hostilities, a world in tatters awaited them. The two young Americans, apprehensive but ready to help, joined hundreds of volunteers working for UNRRA, the United Nations Relief and Rehabilitation Agency. Everyone there knew they were protected by GI's with rifles held in uneasy readiness; God help any former German troops who thought to test them.

Continuing discoveries of immense mass graves steeled U.S. resolve to assist the Jewish people. World opinion declared, "Never again!"

Sweating on the working ends of shovels, Germans living within sight of the camps involuntarily participated in the process of disinterment, opening the most recent mass graves dug and filled in the closing weeks of the Reich. Many stridently proclaimed the innocence of ignorance, somehow blind for several years to the ashes of a people nearly incinerated to extinction that had drifted down all about them, the gray snow of Lucifer's determination.

Sharing a common motive, but still unaware of each other, my parents sought to help the Jews recover from Hitler's megalomania and the complicity of too many of the German people.

To qualify to serve as a volunteer, Mom studied German and Hebrew day and night for months obsessed with going there, a world away, to walk the roads and breathe the air and study the sky where her only brother, Bryant, gave his life. Her parents, both academics, attempted in vain to dissuade her, finally caving in, deciding to support her efforts, hoping to ensure her safety through planning and preparation.

The well-to-do girl from Michigan, rich by the standards of most young people in 1946, educated and outspoken, possessed a natural talent for discussing world politics and considering huge social and historical issues; seeing the big picture. Her newly acquired linguistic skills, as intended, were invaluable tools for questioning survivors, seeking lost relatives from lists compiled at every death camp and ghetto. At first timid, dealing face to face with those she wanted so much to help, alarmed by their quiet desperation, she warmed to them and to the task. Each day gave her a more informed, more complete perspective on the fragile humanity surrounding her. Bringing understanding to displace hatred and intolerance, her political savvy told her freedom could relieve the pallor of cruelty and domination.

The quiet minister's son from Ohio, firm in his convictions but never discussing them, a graduate of reality and human experience whose pockets never jingled, pitched in. Working sixteen-hour days, the CO made hundreds of small but positive things happen, creating change one day at a time for one person or family at a time. Finding the enormity of the crime engulfing the victims of the Reich's attempted genocide inconceivable, he understood the powers of diligence and determination, entrusting the outcome of his efforts to a strong faith that good conquers evil. The eyes of so many of the recently liberated Jews reminded the conscientious objector of a different kind of helplessness common to a portion of the patients in Athens, Ohio. The same plea for help reached outward, demonstrating a haunting, often hopeless, and always pervasive sense of loss, of human beings in pain.

Remembering his years at the asylum reinforced his unshakable confidence that hard work and time, no matter how daunting the task, would repair the devastation of world war, offering a future to a people struggling to survive.

Rivaling the scripts of romantic comedies, Mom and Dad's early conversations lacked any meaning. Every word spoken tripped over the other's lingering stare, disjointed, overcome with the awkwardness of late adolescence but unafraid of misinterpretation. Sheepish, shy, not knowing how to react, but unmoving, stunned by the subliminal spark of germinating attraction, each knew not to walk away–not this time. Nature or Cupid, whatever the overreaching force in the universe that understands the makings of a lifetime of commitment, prevailed. Nothing and everything said between them signaled the beginning of a partnership meant to last half a century; until death do us part and beyond in the heirs of their love.

In bouncing, ping-pong-ball fashion, each topic was served then returned across the net of mere acquaintance between them. The young couple's words probed and questioned.

"Where in Michigan?" he asked.

"Ann Arbor."

"University of Michigan, right?"

She nodded. "You?"

"Southern Ohio. It's wonderful–all little towns and family farms; it's like heaven spaced out between rectangular grids of dirt roads."

"Did you go to a little country school?"

"Sure did," he answered, "and growing up there you don't learn much about big cities or Europe. World issues are just little articles in the weekly paper."

"Okay, then how did you get here?"

Trivial details painted pictures of their pasts, building identities, exposing beliefs. She assumed he served in the military, yet, unlike any other ex-soldier she talked with, he never volunteered information, recounted battles, or shared anecdotes about buddies.

"Do you think David Ben-Gurion will make any progress with the British?" For over twenty-five years, Great Britain had ruled Palestine. Then, with the deaths of British soldiers caught up in the increasing violence of the conflict making their presence there extremely unpopular, the Brits tossed the hot potato of the Zionist-Arab problem into the indecisive hands of the United Nations.

Paul laughed. "Amy, you amaze me. You're going to be a professor of world politics."

Studying her simple cup of coffee, turning it slowly in delicate fingers, she answered, "If that's what you want me to be, then that's what will happen."

Alternating between studying the tin coffee cup in his hand and her eyes across the width of the wooden table in the refugee center, the CO gently steered the subject. "I sure hope something good happens here. These people are still suffering."

"It's a straightforward plan, you know. Dividing Palestine, creating an Arab state and a Jewish state, it'll work. And they want to keep Jerusalem neutral, not aligned with either side."

Not wanting to sound completely uninformed, he said, "I read that the Arabs refused to consider that plan."

"They did, but it's not over yet. If only the United Nations could act. Otherwise I think there will be more attacks back and forth, more killing. Did you have to kill people in the war, Paul? You never talk about it. I'm not prying; I'm only concerned that you're keeping too much of what happened locked up inside. Maybe talking about it is the right thing to do?"

That was when Dad told her about being assigned by the Civilian Public Service office to work at the Athens Asylum for the Insane, that he was a conscientious objector. For long seconds she held back, tears welling in beautiful blue eyes. Thinking of her brother, not even knowing how he died, only told he was killed in action, most likely by a German artillery barrage, she struggled, unable to keep from comparing the CO to her brother.

Her thoughts circled again and again seeking answers to central questions hidden behind two doors labeled chance and choice. Her brother fought and died–chance. Paul Conway didn't fight and lived–choice. Locked tight, neither door opened. Mere mortals lacked the keys.

Did a fundamental injustice lurk in unanswerable questions waiting for explanations to prove if cowardice is evil and killing is all right if you survive to tell about it?

Dad talked about his work in Athens, caring for the patients, how they were so incredibly short of supplies and attendants and nurses and doctors. He told Mom about Dancer, pulling out a small black-and-white photo of Dancer standing with Miss Mattie Bigelow by the front entrance, handing it to Mom.

"But he's just a little boy. What's he doing in a place like that?"

"He's very special. Unique is too small a word. Watching him, I learned so much. Those people are suffering too. Not like the Jews, not like the terrible murders that took place here, but in a lot of ways society doesn't even attempt to understand. It's almost like they're refugees too, pushed aside into a different world and forgotten. In the asylum they do wonderful things to help them, even with crowded rooms and not enough supplies. But it isn't enough. There's so much more that can be done. Shell-shocked GI's from the war are already there being helped–there'll probably be a lot more."

Glancing sideways, studying his eyes as he spoke deeply and sincerely about the patients he'd cared for, she witnessed a kindness and maturity she never saw in the soldiers she met. Their stories chronicled only violence, often exaggerated, spiced with bravado. Paul spoke of life and caring. Her brother had been kind and able to see the needs of others. The war took her brother's life. If he'd survived, perhaps he would have been here helping the Jews too–the world reeled with death and losses, yet this handsome, articulate young man spoke of life. She listened, working to understand her reaction to his choice to become a conscientious objector, absorbing his sincerity, seeing he was more than just the son of a country minister caught up in his father's principles.

"And Dancer ran our errands and swept the long hallways. He's a good worker, almost a comedian about it at times, although I don't think he understands he's funny. I drew a map with all the buildings and put a letter on each one. That helped him navigate. He enjoyed greeting visitors at the door too, and helping them with their belongings. They followed him, appreciating his help, captured by his spontaneity. And, like you, I'm sure some of them wondered about him, about what made him different and why he didn't answer their questions and talk or act or walk like other boys his age."

In the end, she knew he had made a fundamental decision, choosing life over death. Everything he did showed a love of life; all the hatred of war and the act of killing another human being would have destroyed him. The volunteers working around them would find his choice cowardly and repugnant; she accepted that, yet despising Paul for his convictions couldn't restore even one life already lost. Maybe what he did wasn't cowardice at all, but another kind of bravery. Maybe it meant having the courage to say, "I can't do that."

The passing days of the next weeks included quiet times contemplating whether a world at war still held a place for moral courage or if the savagery reduced mankind to a level of viciousness that respected only the courage of brute force.

Swayed by attraction and an inner knowledge recognizing that wars, as monstrous as they were, were temporary, periodic episodes in history, Mom grew to respect Dad's moral convictions. She understood the world needed compassionate, hardworking people to heal, to put the shattered pieces of life back together and move forward.

Dad represented the future. After coming to Germany to help and seeing first-hand the results of war, she longed to put it far behind as quickly as possible; she began to think of her future, of where she wanted to be, and with whom.

In Palestine, the Jews' struggle to establish a homeland, to create a new Israel after two thousand years, became increasingly violent. Theirs was a no-holds-barred fight for survival, although the Palestinians saw it as unprovoked aggression. With the British Mandate set to expire in May, the slaughter of innocents began in earnest as both sides vied to carve out or maintain their territories.

Boatloads of emigrants left Europe on a regular basis, with many turned back. Thousands languished in displaced-persons camps, longing to find their way to Israel, to freedom from oppression. Mom sensed going to Palestine only offered new battlefields, and under increasing pressure from her parents, their letters insistent, almost hysterical with fear, she spoke repeatedly of returning to the United States. Dad listened, sharing the same frustrations, unable, as she was, to do more in the process of relocating German and Polish Jews to a safe, independent nation state.

After months of hard work, their efforts culminated in the mutual realization that, having done their best, only time and the politics of a world attempting to heal the wounds of cataclysm could justly realign its borders, offering sanctuary to these victims.

*   *   *   *   *

The Quadrangle of The University of Michigan stretched south to the visible horizon. Crisscrossing sidewalks divided the view into a series of right triangles diminishing in size from nearest to farthest away. Each three-sided shape illustrated the Pythagorean Theorem's equation, $A^2 + B^2 = C^2$, and created a backdrop capable of engaging the minds of young engineering students. Massive trees, newly barren of leaves as winter approached, were interspersed between the classroom buildings, punctuating the scene. With the annual arrival of spring's new foliage, the trees provided descriptions of stately grandeur for English majors composing essays in nearby classrooms, and promised, by summer, shade for the lovers who reclined beneath them on warm, leisurely days. Neither the aspiring engineering student nor the eloquent English major could possibly understand the motivations of the other as they passed hurrying to class, but, along with each year's summer lovers, they shared equally in the magnificence of this place.

A block away, the bells atop Burton Tower tolled the hour. Their music pealed across the campus, adding a lilting presence, a formal, repetitive melody, to the feeling of tradition surrounding everyone living, working, or studying within earshot, interrupting normal conversation until their echo died away.

After a long morning walk under Michigan's cloudy November skies, crossing the city from the campus to the arched entrance to Nickels Arcade and the stores of State Street down Liberty Street to Main and beyond, the young couple stopped for a treat. The heavy wire legs of the tall cafe chairs scraped the tile floor of the small eating area inside the front door of the Washtenaw Dairy. The benches lining the sidewalk outside the windows sat abandoned to the whims of early winter's weather. Pulling up close to the small round wrought-iron table, Mom and Dad concentrated on bowls of ice cream; one scoop of chocolate for her, one vanilla and one strawberry for him; neither realizing their combination constituted Neapolitan. Coming indoors from a long walk on a chilly day with temperatures hovering near forty degrees to enjoy ice cream seemed somehow very American. It was good to be home. Either Europeans were too practical to have fun, the Germans too Teutonic, or they failed to understand that simple pleasures knew no season and rarely happened if postponed.

"Of course it makes sense, Amy. Everything you say always makes sense. It's just too much for me to accept. It's like charity. I grew up believing each of us has to make his own way in life and nobody said it was going to be easy. I'm supposed to be the provider, remember?"

"That's the point, Paul; you will be the provider, and a far better one, a happier one, when you finish school. Why make it difficult? Besides, it's not charity, it's an investment, and it's not about you, it's about us."

When it comes to understanding the process of love, men often find themselves woefully unprepared for the logic of commitment, hamstrung by notions of role. The dilemma, a throwback to antiquity, lingers in male DNA, the caveman image of the hunter-gatherer ingrained, causing a barrier to understanding. The few hundred thousand years between then and now, and the imposition of civilization, changed the roles nature formerly imposed.

The problem could also be a failure of our language, a misunderstanding of pronouns or the inability of our colloquial phrases to provide specific meaning, leaving our true intentions inadequately explained because of the informality of our speech patterns. After a fire, some say the building burned down, crumbling in flame from the top to the bottom, but others say it burned up, following the direction of the rising smoke and flames that consumed it. Either way, in the end, the smoldering foundation tells us something happened, something's gone.

Hands stretched across the small table, reaching to touch without bidding, spoke of a combination of lives, not individual roles. As nebulous in meaning as the phrases "burning up" or "burning down," the words so often employed to speak of commitment say people "fall" in love. "Join" is a more appropriate verb. People join together in love. But "join" lacks the ring or pizzazz or action of "fall." It does, however, replace the unfortunate negative sense of direction "fall" implies. Thinking about these simple words, you can see how, tragically, our language can lack the accuracy needed to explain human relationships. It's as if ambiguity allows us to avoid the attachments we really don't mean to pursue. But, by doing so, we risk missing out on the ones we truly want.

"Look, Amy," Paul slurred around a spoonful of delicious strawberry ice cream losing its flavor to the seriousness of words. "College is a dream. I've got to go to work and save the tuition before I can think about going to school."

"Didn't you listen to Daddy? He's very serious and everything he said made sense. A college degree is the only way you're going to reach your dreams of helping people with mental disabilities. The cost of tuition is only seed money; you can't miss the opportunity because you're worried about where it comes from. None of those farms in Ohio would ever harvest a crop if they worried about going a little bit in debt to buy the seed. In the long run, you can't worry about the tuition or you'll never reach your goal."

"Amy, I've never been beholden to anyone, not for a single penny. I've always paid my own way. Yes, I know what my dream is, and, somehow, I'll find a way to get there. And, yes, I want the two of us to be together. Maybe we just have to wait."

Squeezing his hand, Mom said, "Paul, if we're going to do this together, they're no longer just your dreams, they're my dreams too, and dreams aren't good at waiting, so you have to accept my parents and what they can do to help as part of the process. We'll all work to make this happen."

The following Saturday afternoon, on the pretext of Christmas shopping, Mom and Dad stood in front of the large windows of Goodyear's Department Store enjoying the arrangement of gift items. Tinsel, cotton snow, and a cherub-faced, four-foot-tall Santa embellished the display's holiday setting. My parents held hands. There's something about Christmas that brings people together, encasing life's immediate concerns in a bigger, longer perspective. Across the street, Dad stopped before the window of Hutzel's dress shop on the corner. He asked Mom if she liked the dress on the perfectly posed mannequin whose gloved hands were raised invitingly. Lost in a daydream, Dad glimpsed Mom in that dress, standing in the foyer years hence, welcoming friends into their home for dinner and an evening of animated discussions. Still clutching Mom's hand, Dad began to feel the connection between the present and the future, understanding that now becomes then in a blink of determination—and then doesn't mean a thing if you can't be together with the one you love.

Looking back over his shoulder, Dad said, "With the university and these great stores this is quite a town. Not too big, not too small, it's really nice. Did you ever notice there's a bank on each corner of the block we just passed? With your dad as a reference, do you think one of them would loan me that tuition money?"

*   *   *   *   *

My sister, Julie, and I have compared what we remember of our childhood Christmases, cataloging images, trying to think back as far as we can. Worth remembering, for us they hold good memories. Foggy with time and overshadowed by the millions of details of our adult lives, we can still go back in our minds to a few early Christmas mornings when we were kids–seeing each other running down staircases in pajamas with feet, kneeling by hearth sides and emptying decorated stockings, gleefully examining their contents.

Mom and Dad and Grandma and Grandpa, retelling anecdotes, provided a glimpse into what the first Christmas my parents spent together was like, the Christmas before they were married. Dad was already working. He'd gone to the office of the Catholic nuns charged with operating Ann Arbor's St. Joseph Mercy Hospital, telling them about working three years at Athens State Hospital. Impressed by his enthusiasm, the credentials his hands-on experience gave him, and unaffected by his status as a former conscientious objector, they immediately hired him to work as an orderly, assisting nurses with patient care.

Finding an inexpensive room to rent on Packard Street, just south of campus and within three blocks of Mom, life again exhibited normalcy, and, for the first time since Athens, a sense of permanence. Always Mr. Pragmatic, Dad set to work establishing himself in his new environs. Mom, the dreamer, spent the weeks before Christmas contentedly planning the holiday and their future together, confident of an imminent proposal of matrimony.

Christmas Eve brought with it the start of new traditions for Dad.

The series of holiday events repeated every year by Mom and Grandpa Mike Porter and Grandma Rebecca, now with the memory but not the presence of Bryant, were destined to also be Dad's for decades to come. Each ritual of celebration fit neatly into a predetermined schedule: dressing in their Sunday best for dinner on Christmas Eve, a candle-lighting midnight church service, Christmas morning gift opening, and a leisurely Christmas Day spent grazing on leftovers and cookies. Every year brought new topics of discussion reflecting the changing lives of all followers of the carefully programmed events. That year was no exception. And even though these family holiday traditions provided history and continuity, everyone participating, after all, was changing and maturing, their lives evolving. That first Christmas, the hand of what's-going-to-be reached back, steering thoughts and plans.

"Paul, the most difficult decisions need to be boiled down to their simplest alternatives. Your stated intent is honorable, to help people stricken with mental and emotional disorders. To best put yourself in a position to achieve that goal, you're going to need some specific qualifications–we just have to determine which qualifications will serve you best."

With a conspiratorial smirk, Grandpa Porter realized his wife and daughter were out of the house on an errand and lit a second after-dinner bowl of tobacco in his pipe. On this holiday occasion he decided to break that rule since his wife wasn't home to reprimand him for smoking up the whole house. The fresh pine scent of the tree also helped disguise his transgression.

"When you talk about the elements of sociology, Dr. Porter, they sound like they fit. I just can't connect them to what I know of the day-to-day operations of the asylum where I worked. Society's groups and organizations are based on beliefs and values. That's what the sociology books tell us. Surely one of those groups is made up of the afflicted, even if they're not a group readily accepted by the balance of society; they're sort of ignored by most people."

"Good point," Grandpa noted. "Now, can you work in the field of sociology, studying the groups of people making up our society, and be able to serve the people you want to help?"

"Wow, this is tough, isn't it?"

"Only if we make it tough, Paul. From what I've learned about you, you're hardworking and dedicated. I'm proud of you for what you've done. I know you worried about what we would think of you being a conscientious objector; Amy told me you were concerned about that. Well, the war's over. Our son died. Nothing's going to change that. Since his mother and his sister aren't here to hear this, and I don't want them to hear it so you can't tell them, there's something about the way he died they don't know. Teaching at the university I hear things. As you can imagine, some of the professors were involved in helping the government with the war effort. One of them, a good friend of mine, came to me with something he learned in Washington and I'm going to keep it as my secret. Maybe I'll tell you about it someday, but not now, and, even if I do, my wife and Amy can never hear it.

"What happened puts a whole new light on how my son died. There were things about the war, ugly and inhuman things that no one wants to talk about. Believe me, Paul, it wasn't all fought honorably and, knowing what I know now, I'll never fault you for your decision."

"I'm sorry about Bryant. I'm sorry about all our losses, Dr. Porter. Looking back now I'll always wonder if I was too young and naive to make the choice I made, and we both know there will always be people who resent what I did."

"That's behind us, Paul. If Bryant could be here today, he'd be talking about his future. But he isn't and his future's gone forever. Our responsibility now is to consider Amy's future and yours. The living, Paul; we can honor the dead, but we have to focus on the living. Understood?"

Dr. Porter rose from the wing-backed chair he'd been sitting in, more fussing with his pipe than smoking it. He walked around the room, studying books on the shelves, allowing the ebb and flow of emotion that always came from speaking about his son to subside before returning to his chair. "We were talking about the differences between sociology and psychology weren't we, Paul?"

"We were and we are, Dr. Porter, especially psychology," the young CO said thoughtfully, his comment's depth visibly pleasing the professor who chuckled in response, lifting the mood of their conversation, returning to the task at hand.

"Your response shows you already appreciate the subtleties of psychology, and, for a lot of reasons, the answer may lie in that field. I'm just an old history teacher, but from what I know of psychology and how the field is changing, it may offer the specific, real-life applications you're looking for. Helping people with mental disorders requires working with one person at a time, doesn't it? Kind of like helping the Jewish victims of Hitler's insanity; Amy told me you did an excellent job of helping them."

"I can see the practicality of what psychologists do, Dr. Porter. And, yes, they work to solve the problems of individuals. I've read about how they study the human mind and work to solve mental and emotional disorders. My concern is that they're practitioners, each working alone, kind of unsupervised, without strong guidance from a central authority. Yes, they do great work, but I'm interested in helping organize the process of providing mental health services and the way psychologists work together–that's what made me think of sociology, sort of a bigger view of the same job."

The professor turned directly to my dad, the look of approval on his face changing slowly to one of admiration; the beginnings of lasting mutual respect. Years later, recounting the conversation, Grandpa would laugh out loud, remembering the turning point.

"What you're seeking is obvious. It's called 'leadership.'"

"I'm sorry, sir?"

"Leadership, Paul. You've seen a great deal of the inner workings of your chosen trade already. You know what went on in the asylum in Ohio, and I'm guessing that some of what you saw didn't seem proper or well intentioned. Knowing how something works, with all its faults, makes a good man want to improve it, to make it better.

That's you, Paul. That's where you're going and what you're going to do." Grandpa stood, transferring his pipe to his left hand, holding out his right. Dad immediately stood up and shook his hand.

Standing face to face with his soon-to-be son-in-law, their eyes level, Grandpa said, "And I'm going to have the privilege of helping you get there."

"Dr. Porter, you're very kind and I don't want to be ungrateful, but I've got to make my own way through school. I'm working now and I'll find a way to pay the tuition."

Suppressing a quiet laugh that caught in his throat and turned grim, Grandpa said, "Amy told me you'd be a little stubborn about this, but now you're going to have to listen to a Dad who's lost his son. I would be helping Bryant through school, but he isn't here. So I'm asking you to let me help you in his memory; he would want you to accept my assistance. And, if it makes you feel better you can pay me back–just take your time doing it, okay? All that aside, I've been doing a little homework and you're on the right track. There's a little present for you in the other room and I think it's time you opened it."

"Won't we get in trouble opening presents on Christmas Eve? Amy sounded pretty serious when she said you only opened presents on Christmas morning, not before."

"Except this one. It's something I wanted to discuss with you and right now is the perfect time. I'll take the blame for giving you this present a little early."

Moving from the small, cluttered library to the living room, Grandpa Mike knelt down and pulled out the gift, only slightly disturbing Amy's neat arrangement of the presents under the tree. From its shape and heft Dad knew immediately it was a book. "Wrapped this one myself," Grandpa said. "Not too neat of a job, I've never been accused of being handy about such things."

Popping the ribbon over a corner of the package and pulling off the wrapping paper as Grandpa continued, Paul held the book and studied its cover. "I wasn't sure if you'd been involved in getting this book published or not," Grandpa said. "So I asked Amy to mention the group to you and she said you'd heard of them but never taken part in their efforts."

"I read their newsletter," Paul said. "The CO's called it *The Attendant* at first, and then changed the name to *The Psychiatric Aide*. I liked the first name better, less assuming. It all started at an asylum in Philadelphia. Byberry, I think."

"The conscientious objectors and their organization, the National Mental Health Foundation, did a great job putting this together, Paul. They made their point, showing the country needs to provide more humane care for people with mental illnesses. The title gets right to the point, doesn't it? *Out of Sight, Out of Mind*, it all sounds like what you've been telling me."

"The patients in Athens State Hospital were very lucky to be there, I think it must be one of the best institutions in the country. That's probably why I knew about the efforts of the conscientious objectors but didn't get involved; it all seemed removed from Athens." Dad turned the pages of the book, scanning its contents.

Walking to the small desk in the telephone alcove and opening its narrow drawer, Grandpa Mike removed a magazine, brought it across the room, and gave it to Dad. "After we talked I went through our magazines from the last year. I knew I'd read an article that talked about these same issues. I saved it for you but I didn't bother to try to wrap it. I'd have made a mess of that."

Paul examined the May 6, 1946, issue of *Life* magazine, automatically turning to the page marked with a three-by-five card on which Grandpa had penned the article's title: *Bedlam 1946: Most U.S. Mental Hospitals are a Shame and a Disgrace*, beginning to read its first page. "Articles like this paint a pretty ugly picture of the conditions in the asylums. Do you think it's really this bad across the country, Dr. Porter? I hope not. I've heard of Albert Maisel. He's a reporter. I read one critical article he wrote about veterans' hospitals; I just never thought it could be that bad."

"I hope it isn't as bad as writers like Mr. Maisel portray it to be, Paul, but it sounds like you're on the right track; there's certainly an opportunity to work in a field that could use the help of smart young people who care about the patients in those hospitals. The CO's even went to Mrs. Roosevelt, getting her to write about the problems in her newspaper column. Have you ever read her column, *My Day*?"

"No, sir, I haven't. I heard some talk about things the conscientious objectors did to bring attention to their concerns, but I didn't get involved."

"I think it's time you did, Paul. I think it's time you did," Grandpa said, turning in the direction of happy female voices coming from the front of the house. "They're back and I bet we're about to take part in more Christmas doings. Are you ready?"

"This has already been the best Christmas I can remember, Dr. Porter. Thank you for the book and the magazine, I promise I'll study them carefully."

Dad certainly did study the book, *Out of Sight, Out of Mind*, the compilation of inputs from nearly half of the three thousand conscientious objectors serving in asylums around the United States. The book became a marker, a kind of reminder of where his efforts all started and why. Sometime during his college years he placed the photograph of Dancer and Miss Mattie Bigelow, already checkered from too many months in his wallet, inside the front cover. As he progressed through the roles of student to practitioner and administrator and then to author and professor, that old book, its cover worn from countless handlings, spent decades residing in the most prominent position on the bookshelves of Dad's many offices. Sometime in the last years of his life he gave the book to Dancer, who, unable to read it, still keeps it on his shelf, unaware of its contents but knowing its worth, aware of its importance to my father. I've watched Dancer take out the small photograph and smile as he gazed at it for long minutes; we've all wondered how much he remembers from those years.

There's something else inside the book's front cover, an inscription by Grandpa Porter. He wrote, "To Paul Conway, Jr., a wonderful young man with a brilliant future–God bless your efforts and light the way to your achievements." It was signed and dated December 24,

1946. The inscription, as much as the book's contents, meant a great deal to Dad. Professor Porter valued and supported Dad's chosen path, casting a learned shadow of credibility on the field as well as his prospects.

Scholarly efforts meant to improve the lives of fellow human beings, especially those chronicled in books written for future students to follow, have a way of staying with us, moving into the future in the thoughts of their readers. The libraries of our colleges and universities are replete with these works. Besides conveying information and theories, they inspire us and remind us, in the overlapping loops of history and progress, that nothing is possible without the concern of caring, dedicated individuals.

It was a very good Christmas; the first of many family Christmases to come.

Five

Following family traditions, each holiday event took place as planned. It snowed gentle, big, swirling flakes on the afternoon of Christmas Day, 1946, accumulating slowly. Dr. and Mrs. Porter's colleagues and friends stopped by, exchanging small presents and staying for coffee and cookies; yet another yearly event.

Standing on chairs, leaning out precariously to reach the highest branches, Mom and Dad spent the better part of a frustrating hour embroiled in the painstaking process of finding the single burned-out Christmas tree light on the long, brittle strings of two-strand wires connecting multi-colored tapered bulbs. In those years when one bulb burned out, they all went out.

Plugged in separately, Dad's favorite lights on the tree bubbled continuously, working flawlessly. Mom teased him about his fascination with the two shorter strings of gurgling, glass tube candle lights encircling the widely spread lower branches. He laughed, but kept going back to examine the colored glass tubes of those lights. Intrigued by how they functioned, he eventually realized the heat of the bulb in each rounded base was warming the liquid in the three-inch-tall, vertical glass tube of each light clipped to a pine bough, causing it to boil. Across town the brave crews of the fire department stood ready to respond to any folly resulting from electrical displays of the season.

That morning, no small square gift box containing an engagement ring waited for Miss Amy Porter under the tree. Unlike the strings of lights gone dark, she stayed bright and animated. She visibly enjoyed giving and receiving presents, sustaining her Christmas spirit on the dual strengths of hope and expectation. To her credit, no reaction, not a sign of disappointment clouded her holiday happiness. Subscribing to a philosophy that good things are worth waiting for, no matter how excruciating the interim, Mom held her breath. She knew the holidays weren't over yet, and she was right.

On New Year's Eve at the stroke of midnight, Dad popped the question. Standing in the middle of the dance floor at the Michigan Union, his arm around Mom as the band leader interrupted a Glenn Miller medley to announce the hour, he deftly pulled the white velvet box from his suit pocket with his left hand, opening the lid to show her the ring.

Lost to the pandemonium of the crowd, Dad's well-rehearsed speech, barely discernable above the noise, relayed its intended message. Missing a few of his words but getting all of his meaning, his bride-to-be understood and screamed, "Yes, oh yes," loud enough for several others paused from dancing around them to hear. The witnesses stopped hugging each other and applauded Mom and Dad, caught up in the moment with them.

Nervous but intent, Dad purchased the gold band with its smallish diamond at Moray's Jewelers on the northwest corner of the intersection of Huron and Main, seriously depleting his meager savings. Mom still wears it.

With the greatest question of their lifetimes asked and instantly answered, the first hours and days of '47 whirled by, individual scenes in a collage of happiness and plans. Initially, the young couple set a wedding date for early June, only to change their minds, settling on the

Saturday after Easter. Weeks of preparation rolled continuously into good times with Dad working long hours at the hospital, spending any precious time off with Mom and her parents, and doing little more than sleeping in his small room on Packard Street. He received his letter of acceptance from the University of Michigan and prepared to begin psychology classes in September.

Mom accepted a position as a clerk in the offices of the political science department, not intending to enroll, but doing so when pressured by her father. "Why not?" he cajoled. "It's what you really want to do, and you can work and take a few classes and see how you like it."

"But Daddy, that means we'll both be in school at the same time."

"That's twice as good as having one of you in school. Darling, don't you remember our talks about 'seed money?' It's smarter to plant twice as many seeds; that way you can benefit from two crops."

Held on a spectacular, sunny afternoon at the old stone church on Washtenaw Avenue, the wedding was attended by both sets of parents and fifty or more family friends and young people there for Amy and Paul. Several young men from the Ann Arbor area who had known Amy's brother came to represent him. Two wore Army uniforms. Their presence pulled at Amy's heartstrings. As she walked down the aisle on her father's arm her thoughts tumbled, convinced Bryant was there smiling at the edge of the shadow where the angle of the sun met the church's stained glass windows, shading the side aisle.

Borrowing Grandma and Grandpa's faded-green pre-war Oldsmobile, the newlyweds' honeymoon took them to southern Ohio at Dad's suggestion. He wanted to visit Dancer and Miss Mattie Bigelow. He hadn't seen them in a little over a year and looked forward to checking on Dancer's progress, showing Amy where he'd worked, and introducing his bride to Miss Mattie.

The small towns of Michigan's southern neighbor rolled by, presenting a continuous display of the tranquility of endless farm fields interrupted by signs of growth with new homes beginning to dot the landscape in small clusters. Post-war America shrugged off the cloak of the gloom of that undertaking and returned to its former vibrancy;

perhaps displaying even greater energy as the young veterans, boys battle-hardened into men, returned to take their places in society. Colleges and universities staggered under the increased enrollment of soldiers home from battle. The war's survivors studied courtesy of the GI Bill designed and pushed through Congress by the American Legion in the early months of '44. New businesses sprang up everywhere and farms expanded, flourishing with the return of needed fuel and equipment. The mood of the nation reflected the optimism of the times.

Athens State Hospital sat atop the hill, the twin towers over its entrance raised in praise of the beautiful little city below them gracing the institution with its name. Spring conquered winter and the farms and orchards on the ridges shone with more new growth than Dad remembered. Walking the grounds together, Mr. and Mrs. Paul Conway, Jr., held Dancer's hands, guiding him between them–or perhaps he guided them; he was, after all, Ambassador of Goodwill, First Class. Dad called out buildings by their identifying letters and Dancer pointed to each one, obviously pleased at having his skill tested by the lesson's original teacher.

Content sitting side by side on the stone carriage steps as Mom and Dancer got to know each other, the three young people enjoyed the incredible view of the ponds and the groomed hillside sliding away across the valley to town, the Hocking River clearly discernable winding through its center. Instantaneous and obvious, the chemistry between Dancer and Mom easily eclipsed the silence imposed by Dancer's almost complete lack of spoken words, replacing it with a natural, easy companionship.

Greeting Dad by name with his excited repetition of, "Paul . . . Paul," within an hour Dancer added a new name to his vocabulary. At first hesitating then concentrating, working to form her name with increasing confidence, Dancer learned to say, "Am . . . ee, Aim . . . ee, Aim . . . ee, Amy," grinning widely as she nodded her approval of his pronunciation.

Exchanging looks and glances, each checking with Dad, searching for meaning in his expression, the young bride and the very special teenager slid smoothly into a comfortable relationship, each of their lives orbiting around the warmth of the sun Dad represented; Dancer's mentor, the CO, and Mom's young husband.

Miss Mattie Bigelow invited the newlyweds to dinner at her home. To their surprise, Dancer sat in the corner of the kitchen peeling potatoes. His paring knife moved slowly and the tip of his tongue escaped through pursed lips, a sign of total concentration.

"Oh, yes," Miss Mattie said. "If the weather's nice, Dancer walks home with me to have dinner; he's here once or twice a week, I guess. Then my husband walks him back to the hospital in the evening. He enjoys spending time with Dancer too, and my old legs are having trouble with all the walking they do during the day, especially the stairs at the hospital. I can hang onto their beautiful old banisters, but those stairs keep gettin' steeper; they're enough for me. One more trip up the hill to the hospital and back at the end of the day and I'd probably just sit down and cry."

"Mrs. Bigelow, it's very sweet of you to take care of Dancer like this," Amy said.

"Darlin', call me Mattie. This handsome fella you married is like family to us and we're so happy for both of you."

The heavy-set woman paused, looked around the room, then focused on Dancer, "Our kids are grown and moved out, you know, so our little house gets lonely and empty. Dancer's such a sweet young man it's a pleasure to share a meal with him and the doctors think it's good for him, kind of like a trial run at being out on his own. Old Doc Henry says someday Dancer's going to live on his own, but I've got my doubts. The hospital's his home and we're all his family."

"Is he happy, Miss Mattie?" Dad asked, still watching Dancer across the room.

"It's so hard to tell. The boy likes to work at most of the projects we find for him–he's good with food and kitchen jobs, you can tell by those potatoes. But the smiling mask he wears hardly ever giving us clues to what he's thinkin' about; that makes it hard to tell."

"It looks like he's grown taller since I saw him, but he's still a little frail; he's not going to ever be really a strong man or well muscled."

Mattie chuckled, "Paul darlin', maybe that's just how he's goin' to be; I suppose a lot of skinny kids end up skinny grown-ups. We're all different, aren't we? Look at me. I never get any taller, but I sure get rounder."

The next morning, the newlyweds said goodbye to Dancer and Miss Mattie in the shade of the front portico of the Athens State Hospital and drove west through Prattsville and McArthur heading for Chillicothe. They spent two days with Grandpa and Grandma Conway at the small farmhouse they were renting outside Washington Court House, Ohio. Dad showed Mom around the area, stopping at the school he attended and driving by the farms where he had worked.

Through three days, two flat tires, one awesome thunderstorm, and miles and miles of two-lane road together as man and wife, laughing and hugging, totally in love, they wound their way north, back to Ann Arbor to begin their life together.

* * * * *

Summer became fall and Mom and Dad's world became busier, juggling the schedules and demands of classes and homework while working as many hours as possible at their jobs. Settling into their new apartment, they scrimped and saved, gradually furnishing its empty rooms with hand-me-down furniture and odds and ends from second-hand stores.

The lesson they learned, the one we all learn if time and circumstance come together to teach us, is that, for newlyweds, money isn't even relevant. The sheer joy of sharing young lives greatly overshadows money's significance.

Just as Julie and I have enjoyed reminiscing about Christmases past, we've compared impressions of what life must have been like for our parents as young college students so soon to be parents and our impact upon their lives—yes, Julie and I came along in their early years together. We complicated their lives in a way no professor or textbook or midnight oil burned studying for a final exam ever could.

Grandpa Mike, the learned history professor, was a tease. He spiced his conversation with phrases that made our parents flinch, pretending panic and rushing to cover our much-too-young ears. Julie and I, picking up on the glint in his eyes and the first crinkled corner of his impending smile, paid special attention to his colorful expressions. Mom said he was a terrible influence. We found him fascinating.

One of his more memorable sayings involved the indelicate relationship between "a pot and a window," forming the basis of his earthy definition of the kind of financial hardships most young married couples endure. Figuratively, the pot in Grandpa's phrase represented the contrivance facilitating the most basic of bodily necessities; the window providing the portal to throw out the contents of the pot. Our parents possessed the pot and the window, barely, and nothing else mattered.

Central to the premise of remembering those years are the questions of how time passes too quickly and the way responsibility can either be accepted joyously or grudgingly. Confirmed by every photograph and loving, teasing testimonial, our addition to their world meant more happiness and lives bursting with activity and laughter during years that meld together in everyone's memories as good times.

Physicist or philosopher, each of us contemplates the substance of time. If a fluid it seems we would hear time gurgling against boulders as it cascades downstream or laps against the beaches of our lives; at a minimum the splash of time against birthdays ending in zeros needs to be audible given their significance. If a gas, we should be able to feel the breeze of months passing, the faint sensation of its movement against our faces, the subtle tussling of our hair as we turn to face the future. But no one ever testifies to any such physical, tangible effects. Perhaps the dilemma is that, whatever the substance of time, whether liquid or gaseous or merely a measure, young parents are carried along with it, unaware of any sensation of movement. Time happens.

Julie was born in the closing days of '48 between Christmas and New Year's, easily eclipsing the traditional, well-choreographed Porter holiday events with the anticipation and excitement of her arrival. I followed in the spring of '51. By all accounts, she was the perfect baby, the darling toddler, a perpetually cooing, smiling, happy child. I, on the other hand, was a challenge. Polite descriptions of my early years include terms like "curious" and "active" and "easily bored." Grandma Porter, by nature always speaking few but earnest and honest words, especially if a lesson could be learned from her portrayals, labeled me a malcontent. She called me a fledgling Dennis the Menace destined to keep everyone on edge, nervously aware of imminent disaster, listening for the next crash of falling dishware or children—okay, you must understand most small boys who read comic books and fashion a cape using a blue towel consider human flight a given. Besides, the garage roof wasn't that high and the bushes were soft and forgiving. I kept them busy.

Busy could be an understatement. The lives of parents of active toddlers revolve within the limited space of their new family's unique whirling dervish, untouched, disconnected from larger worlds beyond theirs. A natural, safe, and normal timeline is supposed to run from the day we paint a small bedroom, turning it into a nursery, to the eventual empty nest. We expect to be able to recognize our place along the length of that line. Sometimes, however, the depth of our involvement in the process means we can't objectively sense our position.

By comparison, passengers in hot-air balloons are immediately aware of the stillness of the air, as if there were no wind aloft, yet realize they're moving, propelled along by the wind at the whim of its currents. Most young parents, so occupied by daily events, are completely oblivious. Functionally, they're removed, isolated by their responsibilities from the movement of wind or time, immune to changing calendar pages, living day to day as life carries forward in a non-stop series of tiny events, diapers, toys, precious moments, and all the expected good things. There is no room in the process for bad things to happen.

Pilots of engineless gliders, like the occupants of the gondolas of those hot-air balloons, ride the skies enraptured by the same silence, the same perception of a lack of air movement. Their planes, towed to altitude and released, ride the crests and troughs of air currents. Lifted by thermal updrafts, they slip sideways cross-country, dipping a wingtip to salute the sky's beauty, and expend height in fair trade for distance. As they seek the next rising column of heated air, they move with the air like young parents riding the swells and dips of time.

Gliders and hot-air balloons aren't supposed to fall from the sky, but occasionally they do. Time, aloft on its wings of happiness, isn't supposed to crash, but, when least expected, it can.

Mom and Dad, as typical young parents, unaware of time passing, relished riding those air currents until '55 when polio stopped time. The disease blasted a huge gap in the unnoticed continuum of months and years, indelibly marking the occasion, changing their lives and its victim's future.

At the age of seven, their angel baby, the little girl encased in billowing clouds of sugar and spice, skipping and jumping and dancing in spinning circles of girlish delight, fell victim to a monster. Months later their darling daughter remained, but her life's dance steps stopped. A series of hinged metal braces and leather straps, changing in size and complexity as she grew to adulthood, captured and constrained the vitality of her step, but could not diminish her spirit.

The monster was polio, completing its reign of anguish nearly forty years after its first epidemic in the United States in 1916. It even crippled a U.S. president. Franklin Delano Roosevelt contracted the virus at the age of thirty-nine, twelve years before his first election to the White House. Always open about his affliction, FDR concealed the extent of his disability.

A knight of medicine, the doctor intent on slaying the dragon of the disease of the times, did his work right in Ann Arbor. Dr. Jonas Salk's miracle vaccine came along in time to save thousands of children from the horrible effects of the virus. Unfortunately, my big sister Julie somehow missed being among the two million children taking part in the first field trials of Dr. Salk's injected vaccine of inactivated virus.

My big sister Julie, the phrase always limited to acknowledgement of age not height, not only survived the sharp teeth and flaming breath of the dragon that crippled so many children but, after several dark months, thrived. If anything, the physical inconvenience of her shriveled left leg steered her life, focusing her attention on her future—the hospitals and doctor's offices and medicines and physical therapy she endured inspired her, creating a love of the healing arts, a central reason for being. In addition to the influences of caring people during her experiences as a polio patient, she no doubt absorbed some of her spirit, the need to help others, from our father by simple osmosis.

Julie also had a little help from a friend. Dancer came along to give her the patience and courage to get beyond the disease itself.

When he came into our lives, Julie was wrapped tightly in the grasp of a seven-year-old's kind of fear. Little kids can't understand the clinical, medical terminology spoken between the adults surrounding them. Doctors and parents and family members, intent on helping, infrequently realize they must paraphrase when explaining the effects of an illness to a child whose vocabulary and level of understanding are nowhere near their own. Sometimes adults can be too busy or too self-important to understand when and why a child *can't* understand. Dancer understood. His eyes showed his concern, clearly expressing empathy without the burden of big, foreign sounding words.

Over the next months, as Dancer became a regular visitor to our Ann Arbor, Michigan home on weekends, his affect on Julie was remarkable. Each time he found her struggling, her spirit so damaged and dejected by her situation that the joy and animation of her life were turned off, he naturally gravitated to her side, somehow aware of her suffering, sensing her need to be comforted.

Gently prodding her into a smile, tilting his head as he studied her face, his own smile coming first, he radiated a glow of life, a contagious human sincerity reaching out to her in her sadness, dispelling the gloom. Eventually his quiet, wordless counsel straightened her stance as she learned to walk in metallic supports, taught her to hold her head up even if her foot dragged, and returned the sunshine and confidence to her face; his contribution, as always, impossible to concisely explain, but obvious.

Six

year before Julie contracted polio, changing her life and perhaps setting its course, Dancer's life changed too; not as severely and nothing permanent, Dad intervened to ensure that. No crippling virus sickened him or ran unchecked through the ranks of the patients. Still uniquely Dancer, he remained almost the same; his luster only slightly tarnished by circumstance.

Like Julie, Dancer's resilience in the aftermath of adversity proved strong, foreshadowing responses to future challenges. As a child, Julie's destiny was affected by a cruel virus. Dancer's destiny would evolve over decades as he continually encountered cruelty at the hands of others; some well-intentioned, some not. Julie faced physical challenges due to the atrophy of a limb; Dancer faced discrimination in a society often bereft of human understanding.

During Julie's recovery, Dad received a letter from Mattie Bigelow. Unsure of how best to approach the situation she described, weeks passed. He found it difficult to consider Dancer's future while under the stress of his little girl's illness. Once able to think clearly again, he went to work evaluating how to help Dancer. He knew personal involvement tended to blur the edges of professional judgment.

Dancer, however, defied logical analysis; he was Dancer and he was very special. Something was there, intrinsic to his uniqueness, subliminally convincing Dad to continue his ties with Dancer, to strengthen them; not so much fearing a loss if their bond of friendship succumbed to time and distance, but recognizing Dancer's ability to help others, the way he gave so much back to those around him.

Attrition at Athens State Hospital had thinned the number of people looking out for Dancer's welfare. Unable to climb the hospital's long flights of stairs or walk its never-ending hallways, advancing arthritis forced Mattie Bigelow into retirement. The wonderful old nurse stayed in contact with her friends working at the hospital. Because of her love for Thomas "Tommy" Daniel Higgins, the gentle young man she called Dancer, she diligently monitored his welfare.

Within a month of Mattie's retirement, old Dr. Henry died of an apparent heart attack late one afternoon while sitting in his office in his battered oak swivel chair making notes on patient charts. The nurse who looked in on him twice thought he was napping, his head slumped forward, chin on chest, his fountain pen in his hand, stopped mid-sentence. The loss of his easy-going, grandfatherly guidance left the entire wing of the hospital he supervised without a sense of direction and cast Dancer's fate into new hands. Those now in charge of Dancer's life and duties, by some unfathomable determination, perhaps because they recognized he would perform any task without complaint, assigned him to the kitchen as a full-time dishwasher.

The nurses Miss Mattie worked with for so long kept her up to date. Through them she knew Dancer now endured long hours every day, overworked in a hostile if not dangerous environment. Limping on a cane and supported by her husband walking at her side, she went to visit Dancer on a rainy Sunday afternoon. Sitting together on a bench in the administration building's main hallway, what she found confirmed her suspicions. Pale and withdrawn, the young man responded to her calm voice, clearly pleased to be with her. Concealing her dismay, she observed the many fresh burns on his forearms.

Holding his pink and scalded hands, she hoped he would move

and sway in his private world of dance–but he didn't. Dancer's private orchestra rested, muted, waiting in silence for him to again direct their melodies. Beyond her concern for his physical condition, the old nurse, after hugging him goodbye, left in tears, alarmed at the deterioration of Dancer's spirit, the dimming of his natural spark.

* * * * *

A distinguished graduate of the University of Michigan, his diploma burnished with achievements as an honor student in psychology, Dad's career path had already taken him through three years with St. Joseph Mercy Hospital. Even in these early years his dedication was being noticed. After progressing through several more responsible roles since starting there as an orderly, the young manager established an office to coordinate the treatment of patients exhibiting mental and emotional symptoms. The procedures he originated moved patients seamlessly through a process guaranteeing complete medical treatment and a timely and humanely administered transfer to an institution devoted to their non-medical afflictions.

Two months before he received Miss Mattie's letter, and highly recommended by St. Joseph Mercy based on his work there, he'd accepted the position of assistant administrator at Ypsilanti State Hospital, a new institution on Willis Road in a rural area south of Ann Arbor.

Wanting to intercede on Dancer's behalf, he made calls and wrote letters seeking advice, grappling with the many legal and jurisdictional complexities he faced. Under the laws of the State of Ohio, Dancer was a ward of the state destined to reside permanently at Athens State Hospital. Unless deemed competent to live on his own by its physicians, his release into anyone's custody required the consent of one or both of his parents or a legal guardian acting on their behalf.

Fearing securing Dancer's release in order to move him to Michigan under his supervision was impossible, good news came as a result of Miss Mattie's diligence and the love the nurses at the hospital felt for Dancer. At her request, a nurse working on the floor Dancer occupied spent several quiet evenings, the patients already in their rooms, scouring every page of Dancer's records. On his yearly evaluation reports, the names of visitors he received, compiled from hospital guest records, were duly noted under a category titled Family Contacts. Mr. and Mrs. Paul Conway, Jr., were listed as family in '47, '50, and '53. Going back ten years in his file, Mattie's friend found a woman's name on the list at least once every two or three years.

Faulting age's heavy hands exerting their pitiless choke-hold on memory, Miss Mattie admitted completely forgetting the quiet, poorly dressed woman who visited Dancer, having met her on one occasion several years before. Together, Mattie and her friend pored over the hospital's old guest registry books searching for details accompanying the name. Mrs. Alice Freeman listed an address with each entry, a rural route outside Ellenboro, West Virginia, less than twenty miles east of Parkersburg. On one of the guest book entries three years earlier, Mrs. Freeman, in a strong, flowing script, identified herself in the Relationship to Patient column as "aunt." The search began; Dad's hope of locating Dancer's parents stirred by a single word inked on a line in an old guest register at the hospital.

*   *   *   *   *

A ham-like hand preceded the huge forearm reaching into the early afternoon sunshine from the porch's cool shadows, stretching around from within the doorframe, holding open the screen door.

"Yessir, she's right here, been expectin' ya'll," a deep voice offered in deference to Miss Mattie's struggling ascent of the narrow steps aided by my dad, the young man intent on assisting her.

"Thanks for seeing us, Mr. Freeman. I'm Paul Conway and this is Mrs. Bigelow who wrote your wife the letters asking about Tommy Daniel Higgins's family."

"Come right on in. Alice's waitin' there by the parlor. Just a bit nervous is all. She's been loyal to her sister these last years when it came to checkin' on the boy and stayin' in touch. I guess it's been a burden she didn't go lookin' for, but had to take care of, lovin' her sister like she does."

Alice Freeman finally came forward, standing timidly in her husband's shadow. The man, owner of the muscled forearm, introduced himself as Joseph, saying everyone called him Joe. The misshapen fingers of Mattie's arthritic hands gripped the woman's hand in quiet, firm appreciation. "This means a lot to us, Miss Alice," she said sincerely. "A whole lot. And my heart tells me you're doing the best thing for your sister's boy. Since you've seen him, I know you know what a very special, grand boy he is."

"The boy's gentle, been harmless all his life. Emma wrote me about him and, yes, I've seen it myself," Alice Freeman responded, her voice near breaking. "I've been checkin' on him and writing to his mother since she took him to Athens. It was the best thing for him and her–but havin' to take him there's been a weight on her heart, you gotta understand that."

"She did the right thing, Mrs. Freeman," Dad said.

"Call me Alice, please; we're not real fancy folks. And I've read Miss Mattie's letters over and over so I'm pretty sure you and her both love the boy too. You're sure welcome here, carin' for him the way you do."

She continued, as if in explanation of her feelings. "Emma was so beautiful nobody here ever rightly got over her runnin' away with Tommy Higgins. The pastor'd say I'm speakin' poorly of the dead, but that no-account only cared for drinkin,' n'he surely treated Emma and the boy poorly."

"I hope I wasn't too strong in my second letter, Alice, but after you wrote me about what happened to her husband, I had to write you what we remembered at the hospital from the day your sister and Tommy Higgins brought us the boy. We wondered if he was the boy's daddy. Then, havin' watched the boy for so long, I'd bet my stars he wasn't. That boy's too kind."

"My sister fooled our folks, both of 'em goin' to their graves believin' it, but I figured out her secret soon after she left here with

Tommy Higgins. Ellenboro's too tiny a place. Right after Emma got married and moved away, I caught the boy's real daddy staring at me and momma and daddy in church, his eyes all teary. Keepin' a secret's a lot easier than hidin' a broken heart. He was just a boy himself; too young for my sister."

"Does he still live here, Miss Alice? Does he know he has a son?" Dad asked.

"He mightn't have known for sure with Emma takin' up with Tommy Higgins and all, but he must have suspected when he heard Emma birthed a boy so soon."

"It don't matter now, anyhow," Joseph Freeman interjected. "Daniel's been gone for ten years now."

"He moved out of Ellensboro? Do you think he's still in West Virginia?"

"Nope, I mean he's gone, died goin' ashore at Normandy, June of '44 that was. Might've been twenty-nine or thirty years old but he was just a slip of a fella. Kinda bookish all his life; never married, a schoolteacher like his momma, never suited to heavy work let alone the army. One soldier who lived near here was there and said Daniel come out of the landin' boat packed in a bunch of soldiers and went down in water over his head. Never came up. Never got to the beach or fired a shot. Drowned right there. Carryin' all that stuff killed him before the Germans could."

"Does your sister know you know her secret?" Mattie asked Alice.

"When Daniel died in the war I wrote to her, not saying right out that I knew but she has to think I do. Either way, what's done is done and Emma's got a good life where she is–it just didn't start out the way anyone would have wanted it to. I've written to her about what you're askin' for and she wrote back. Got her letter right here," she said, handing the envelope to Dad. The postmark was Blissfield, Michigan.

"She's in Michigan?"

"Sure is, moved there with a woman named Flossie Duncan, an older woman from Cincinnati. Emma surely loved that woman."

"Miss Mattie mentioned a kindly woman helping your sister, you wrote about her in your letter, but you said 'loved.' Has Miss Duncan passed away?"

"Oh, yes, several years ago now, meant the world to Emma though, like a momma to her, more of a grandma, I guess. That dear lady bought a farm in Michigan and set my sister up with a new life after Tommy Higgins died; everyone there thought Emma was kin of Miss Flossie's sister's husband. Like my letter said, I never knew for sure what happened to Tommy, only somethin' about him getting' drunk an' tryin' to stick a knife in a man who used to be a policeman. Got hisself killed. There I go again, speakin' poorly of the dead, but he was a devil, a regular bag full of devils that one was."

"Your sister, Emma, does she still live on Miss Duncan's farm in Michigan?"

"Oh, no, she married a fine man from right there, a widower. Two little girls he had, real young ones, and his wife died. Emma wrote he came courtin' her with flowers and he's been the most wonderful husband since; no reflection on you Joe Freeman, you've always been the best husband for me, I'm just tellin' how Emma found her a good man."

Dad read the letter from Dancer's mother, Mrs. Freeman's sister Emma, slowly evaluating its contents, then turned to Miss Mattie.

"She says she'll talk with me about Dancer, that her husband knows about him and it would be good to have him closer so she could visit him."

"Why do you call him Dancer?" Mrs. Freeman asked, a perplexed look on her face.

Mattie clarified. "That's what we've always called him at the hospital, Miss Alice. It's the name the other nurses and I gave him. Nothin' wrong was meant by it, it was just our way of lovin' him for the cute way he stands and dances by himself."

Alice Freeman began crying and turned away from her guests and her husband. Short, sharp sniffles strengthened into long sobs that wracked her until she regained control, holding a handkerchief wet with tears to her face.

"I'm sorry," she said, wiping her eyes. "It's just that Emma wrote me over and over about that years ago, when Tommy Daniel was little, about how she could soothe him when he was afraid, holding his hands. He'd hold her hands and dance with her."

"So that's how it started. We named him right, didn't we?" Mattie said, near tears herself.

"Joseph, can we drive to Michigan so we can be there with Mr. Conway when he talks with Emma? It's a long ways but I'd really like to see my sister; it's been too long."

∗   ∗   ∗   ∗   ∗

Dr. McClennan came through the latched, wooden-slat arbor gate in the fence in the side yard of our home in Ann Arbor, ducking and turning his head to stay below the tendrils of its flowering vines, his black two-door businessman's coupe parked at the curb. I can still remember him driving up in that car like it was yesterday. I think it was a '50 Ford sedan; plain looking, its hood and trunk square and stubby, its roofline slightly rounded, utilitarian not stylish, almost devoid of chrome trim. There was nothing ostentatious about our wonderful, caring, friendly pediatrician with a clear deep voice that seemed to rise from the bottoms of his shoes. I heard that voice again forty years later. Somehow old Doc McClennan bequeathed it to a country singer named Randy Travis. And, yes, he did make house calls; people have trouble believing that in today's world. Now specialists practice medicine in large office buildings, hiding in rows of little examining rooms, sequestered behind high counters staffed by scurrying clerical help all silently cursing the needless complexities heaped upon them by medical insurance providers.

Tall, silver-haired, and thin, the good doctor was always there for Julie and me when we were kids, his voice soft and low and reassuring, just a natural part of our lives. Somehow he gave us those childhood immunization shots without letting them hurt and treated our bad colds and ear infections and watched for the normally anticipated diseases like chickenpox. He diagnosed Julie when polio struck, and, like every polio case he saw, Julie's broke his heart, chipping it away a bit at a time.

Calling out to Julie, who was being rolled about the tall green grass of the backyard in her wheelchair by Dancer, Dr. McClennan approached and knelt down in front of her, reaching to hold her hand, studying her eyes. "Is this young man taking good care of you, honey?"

"Oh, yes. This is Dancer, he's my friend," Julie answered, unbridled joy in her expression. "Dancer lives where Daddy works, but he can come and play. We're going to the park after lunch."

The doctor stood up, appraising Dancer, whose gaze locked on his face in unblinking fascination, reacting to Julie's obvious happiness in seeing the tall man, quietly awaiting whatever came next.

"Well, hello Dancer," Dr. McClennan said. "I happen to know your real name is Tommy Daniel, but I'll be glad to call you by whichever name you like best."

"Dancer," the young man said to the sky, recognizing his name and repeating it, looking away, addressing neither Julie nor the doctor.

The doctor paused, observing Dancer's response, obviously considering its implications, then answered.

"Dancer it is, son," he said, reaching out to give Dancer a hug. "I think you and Julie make a good team. I want you to have fun, but I want you to be careful too. Can you do that for me?"

A resounding "Yes, sir" came from the darling little girl in the wheelchair. The young-looking man in his mid-twenties held the wheelchair's grips as the doctor waved, leaving the yard by the same gate he entered. His visit showed his concern. It was his way of checking up on Julie's progress; most likely he glimpsed her in the yard as he drove by headed for a house call in our neighborhood.

After lunch, Dancer did wheel Julie through Burns Park. I tagged along on my bike, trying to maintain my balance at a very slow speed as I accompanied them, the balloon tire on the front wheel of my Schwinn jerking back and forth. The park was huge, or at least it seemed that way then; it looks much smaller to me now. Off in the distance was the round top of the big hill, its summit bald, its grass worn off showing tan clay. The big hill wasn't that big but it was by far the best sledding hill, much higher and steeper than the nearby flat-topped little hill next to our favorite softball diamond over by the Granger Street park entrance. A large, covered sandbox watched over the expanse of open fields where the ice rink, surrounded by its wrinkled enclosure of heaped, plowed snow, dominated the landscape in winter. The old log cabin was still standing then, years before the new brick Parks and Recreation building was built on almost the same site. Over along Wells Street, the bookmobile stopped two afternoons a week all summer, a regular attraction for Julie and me. We grew up roaming those streets together as I piloted her wheelchair or, later on, as we walked slowly together at the pace mandated by her leg brace.

Hurrying to where Dancer wheeled Julie under the shade of a large tree near the three-story brick school building, I let my bike fall, fenders clanging, over on its side. I joined them as they stared at the gate of the empty wading pool encircled by chain-link fencing. Julie was explaining how it used to be filled with water so the neighborhood kids could cool off on hot summer days, running in the mist of the tall pipe fountain which sprayed water straight up in the center of the shallow concrete circle. Dancer listened intently.

Back then, we never questioned whether he understood what we were telling him. It really didn't matter; he was always there for us and he listened as if our words carried directions to pots of gold at the ends of rainbows. Julie missed the splashing water and loud happy voices of children cavorting in the wading pool, wondering why it sat empty and abandoned, with grass growing in cracks in the concrete. Years later, as a physician, she understood. The virus of polio lived in those innocent-looking waters in the '50s, attacking laughing children playing in the summer sun, so the wading pools had been drained, their gates chained and locked. Dr. Salk came along, but it was too late for too many of the kids who frolicked there.

Leg braces and wheelchairs didn't seem to register with Dancer as sources of heartbreak or anguish. Perhaps his years at Athens State

Hospital, surrounded by people with crutches and wheelchairs and handicaps inflicted by life and the caprice of war, kept him from noticing. Perhaps in his simple way of loving others, such inconveniences didn't hold meaning. He cared for Julie and enjoyed being with her, no strings attached to his sense of companionship, and displayed devoted concern for her welfare.

To him, she was no different than anyone else, and his perception of that quickly rubbed off on her. She would learn not to be different. She had already unquestioningly accepted Dancer–her daddy loved Dancer so it must be all right even if Dancer never talked like other grownups.

*   *   *   *   *

The informal tour took the two men down the long hallways of Ypsilanti State Hospital until they ended up in Dad's office in the administrative wing. Twenty years older, Dr. McClennan, always tall and healthy, showed no signs of fatigue. Their conversation had kept pace with their long walk, interrupted only when Dad said hello to doctors and nurses or checked quickly on individual patients who called out to him. First impressions of the huge institution usually centered on the scale of its buildings and the expanse of its grounds, later including a golf course, off Willis Road. The wise old pediatrician, like my dad, considered the bricks and mortar and acres of land of any facility as only a physical means to an end; the staff and the patients were the real life of the hospital.

Finally able to speak without interruption or eavesdroppers, Dr. McClennan asked, "Paul, how did you manage to get legal custody of Tommy Daniel?"

Dad laughed. "It was a lot easier than I thought it would be. His mother moved to Michigan in 1938 right after she left him at Athens State Hospital. I met Dancer four years later when I started working there." Dr. McClennan knew Dad's history as a conscientious objector.

"It's quite a story, but her first husband wasn't Dancer's biological father, and he's long dead anyway. It took the original birth certificate his mother had kept, and the help of her lawyer. He's a real old character; we drafted a custodial guardianship that lets me act on Dancer's behalf. He has a full power of attorney from Tommy Daniel's mother."

"Has his mother visited him? Doesn't she care about him at all?"

"Oh, it wasn't like that. She loved him, still does, life just got in the way. She couldn't make a go of it with him along. Since I moved him here, she's been to visit several times. I'm not sure he recognized her at first and then, as they sat together and she talked to him, I could see the awareness, the connection come back to him. He knew. He might not have remembered what those early years had been like, but he knew. She knew too; I think it must have been pretty tough leaving him at the asylum."

"How did it happen? Why would a young mother abandon her child like that?"

"Life forced her to give him up; she realized she wouldn't be able to care for him. Her husband was no good and, given some good advice about her own future and the boy's, she made the only decision she could."

"That must have been excruciating for her. I stopped to check on Julie one afternoon and Tommy Daniel was out in the yard with her. He seems kind and gentle, but he's got some obvious learning and speech impairments. Without examining him, I can only say he looks healthy, maybe a little too thin, and his arms have recent burns on them."

"You're having difficulty with his nickname, Dancer, aren't you? It really is okay to call him that, he responds to it."

"Forgive me. I'm just not used to it. It's probably easy for you. You've known him for what, twelve or thirteen years now?"

Dad laughed again. "You're right. The years have reinforced it for me. But there's a story to the name Dancer. His mother said it came from behavior he exhibited when he was a very small child. He dances. And when I first saw him in 1942, I can remember him standing at a window, leaning on the sill and looking outside, and suddenly he began to sway and move. The music's inside. I've often thought it meant he was happy or content or felt safe."

"Does he still do it?"

"Not often, but I saw him begin to shuffle his feet one day when he was holding the grips of Julie's wheelchair. He was that happy just being with us. The music in his soul played and he responded. We were standing at the curb waiting to cross the street. He's happiest when he has a job to do. The burns you saw came from the dish-washing he was doing. After too many hours, I suppose he'd get too tired and bump into the hot dish racks."

"And you have absolute trust in him, even when he's around your children?"

"Yes, I do. He *is* a child, always will be, but a very unique child. When he interacts with others, neither age nor gender seems to even register with him. He's just there for whomever he's with and he connects with people instantly. I've seen more than a few adults become a little unnerved by it. If there's any risk, it's probably to Dancer. *He* could be much too trusting in the wrong situation."

"Sorry if I was prying, Paul, but I had to ask. You've trusted me to care for your two beautiful children and suddenly this new person, Dancer, see I can say it, well, he comes along and I guess I was just concerned."

"You weren't prying. And remember, you were the shoulder we leaned on when Julie came down with polio. We couldn't have gotten through it without you. This is difficult to explain, but you had an able assistant in your treatment of Julie. Dancer's been so good for her–that's the psychologist in me speaking now. I've stood in awe of the way he's turned the shining lights in that little girl's eyes back on, and you know it was difficult for her, polio doesn't leave a child much to smile about."

"Julie was bright and excited when she introduced Dancer to me. To say she's comfortable with him would be an understatement," the pediatrician said.

"When I decided to help Dancer and move him to Michigan, maybe, somehow subconsciously, I was aware of how he'd affect Julie. Remember, I'd known him in Athens and watched him greet visitors and run errands. I saw him sit with shell-shocked soldiers, calming them. And I must have told you the story of the young GI with the pistol. What Dancer did that day was amazing. I still can't understand how he stood in that hallway, facing a gun, and saluted, but he did. There's something there, something special. I don't think anyone's written a thesis about it, probably because we have yet to understand the world he lives in. Who knows, perhaps that's what I'm supposed to do someday."

"Listening to you describe Dancer, I'm beginning to think he's a good teacher. You and I and a lot of others need to be better students. The world of medicine needs to learn from him. We're too quick to categorize people, putting labels on them. There's been a lot of progress, especially lately with new pharmaceuticals. I'm very proud of you for what you've done in that field. And the lobotomies have ended. No matter what method was used to perform the procedure, they were horrible. We can't let abuses like that happen again."

"We have a long way to go," Dad said. "When I watch Dancer interact with my wife and children or the patients and staff here, the sheer goodness in him makes me recognize how critical our task is. A lot of people like Dancer can't speak for themselves and they deserve good care and protection."

* * * * *

They were two idealists, a respected pediatrician and a young psychologist who would become a great professor. The exhilaration of a nation back from recent wars had spawned a generation of young men like my father. They were eager to help others. Dr. McClennan had already established his credentials in that noble regard. Dad went on to pursue a lifelong career dedicated to those he cared for; Dr. McClennan continued his. Each man put the trauma of the global conflicts of WWII and Korea in the past. Both men would strive to keep their word, toiling for decades, committed to caring for others, those often unable to speak for themselves. Both succeeded.

Seven

Our pediatrician, Dr. McClennan, and Dad both lived up to their personal convictions, each in their own way, over years and years of caring for others. Dad recognized the need and came right out and stated it that day long ago in his office at Ypsilanti State Hospital, identifying his purpose in life. Each man cared for and protected those they served, their personal contributions remembered by hundreds, perhaps thousands.

Years later, when Dad died in 1994, many came to the funeral home out of respect to stand near his memory. Friends and associates in attendance knew they would miss being with him until the day they too received the call, joining him at the same ultimate destination–a destination he was always aware of even if we didn't recognize the clues he gave us.

When parting, some say, "See ya." Dad always said, "See ya when we get there," looking down over the tops of his glasses and making a silly hand motion like Roy Rogers casually firing a chrome-plated six-shooter into the air. As kids, we found this habit, this different turn of phrase, annoying; another grown-up trying to be cute. We asked ourselves why he couldn't just say, "See ya" like everybody else.

The wisdom of his words, in retrospect, is a paradox, and he no doubt knew it. Now he was *there*. He beat us to the destination he always alluded to. He didn't wear his faith on his sleeve, but it was always just below the surface of life's lessons as he taught them to us.

Thinking about it, that was the way it was supposed to be, he was destined to get *there* first. Any other sequence would have been unnatural. Children aren't supposed to predecease parents like Mom's brother, my uncle Bryant, who died in WWII. And, as I learned when Dad passed the secret on to me, Uncle Bryant wasn't killed in action.

In the closing months of the war, my grandfather, Professor Michael Porter, found out from fellow university professors who worked with the Department of Defense that his son, Bryant Porter, had actually been murdered by the Germans along with over eighty other unarmed U.S. Army soldiers captured in Belgium. The massacre took place at Baugnez Crossroads, an intersection of rural roads the Americans called Five Points, outside the tiny village of Malmedy in the Ardennes Forest in Belgium. The Malmedy Massacre; it was the second day of the Battle of the Bulge.

For most of her life, my mother, Amy Porter Conway, believed her brother was killed by German artillery fire, the forest around him blasted to smoldering shards. We deceived her. Dad knew the truth and made me promise never to tell her what really happened. I kept my word. He believed knowing members of a German SS battalion murdered Bryant in cold blood would only deepen her sense of loss and obscure her memories of her brother as a soldier killed fighting for his country in a just war.

Dad knew that hour, those terrible minutes just before one p.m. on a Sunday afternoon in mid-December 1944, represented a black hole in human history, a savage time when even the rules of war were displaced by blood rage–and the rage went on. Four days later Fragmentary Order 27, issued by HQ, 328th Infantry, directed that SS troops were to be shot on sight. Sixty German POW's were executed. Atrocity bred atrocity. Grandpa Mike told Dad and Dad told me. Another of history's dirty little secrets stayed alive passed to yet another generation. The men of Battery B of the 285th Field Artillery Observation Battalion, Uncle Bryant included, would never be forgotten. Maybe Dad, the conscientious objector, was right about war all along.

The year before she retired, a fellow professor researching a book on WWII came across Bryant's name on the list of U.S. victims of the Malmedy Massacre. With good intentions, he expressed his condolences to mom about the tragic way her brother had been murdered. In her wisdom, she accepted the truth and forgave us for keeping it from her all those years; she'd always known the ugliness of her brother's war, but it had finally come home to rest on her personal loss.

Dr. McClennan couldn't join us in our celebration of dad's life when it ended. He had received the call and bid us farewell years ago. There in spirit, he floated through my thoughts and Julie's thoughts as we looked at all the faces around the room, aware of those remembered but outlived. Some countenances showed seriousness, some wore smiles. An occasional laugh erupted and turned heads when someone recounted a memory that, by reflex, necessitated a sincere guffaw in loving appreciation.

Although we wished he were here, the wonderful, ageless, tall gray-haired pediatrician with the deep voice slipped out of our lives gradually until he was gone and we hadn't even noticed his departure. I think the last time I went to his office for an appointment was for a physical exam so I could play football in junior high. Then the years snuck past and I grew up and went off to college and married. He was replaced by other doctors in other places, my childhood caregiver relegated quite naturally to memories of childhood. Years later, before he passed away, Grandpa Mike told me that when Dr. McClennan retired, turning his office in the old house on Hill Street over to two young pediatricians, he packed up everything and moved somewhere out in the vast, arid Southwest. For several years he worked as a doctor on an Indian reservation, continuing to care for children, continuing his life of service to others, his only remuneration their love.

Sadly, I lost track of him. Doing so wasn't any kind of a lack of respect on my part, only an accumulation of years and distance and circumstance acting to pull our lives apart. He was memorable; his was the kind of integrity taken for granted in those years and often sorely missed today. He stood out, setting an example worth emulating. I really did wish he could be here for Dad, and, selfishly, for Julie and me, but since we thought of him, maybe he was.

Others came to remember Dad who displayed the same fundamental integrity as our pediatrician, although in very different ways. Those in attendance included past presidents of the university, members of its Board of Regents, fellow professors, students who pursued careers in psychology and continued to hold him in esteem, nuns from St. Joe Hospital, doctors, lawyers, bankers, and Dancer. Dancer lacked the words to tell stories about Dad, but his life and his role in Dad's career and the magic he brought to all our lives represented an integral part of Dad's life story.

Two small children holding hands, a boy and a girl younger than Julie and I had been way back then, darted through the legs of the crowd standing about the large room in the funeral home where no funeral was being held. It was a remembrance, just the way Dad wanted it, his physical presence reduced to ashes in a simple green, corroded copper can from the shelves of a long forgotten room in the basement of Athens State Hospital. As family, we knew the story of the unusual container.

For decades the patients who died at the five-hundred-room facility were buried in hillside cemeteries on its grounds, their resting places marked with simple markers bearing only a number. In the early years, separate journals were kept for men and women. Too late, someone realized the numbers on the markers were being duplicated, the same number given to a man as to a woman and vice versa. Two markers with the same number stood at separate burial spots, leaving family members who came to visit the graves of loved ones unsure of their location; perhaps adorning a stranger's resting place with fresh flowers.

Over many years and thousands of patients, as the little cemeteries filled up, cremation became a popular alternative. The asylum stored the cremated remains of patients in copper cans on the shelves of basement rooms with their numbers, like those on the tombstones, each recorded in a registry and marked on the lid of a copper can. Copper, not tin; they didn't want them to rust. With an amazing, ironic similarity, over years of storage in damp, subterranean rooms, carefully inked numbers disappeared, obliterated in the accumulated coating of green corrosion claiming each copper can until, once again, like tombstones with duplicated numbers, it was impossible to tell whose remains were in which can.

The patients, most of whose identities were already casualties of their years of residence in the institution, abandoned if not forgotten by their families, crossed into a greater abyss, their identities lost to eternity. Living in the unique, separate world they lived in and exiting it without fanfare, they may have preferred anonymity.

Dad looked at life as a transitory condition to be lived to the best of one's abilities; its physical trappings, the flesh and blood of life, of no importance when life was finished. To Dad a person's principles mattered, and what they accomplished if it could be measured in how it helped others.

He chose to be cremated, asking that his ashes, until sprinkled along his favorite footpath through the woods, be stored temporarily in one of the unused copper cans from a shelf in Athens, Ohio. Those of us who knew the story smiled as we looked at the green can resting on a table in a corner of the large room. It was history and Dad had grown into his new role as a part of that history, not lost, not forgotten, only different; moving on, making room for us to step up to our own destinies.

Those unaware of the story of the copper cans studied Dad's with bemused expressions, nonplussed, confused by its grimy surfaces and plain, cylindrical configuration as if fearing it was part of a new trend, a sacrilegious display of earthly remains, sinfully presented in ancient popcorn tins.

As more and more people came, two men in dark suits slid back the folding partition between two viewing rooms to open the area to accommodate the crowd. I continued watching the little boy and girl. Dad was watching them; I felt his smile in the room as he watched and listened.

From one end of the room to the other, a steady hum of voices created a sense of activity, told stories about him; anecdotes were shared and cherished memories recounted. His friends and colleagues stepped back in time to visit the occasions where Dad's presence, his life, changed their lives and their futures, often steering their careers.

Lives intersect and each moment of passing becomes an almost tangible experience, remembered even when one of those involved is lost to the normal cycle of living and dying. The way in which a person is remembered, in Dad's view, represented the only form of immortality any of us should ever hope for–he believed we live on as long as anyone still alive remembers us fondly. Then, and only then, do we slip quietly into the realm of those who came before, our faces smiling or serious in grainy family photos with our names penciled on the back, relegated to a dusty cardboard box with thirty others.

Many in this room would go on remembering Dad for years to come. Both my sons would cherish his memory. My oldest, Tommy, fourteen, and my youngest, Danny, eleven, both idolized their Grandpa. He'd been there for them and, although they were still too young to understand it, they'd been there to round out the last years of his life, giving him back so much of the joy he'd given us all. Yes, my wife and I named them Thomas and Daniel after Dancer, Thomas Daniel Higgins. Each carried the same middle name, Paul, so that Dad's legacy moved forward through their names as well as their smiles and tiny facets of the look of their eyes and the shapes of their facial features. My sons would be able to look back on childhood memories of Dad just as Julie and I remembered Grandpa Mike and Grandma Rebecca. The strength of generations would again act, fostering a sense of permanence and origins in everything my boys remembered, every shared event of their early lives connected to a prior life; the past moving easily and naturally through time with them.

Sometimes events are seen clearer in retrospect than they ever could have been seen at the time. Ralph Waldo Emerson said it beautifully: "The years tell us much that the days never knew."

Emerson made us think with his words, Dad made us think with the changes in the world of health care accomplished through his initiatives. Many more mentally and emotionally challenged patients now received care as individuals of worth, not society's castaways. It wasn't perfect, nothing is; mistakes are still made and some calloused people still end up miscast as caregivers and bureaucrats still push paper. But Dad's life made a difference. Progress was made on his watch. I was proud to be his son.

I walked to the center of the long rectangular room and stood on the spot where, a moment before, two little children frolicked. From that vantage point, trying not to be too obvious, I turned in a slow, continuous circle, scanning the faces of all those in attendance. The clear feeling of Dad's presence and the wisdom of Emerson's words struck me, carrying the soft impact of understanding, each meaning more significant by the occasion. The maturity forced upon each of us by the passing of generations made its way to me and I was ready; Dad's lifelong teachings had prepared me well. I stepped forward, accepting the baton handed me in the foot race called life, knowing suddenly I, too, must begin to consider its approaching finish line.

* * * * *

As I studied faces, I wondered whether Dad ever really understood the positive effect his life had on others. He told me several times in his should-have-been-retired-but-wasn't years, aware his health was declining, that time seemed to have gotten away from him. His concern always returned to dwell on his role as a father, worried his career took too much of his time, causing him to shortchange his children. A great many fathers look back over their lives and face the same question. We reassured him it was all right, that he was there for us when we needed him, telling him, in turn, how perhaps we went off on our own too early, that, conversely, we weren't there for him and Mom when they were older and needed us.

It was true he found himself unable to retire gracefully. The thought of sitting idle in life's rocking chair offended his work ethic. With no mandatory retirement age for full professors, Dad kept going, cutting back his class load after his seventieth birthday only to use the hours it gave him to further his research and complete yet another book, until God tapped him on the shoulder and time was up.

I looked across the room and found Mom talking to my youngest son, Danny. She spotted him sitting alone, much too alone, in a far corner of the room, eyes downcast, studying the toes of dress shoes purchased for the occasion. Before I could wind my way through the crowd to reach them, she took his hand and asked him to accompany her. I intercepted them as they reached the corner display of photographs flanking Dad's ashes in the old copper canister.

"Danny," she said as much to me as to him, "this is going to be hard to understand, but I know it will make sense to you someday. Look at all these wonderful photographs. Look carefully; take a real close look at your grandpa."

In the sidelong look of a child reaching to be older than his birthdays, he glanced up at me and moved to stand so close to my side I could feel the weight of his body against my hip. I put my arm around his shoulder. He continued to hold fast to his grandmother's hand, leaning forward at the waist to study the photos, a force of will holding back tears.

"Your grandpa loved you and Tommy with all his heart. Now he wants you to know he'll always be with you–that he's only gone physically and he can never be taken from our thoughts and memories. See this picture of you and Grandpa in the sailboat, the little one he used to teach you boys to sail? I think you were about six years old. He's right there, Danny. He's in the picture and he's in your heart and mine and your daddy's; he belongs to all of us."

*   *   *   *   *

If the good friends and acquaintances who came to celebrate Dad's life showed consternation over the green, corroded can containing his ashes, it was nothing compared to their reaction when the Yoopers arrived and the real show began. First impressions really can rock. Dad's other world would prove alien to most of them with the exception of several close friends from the university who had stayed with him and Mom up on Lake Huron.

I knew the doors would be opening at any moment. Just after the shriek of worn brakes, I heard the low, grinding, rhythmic hum of the high-mileage diesel engine of a casino bus idling under the portico entrance at the side of the funeral home. Glancing outside through the main hallway, my suspicions confirmed, the garish lettering on the airport shuttle-sized bus was final proof of their arrival. Gurgling and grumbling, happy at surviving its six-hour run, the bus leaned forward on exhausted front wheels catching its breath. It was just like Thompson to leave it sitting there running while he escorted his dozen passengers up the short flight of stairs and in the door–some habits die hard. I wondered if he thought to check the overhead clearance and doubted it; the practical things that bothered us Trolls didn't even occur to Thompson Crow. Yes, he was a lifelong Yooper, having been born and raised in the Upper Peninsula, a child of its wildly changing seasons, while, in his vision of life, we were new settlers. Yoopers less than graciously applied the title Troll to anyone from Lower Michigan, those unfortunate enough to have been raised under the bridge, or below the bridge as the Yoopers would say. The bedraggled delegation filed in quietly, nodded to my mother and, sensing as much as seeing the focal point of the occasion, immediately moved lock-step toward the display of photographs in the corner.

Dr. Marshall, Dad's loyal office and fishing partner of many years, a regular summer visitor to the U.P., turned to observe the spectacle. A few years older than Dad, he stood waiting, stooped with age, his hands clasped in front of an ample belly. With only a wispy fringe of gray-white hair on his head, a massive white furry eyebrow traversed his forehead, a B-movie caterpillar paused above still-sparkling eyes. Dad always said old Dr. Marshall could mesmerize a classroom; his students loved his way of bringing psychology to life. Enjoying the scene, the diminutive old educator swallowed a chuckle, knowing what was coming.

Conversations stopped mid-sentence, heads turned. PhD's accustomed to speaking to auditoriums full of attentive, respectful students found it impossible to prevent their jaws from dropping for a second, but, to their credit, instantly regained professorial composure.

Dancer stood and smiled, saying, "Chief," in a loud clear voice when Thompson Crow entered the room; his appellation startling, but perfectly correct.

Thompson's western-cut jacket, pressed plaid snap-button shirt with oversized collar, and bolo tie secured by a large, silver eagle medallion were worn out of respect. Pulled tightly back and fastened into a long ponytail, coal-black hair showed not a trace of gray, although his weathered face spoke of late middle age. Faded blue jeans were worn out of necessity; the only kind of pants he owned. Sharp-pointed, shiny silver toe caps on his western boots peered out under the long, straight-hemmed bottoms of his jeans; a nice touch completing an ensemble few men could wear convincingly.

The lights of the room bounced off the visible pattern of scales on his boots for which a very large snake forfeited its life and for which Thompson paid more than the balance of his wardrobe. Walking directly to my mom, the chief, tribal council president, and casino operator clasped both her hands in his and, eyes glistening, slowly nodded as he studied her, gauging her strength in the face of grief. His wife, Kathy, still beautiful with a touch of silver in the hair at her temples, stood with him waiting to give Mom a hug.

"It is a loss to all of us, Dr. Amy." Thompson Crow could never call her just by her first name. "He became one with our people, part of our family, too."

"Thank you, Thompson." Mom didn't share his sense of required formality. "He's at peace. He learned much of that peace living in your community on the lake. You accepted him, and Dancer, and us, and made it possible for him. You were a great friend."

"Chief," Dancer said again, causing Thompson Crow to turn in his direction.

"Hello, Fawn Talker. It is good to see you."

By then, I'd joined the clustered group of Yoopers admirably led by Chief Crow and his wife, bringing with me the first contingent of Dad's fellow professors to begin making introductions. Dancer instinctively turned to face us, joining ranks with his Yooper friends.

Life is full of surprises, and men and women and their families can successfully live in two worlds. Our family did. And in Dad's last years, I believe he was actually more comfortable as a Yooper, relishing its tranquility, sharing Dancer's world just as Dancer shared his world for so many years. They were both at home on the bay on Lake Huron. Now Dancer lived on, a confirmed Yooper, responsible for sunrises out of the open waters to the east and sunsets over the Les Cheneaux island chain. Oh, yes, and for being there for all the animals who vied for his attention.

As Thompson Crow acknowledged when he renamed Dancer, the remarkable little white-haired man of few words spoke at length without words with the fawns and does of the surrounding woods. His ability to do so, even under the aloof but watchful eyes of heavily antlered bucks, astounded our fellow Troll settlers and set him apart to the members of Chief Crow's tribe, marking him as a man to be respected; his unspoken words close to the land and sky.

* * * * *

Flushed with pent-up anger, Harold Burnette's face, as usual, barely constrained caustic commentary due to explode.

"How was the trip?" I asked; a poorly chosen straight line I immediately regretted.

The old couple, neighbors on Bay Drive, cringed. Harold's wife sought a quick escape from the impending storm, found one, and slunk away out of the line of fire. The explosion came.

"Crazy bastard ran the left lane of I-75 most of the way. Then he'd pass on the right, running right up the taillights of a semi before cutting back in. We almost jumped ship at the Big Boy in West Branch. God help us."

He paused momentarily to catch his breath, "You riding home with us, Dancer?"

"Yes, he is," I volunteered, answering for Dancer as Dad had done for so many years.

It turned out my rush evening drive north the week before to pick up Dancer, bringing him back the next morning, was absolutely the right thing to do. The doctors at the hospice tactfully avoided predicting how much time Dad had left and I didn't want to ask them; based on intuition and a feeling Dad's strength was waning, I figured it was time and they should be together.

During his illness, I witnessed Dad's effect on the nursing staff at the hospital; they all fell in love with him. The combination of Dad and Dancer, the small, quiet man sitting patiently by Dad's bedside all day every day at the hospice, was overpowering. The professor who smiled even when the pain medication couldn't cut the mustard and the little man who kept wordless vigil over his friend captured their hearts. Everyone except Dancer wept when Dad closed his eyes for the last time–I genuinely believe Dancer understood, knowing his lifelong friend and mentor was stepping into a better world, his responsibilities here finished. He'd been by Dad's side until the end when Dad left us to go *there*. Now it was time for Dancer to return to his home in the woods and his duties, watching nature's creatures. His extended family from the shores of Lake Huron would take him home and make sure he was settled in and safe.

His feathers really not ruffled by Harold Burnette's venting, Thompson Crow still felt the need to retaliate, struggling to suppress a grin. "Come on, Harold, I'm a good driver, you know I watch NASCAR all the time. I'll make it up to you–when we get home I'll tell you which dollar slots are set loose."

"*If* we get home," Harold Burnette said, mumbling the Lord's name in vain and offering in colloquial terms loud enough to make the minister flinch ten feet away that Chief Crow's mother had fleas, chased cars, and was known to bark at the mailman.

"I always thought the slots were fixed," I responded to no one and everyone.

"Jesus, Conway, we've always known Thompson keeps them tight. It's payback for our economic oppression of his ancestors," Harold Burnette, Bay Drive's curmudgeon, grumped aloud, the fire in his words quenched.

For the next twenty minutes the diverse group mingled, always on the edge of an oil and water separation, requiring frequent stirring to maintain their forced combination. Finally, comfortable in the unanimous realization that everyone there, regardless of wealth or status or intellect or education, or lack of any of those qualities, came to honor Dad, they turned in unison when the minister walked to the lectern and spoke up, gaining their attention.

The short service was exactly what Dad would have wanted; long on sentimentality, short on praise for his accomplishments. Even Grandpa Conway, a minister from southern Ohio, would have approved, although, by lifelong habit, feigning umbrage to the group's casual approach to eulogizing Dad, favoring a stricter, more traditional flavor. He would have done it by The Book.

Eight

"Hi, Sis," I said, taking Julie's hand. She'd walked back in from the funeral home's main entrance to join me, the few remaining surgeons having said their goodbyes.

"Pretty amazing, wasn't it?" the tiny woman said, scanning the room to see who stayed after the memorial service.

"Good word, 'amazing.' Yes, I think it was. Think Dad would have approved?"

"Approved?" she said. "He'd have loved it. I can see him working the room, chatting and laughing and listening to everyone's stories. How would he have said it . . . oh, yes, he'd have been 'like a pig in poop.'"

"That's funny. Not the poop thing, I mean, the idea of him being in the room. The same thing occurred to me; I felt it too, the sensation he was here moving through the crowd."

"Maybe he was," Julie said, putting her arm in mine. "I need to say hello to Thompson, I couldn't get away from the group from the hospital. Walk me over there, okay?"

We moved across the room together, arm in arm. Walking together drew attention away from the gentle, side-to-side swaying of her gait, the rolling of her shoulders, but it didn't matter. She'd never been self-conscious, although her small stature and unsure stance posed problems for her early in her career as a surgeon. Initially, she had to face the physical issues it caused, the awkwardness as she moved around an operating table. Once accepted in her realm, and her great skills recognized, the residual challenges of polio were quickly overcome. To this day, she performs surgeries standing on a stainless steel stool with a treaded rubber top plate. A spare, identical stool is kept in the operating room ready to be placed for her as needed, enabling her to reach the patient from each side of the operating table. Once, I asked her if the stools caused her any problems. She said they didn't, but a few of her fellow surgeons had tripped over them over the years. They caused them a problem, she said.

A renowned cardiologist, my pride in her achievements as a surgeon was almost as great as my admiration for her spirit. Both aspects of her life were equally incredible. She was a walking, talking lesson in what a person can accomplish in spite of what others see as physical limitations–a lesson she'd taught me and her surgical interns. Most of them learned to avoid tripping over the little stools too.

"Dr. Julie," Thompson Crow said, bowing and twisting to kiss her cheek. "When can you do this surgery for me, you know, the new operation to install a heart? Harold says I'm heartless."

The relationship between Julie and Thompson Crow spiraled in an unending circle of jokes and self-perpetuating mischief dating back years and years. He could even tease her at the memorial service for her father and she would smile, which she did.

"I didn't say heartless," Harold Burnette interjected, feigning anger. "I said brainless. Have they got a transplant for that, Doc?"

"Can't say I'd want a brain donated by any of the old Yoopers who cash their social security checks and drop the money into slot machines," Thompson offered. "Those brains can't be working too well, can they? I think I'd want one of these smarter Troll brains they have around the university here; now those are great brains."

"Now, children," Julie said, scolding. "Can't we all just get along?"

Hugs were exchanged and several hands unashamedly wiped away tears.

"He was a wonderful man, Dr. Julie. We're just being smart-asses, you know we really are so sorry for your loss," Chief Crow intoned, suddenly serious, the gift of laughter given, received, and, as quickly, taken away by the occasion. "I will always see your Dad walking slowly down Bay Drive with Dancer early in the morning just after sunup. They watched everything: the sky, the woods, the lake, every bird and animal moving around them. Dr. Paul would point at something and Dancer would nod, or Dancer would step into the edge of the woods to study something and your dad would wait patiently for his friend. They really didn't need words. In many ways, the years braided their lives together, leaving them too close for words."

Whether Thompson Crow's comment registered with Dancer or not was, as always, a matter of conjecture. Standing with us, listening to every word, the gentle, slightly built, sixty-four-year-old man gave no visible sign of understanding. His gaze moved from face to face, pausing on each, reading emotions, but, given his cognitive limitations, probably not grasping the detailed meanings of our words. Maybe Dancer was wiser than words. Maybe in his world the details the words described were too small and really didn't matter. Maybe what he saw or felt mattered more than details.

Since Dad's death three days before, an aura of sadness settled around Dancer, its presence unmistakable; Dad's death wasn't a detail in Dancer's world, Dad's absence would leave a huge void.

In times of sadness and grief, words may not play that important a role for anyone, especially Dancer; somehow the communication of those feelings changes, becoming more subliminal, more subtle. Known for communicating without words, I was sure Dancer understood. Yet it wasn't the words, it was the message. This time I worried the message might be too much for him; too big, too close to home.

Intuitively, I believed Dancer sensed the loss we all felt; he must have. But his lack of tears was daunting, part and parcel of his form of comprehension, the mystery of his ability to relate. I knew he understood, but without visible expression, the observer is left without feedback and confirmation.

Dancer must have felt loss because loss is the reciprocal of love, the opposite of his ability to care for others, to give love in his unique way. Love wasn't unilateral; one emotion couldn't exist without the other. With Dad, his closest companion, gone, the duty to look after Dancer fell to me, especially in the coming months, making sure his loss didn't translate into depression. His attachment with Dad went back fifty years. Describing the depth of their friendship seemed difficult, if not impossible, so, conversely, I knew I must not underestimate Dancer's ability to grieve or ignore it just because his very uniqueness made it hard to gauge.

* * * * *

Back at the house, resisting my wife Laurie's attempts to help, Mom busily crafted a pot of coffee, rattled about the kitchen gathering cups, saucers, spoons, napkins, and cream and sugar and served us in the sunroom. The activity invigorated her, establishing an immediate purpose after a long afternoon spent reminiscing within the cocoon of sadness the remembrance at the funeral home spun around her. Walking to the car with us, crossing the empty parking lot beside the funeral home, Mom finally felt the separation, leaving Dad behind. Now she sat quietly, blowing across hot coffee, watching the steam rise, twist in ghostly columns, and dissipate. Her eyes focused beyond her cup, moving about the room, glancing at the familiar setting as if it were suddenly unfamiliar; as if, without Dad, the room somehow turned several degrees away from years of everyday memories, out of sync, the axis of normal altered.

"Do you think we should call Isaiah?" she asked, cradling her cup in both hands, absorbing its reassuring warmth. "He was pretty shook up."

The matriarchal survivor, the focal point of our family's grief, she was predictably worrying about someone else. After nearly fifty years together, Mom's perspectives, her sense of caring, closely resembled those of her lost mate. I tried to remember the adage about couples eventually beginning to look alike, or was that people and their dogs? I was at least certain they could grow to think alike.

Laurie looked at me from the comfort of the sun-faded, blue-and-white-striped couch, her eyes expressing hesitation, silently imploring me to keep Mom from continuing the day's activities; seeking surcease from its anguish.

"Well, you have to admit it's probably not healthy for a man of his age and health to display such deep emotion; he just completely broke down," said the new widow.

"He cared, I guess he cared a lot," I replied, trying not to sound calloused, seeking only to avoid further discussion, to stifle speculation. If I'd possessed Dad's unique skills of observation, their powers integral to his expertise in psychology, I would have known Mom needed to go on talking. I would have understood her immediate involvement was medicinal, a soothing activity, not unlike the busyness of making coffee. But sons are not their fathers, nor should they be. Although abilities may not be hereditary, an appreciation of having or lacking them is genuinely helpful; at least I recognized she needed my support.

"Hand me the phone, will you Laurie? I just want to call and see how he's doing."

Accepting the inevitable, Laurie complied and we sat, enjoying our coffee, obviously eavesdropping on Mom's conversation.

"Hello, Isaiah. Amy Conway. We're home and things have quieted down. I just wanted to talk with you. Are you all right?"

She paused while he responded at length. "Of course it's upsetting, and, no, you shouldn't be embarrassed." Another pause. "Good friends are allowed to shed a few tears, you're absolutely right about that." A break. "You're sure you're all right? ....Good."

Isaiah O'Connor was more than all right. He was spectacular. My earliest memories of him, however, don't include his Biblical first name. When I was ten or eleven, I thought his first name was Thatsonovabitch; some kind of strange Russian or Eastern European name, pulled from an ancient, Cyrillic alphabet, bubbling over with consonants.

His last name was another story. Even as a boy, I knew O'Connor was a good Irish name, but that didn't fit Dr. O'Connor either. Thatsonovabitch O'Connor, a psychiatrist, worked at Ypsilanti State Hospital with Dad, but his occupation was the only easily definable thing about him.

Replete with Irish jokes, the 1950s put a sharp edge on ethnic barbs. Sarcasm stretched itself to hurtful limits. Thinly veiled hatred swirled in the shallow, dirty water of dislike, and prejudice lurked within joyless smirks, speaking in the quiet coughs accompanying knowing laughter. Mick and Mack struggled under the abuse, part of the language of those times, precursors to the Polish jokes of the 1960s. Yes, eventually I would hear about the two-hundred-eighty-pound Polish guy who had never heard a Polish joke and suffer through learning the reason Polish girls shouldn't wear pantyhose. And the stories went further than just heaping tasteless humor on the doorsteps of our Irish or Polish neighbors.

In our early teens, we wondered at the origins of the controversy surrounding our new President, John Fitzgerald Kennedy. A handsome young man without a hat, he stood before the formal top hats of the past at his cold, windy inauguration. Speaking to the future, he urged us to think independently, asking us to contribute to our country, to avoid the easy, self-centered route of thinking about what our country somehow owed us. Kennedy's Irish name brought with it whispered questions about his loyalty to the Pope in Rome, hinting of other, perhaps deeper, prejudices.

Later, when I was sixteen or seventeen, Dad shed light on the concepts of prejudice and discrimination, passing on what he had learned from experience. He told me his definition of discrimination and it has served me well. Dad said discrimination is the unequal treatment of equals. His explanation rang true, clear, short, and logical. The problem, he said, begins when one group of people, for whatever reason, believes they are superior to another group of people.

Earlier, in my preteens, when contemplating names, I struggled with their supposed connections to nationalities or ethnic groups. During those years, understanding Dr. Isaiah O'Connor posed even greater conundrums than the undercurrent of doubts surrounding President Kennedy. The obvious Irish lilt of the last name O'Connor contradicted the shiny, coal-black luster of his skin, his bony, equine features, and the bulbous shape of his sculptured hairdo, his then socially inflammatory afro. Dr. O'Connor is black, although back then we said colored.

Once, when queried, he boldly and confidently stared the questioner squarely in the eyes and said he was African-Irish, establishing that the question spoke more about the inquisitor's ignorance than his own ethnicity. I still like the way he responded; a preview of Dr. O'Connorisms to come.

And Dad, with his way of getting to the heart of issues, set down another of life's lessons in his definition; discrimination clearly is the unequal treatment of equals. Ever since I've been wary of people who somehow believe they're a little more than equal.

Nothing about the man fit the stereotypes of the times. A cultural, ethnic enigma, Dr. Isaiah O'Connor's identity bounced off the walls of classification and defied attempts to apply labels.

During their first years working together, each of Dad's rants about him included the same preamble, a declaration, "Thatsonovabitch O'Connor." Dad forcefully exhaled the phrase, each utterance more in frustration and annoyance than anger. Dad could rant and rave over individual instances, the daily disagreements born of their different approaches to patient care, but the scope of his intellect prohibited lasting anger. During those years, given Dad's vehemence, a simmering animosity best described their relationship.

One remarkable meeting, however, would alter differences, combining them into the strong mastic holding a friendship together, defining the degree of expertise and concern each brought to their profession. Thirty-some years later, the aged psychiatrist, the circumference of his long ago afro reduced by time to a thin fringe of white around a bald, glistening scalp, wept uncontrollably at the service held in memory of the colleague he came to love and respect. Dr. O'Connor sobbed as he mourned the loss of the professor of psychology who so adamantly debated his ideas all those years ago but came to his aid during his most troubling years when the mental health community turned against psychiatry's goals and practices.

Yes, Dad set Isaiah O'Connor up. He probably felt no guilt, maliciously relishing the comeuppance of a nemesis after several years of anecdotes begun with Thatsonovabitch, the expletive glued to my memory. Perhaps the contentious psychiatrist deserved it. Either way, when Dancer wheeled Julie out on the stage in the University of Michigan lecture hall in her wheelchair, Dr. O'Connor never suspected he was about to be had.

Curious students filled the steeply tiered rows of seats, anticipating Dad's controversial presentation on the then-current debate between the relative benefits of psychiatry versus psychopharmacology and the new miracle drugs lessening psychotic symptoms. The two men stood at separate podiums. Adjusting his microphone, pulling the flexible stem toward him, Dad began with an introduction summarizing the benefits of lithium and Thorazine, the new wonder drugs being used to control numerous thought disorders, hallucinations, delusions, and symptoms of mental agitation.

Studying Julie in preparation for his retort, Dr. O'Connor, totally oblivious of Dancer's presence, leaned forward, ready to object.

"Surely, Dr. O'Connor, you must admit that psychiatry alone simply cannot adequately address all the conditions encountered in the wide range of today's treatment programs."

"Dr. Conway," Dr. O'Connor said, "I must protest this outrageous sham."

Condescension dripped from each syllable, disdainfully knocking my father's PhD in psychology while intoning the superiority of psychiatry.

"I beg your pardon, Dr. O'Connor. The patient I'm going to introduce doesn't require treatment with any of the new psychotropic drugs, although very small doses of Thorazine were tried to alleviate minor symptoms of agitation, but has also shown no benefit from any psychiatric intervention. The psychiatrist examining this patient concluded that the signs of agitation most likely represented positive responses to environmental stimuli."

"That should be obvious, Dr. Conway. Without examining her myself I can offer no professional psychiatric opinion, yet it seems ludicrous that she should ever have been treated with any mood-altering drug. The little girl obviously suffers from some form of physical ailment such as paralysis from polio or spinal injury."

"Excuse me, Dr. O'Connor, I thought you already knew my daughter Julie," Dad continued, gently tugging the line to set the hook. "And, you're perfectly correct, Julie is being treated for the effects of polio. The patient I wished to discuss is Tommy Daniel Higgins, a residential patient at Ypsilanti State Hospital. He's pushing my daughter's wheelchair."

Isaiah O'Connor, suddenly perplexed, had completely ignored Dancer, never noticing anything unusual about his appearance or movements. The outspoken and opinionated psychiatrist wriggled and flopped helplessly at the end of the line, slowly reeled in as Dad prepared to net his catch.

Pins could have dropped, their impact on the floor echoing across the silence gripping the auditorium as Dancer moved forward in response to Dad's hand motion. Stopping in front of Dad's podium, swinging Julie's wheelchair so she faced the audience, he stepped back and stood beside my father, perfectly executing the pattern they rehearsed before the meeting.

Dressed in the tailored dark-blue suit, white button-down Oxford shirt, and striped collegiate tie Mom and Dad purchased for him at Van Boven's men's clothing store on State Street, Dancer looked like a young graduate assistant at the university. Moving away from Julie's wheelchair, suddenly without the support of its handles, Dancer's footfalls reverted to an unsteady shuffle. His facial expression unconcerned and slightly vacant, he ignored the audience before him as his eyes rolled up and over, taking in the height and scope of the tall, narrow auditorium.

Dad turned to Isaiah O'Connor, excusing himself momentarily, and stepped forward to kneel beside Julie. "This is what the classes in medical school look like, darling. Someday I hope you're able to sit in one of those seats up there and learn all about medicine."

"That's what I want to do, Daddy. You know that," Julie said, the clear bell-like sound of her voice met with instant applause from the rows of students.

After wheeling Julie off-stage to Mom who was waiting in the wings, Dad returned to his podium and placed his hand on Dancer's shoulder. Dancer never flinched.

"Dr. O'Connor, Tommy Daniel Higgins has been a custodial patient since he was eight years old. His case provides clues, or I should say insights, into a variety of mental afflictions, yet, as I mentioned, he does not respond to psychiatric or psychotropic medicinal treatments. I brought him here today to illustrate the necessity of our two specialties working together."

To his credit, Dr. Isaiah O'Connor was smiling ear to ear, enjoying Dad's ruse even at his expense. "Dr. Conway," he laughed, throwing his head back in relaxed appreciation of the skill involved in the deception, "I look forward to working with you. Perhaps we can find a synergy in the combination of our disciplines." His words were prophetic.

The students broke into applause again as a new friendship was forged on the academic stage. And Isaiah O'Connor, who broke down and wept at Dad's memorial service, remembering his friend and unashamed of his tears, was true to his word. Their work together in the coming years would help resolve many of the controversies surrounding the choice of appropriate, effective treatment regimens utilized to care for patients with mental and emotional impairments. On a personal level, he eventually became Dancer's friend and a mentor of the little girl in the wheelchair, my sister, the future heart surgeon, Dr. Julie Conway Church.

Nine

y the time Dancer was admitted to the Athens Asylum for the Insane in 1938, the huge institution had served its patients for almost seventy years. The large "1868" at the peak of the gable high above the administrative wing already bore the stains of decades of weather. Its grand front entrance had witnessed the arrival of thousands of souls brought there for treatment since the asylum's completion in 1874. Like a great many of his predecessors, it became Dancer's home and refuge.

Situated where southern Ohio nestles against the deeper, more dramatic valleys of West Virginia, the imposing Kirkbride design of the facility looked down from atop steep ridges. Its twin towers cast their shadows on the Hocking River, the little college town of Athens, the patients coming through its doors, and the families bringing them there. And, as the sun traversed the sky year after year marking the seasons, the towers' shadows moved slowly through the trees growing tall across the grounds, dappling leafy images on the hillside cemeteries holding the remains of the patients who, unlike Dancer, never left. Between arrival and departure, even if only to the peace of eternity beneath a plain-numbered marker on a nearby slope, the quality of patients' lives and the particulars of the treatment they received varied widely according to the severity of their symptoms.

Hundreds of soldiers returned from the Civil War maimed in body and mind to find a sense of security living and working at the giant institution, unable or unwilling to rejoin the world beyond its boundaries. As a child and adolescent, Dancer captured the hearts of Athens' patients and staff. His legacy included stories of the little boy, the Ambassador of Goodwill, First Class, who greeted visitors, ran through the hallways and up and down the stairs, played on the buggy steps, and faced down a deranged veteran with a gun. Dancer was remembered.

Removing "asylum" and "insane" from the great institution's name during WWII, in Dancer's early years there, lessened its ominous tone. It did not, however, substantially alter the treatments of the times which, by today's standards, would raise eyebrows. Primitive chains and metal manacles, used as physical restraints, would cause cries of cruelty. The history of the treatment of patients exhibiting severe mental disorders has never been pretty. Restraints were followed by ice-water baths and straitjackets and wrapping patients in wet bed sheets. Technology brought with it electroshock and, eventually, the invasive techniques of lobotomy, the most gruesome, inhumane episode of all. Over the decades, the means utilized represented those available and thought effective. If deemed incurable, patients were sterilized to preclude the possibility they would parent children, passing on their disorder. Although generally unsuccessful, asylum physicians attempted to induce a state of tranquility in agitated patients by treating them with bromides and other drugs. Insane patients, given the futility of treatment, languished under a life sentence of virtual incarceration, victims of early medicine's learning curve.

As bad as conditions were in the asylums in the 1940s, a century and a half earlier, in the late 1700s and early 1800s, the l-u-n in the terms "lunacy" and "lunatic" mirrored their etymology, their origins in the word "lunar," in the influence of the moon and its purportedly inexplicable effects on man. Back then, scholarly, sincere discussions of symptoms included beliefs about evil spirits and the feared tendrils of witchcraft reaching out to possess its victims. Asylums established around the nation removed the "lunatics" from their communities, believing they could only be restored to health in a therapeutic, custo-dial environment. As the asylums filled with patients, most attempts at providing therapy were overwhelmed by the basic custodial con-cerns created by sheer numbers.

Although the giant asylums were built with federal funds following the Civil War, the State Care Act of 1890 transferred responsibilities for their operation to the states. The belief at the time considered the change key to ensuring higher standards of care. In reality, it was the end of central control and the beginning of differences in treatment from state to state. Federal funding ceased. As they grew, asylums took on the care of the indigent, the elderly suffering from senile dementia, and those made insane or paralyzed by syphilitic paresis resulting from venereal disease; what television comedian Johnny Carson later called "the gift that keeps on giving."

The first signs that biology held secrets of treatment for mental disorders came from a technique utilized to treat syphilis. To halt the progression of paresis doctors infected patients with malaria by injec-tion and then treated the resultant disease with quinine. It worked. Used on patients with a wide range of mental disorders, however, the process was not successful.

This glimmer of the possibility of using medicine to treat mental disorders offered hope and helped motivate the rise of scientific med-icine. If science could identify causes and develop interventions that worked, patients suffering from acute symptoms could be treated, perhaps even returned to productive lives in society.

The 1900s brought with them Freud's new method, psychoanal-ysis, which saw symptoms as the outward manifestations of the nega-tive influences of childhood events or adult stresses. By looking into their inner lives, patients, especially those in group analysis, recog-nized they were not alone in their difficulties.

In 1944, as the Allies were pushing toward Berlin and the U.S.

Army, Navy, and Marine Corps retook the Pacific bloody island by island and a fourteen-year-old boy named Dancer lived happily in Athens State Hospital, Dr. William Menninger was chief of Army neuropsychiatry. He reacted to the shortages of professional mental health personnel and the inability of mental health treatments to keep up with medical science. The National Mental Health Act of 1946 resulted from the Federal action he initiated. One man could bring about change. Inspired by the news articles of the times, the mentoring of his father-in-law, Professor Michael Porter, and his experiences living within the walls of the asylum in Athens, Ohio, caring for the afflicted, Dad found his future.

A dozen years later, as Dad, now Dr. Paul Conway, entrapped Isaiah O'Connor on a University of Michigan lecture stage, the process of combining medical treatment with psychoanalysis was still a work in progress. The 1950s were, however, pivotal years in making possible a lasting partnership between medicine's dependence on antipsychotic drugs and psychiatric intervention. The majority of the infighting between the two disciplines ended, not only in Ann Arbor, Michigan, but across the nation. Only small groups fought the merger, those with extreme views one way or the other, and, as Dad discovered, those who were just plain mean-spirited or held an economic interest in either discipline.

∗　∗　∗　∗　∗

The day-to-day world Dancer lived in changed subtly as he grew older. Things happened. Not all of them were pleasant, like long hours washing dishes in scalding water at Athens State Hospital. But Dancer kept on keeping on. His ability to find his form of quiet happiness in each new environment proved not only his versatility or adaptability, but spoke of small acts of courage, humility, and achievement. The child who ran gleefully up and down the hallways of Athens, Ohio, became the young adult working with the grounds crews at Ypsilanti State Hospital.

Dancer loved the outdoors; this obvious affinity for nature central to his eventual acceptance by the maintenance workers at Ypsi State. The medical staff and orderlies had grown to trust him to remain close to his building. Understanding the value of sunshine and fresh air, over time they bent the rules more and more, allowing him to go outside whenever possible. Dad told them about Dancer's role as the hospital's messenger in Athens, and how, with ample instruction, he could be relied upon to stay close by. Dancer never once got lost or ran away. Why should he? He was home.

The teenager with curious eyes set in a kind face began tagging along with maintenance personnel weeding flower beds, trimming shrubs, and manicuring great open stretches of lawn. Sometimes he stood so close to the men as they worked, observing their actions, they appeared to be tutoring him in their methods. He watched and smiled and learned. Dad always said Dancer learned in his own way and in his own time and that he possessed a strong work ethic. Years later, Dancer's vegetable soup confirmed the accuracy of Dad's observations.

Slowly and unobtrusively, Dancer began to help. His small hands deftly moved through the flowers, expertly removing even the smallest weeds while smoothing the soil, leaving picture-book gardens of blooms. The grounds workers readily accepted the assistance of the young man without words, giving him instructions through easy ges-tures and nods. Dancer followed them throughout the day, moving indefatigably from task to task, beginning each new assignment with enthusiasm. His hair, cut short in a crew cut, and his fair skin left him easily sunburned, so they bought him a straw hat. Augmenting his charm, he never complained, and the men smiled at his easy-going, ready-to-help nature; the glow lifted their spirits as it brightened their days. Of course he lacked the words to complain, but it was more than that; he could have shown reluctance or fatigue through his actions, words weren't necessary. Many of them tired in the hot sun and slowed down and dragged by day's end, but not Dancer. He smiled and worked.

Rewarding his steadfast dedication and hard work, they occasionally allowed him to ride on a tractor as they mowed the acres of grass. He always hung on tightly to the seat's crossbar as instructed and never touched any of the controls and always waited for them to stop and shut off the motor before he climbed down. Thoroughly entranced by the adventure of moving across the slightly rolling open fields, he pulled his straw hat down tight. The triple gang of giant reel mowers towed behind the tractor smoothed the shamrock-green grass, emitting a continuous metal-edged growl audible above the engine's exhaust note. Dancer grinned in pure joy. A life without complications can be beautiful to watch.

The smallest of the groundskeepers, Roscoe Perkins, asked his wife to mend his old uniform shirts and pants when the plant manager issued him two new sets. Asking politely if it was all right, his boss smiled and granted his request that Dancer be allowed to wear his hand-me-downs. So began Dancer's new role at Ypsilanti State Hospital. The former Ambassador of Goodwill, First Class, from Athens, Ohio, became an informal, but uniformed, member of the grounds crew.

Out working with the others, he was now indistinguishable except for the huge white name tags Roscoe's wife sewed over his shirt pockets. The name "Dancer" stitched in bright red letters stuck out a bit and, rain or shine, he always wore his big straw hat. And, yes, he did sometimes prefer skipping in lieu of walking; maybe because he wasn't all that good at walking, and skipping was more fun. Skipping required big, bouncing steps like Tigger in the Hundred Acre Wood in the storybook the CO, Paul, had read him, and motion, lots of motion, almost like dancing.

Well, maybe he wasn't all that indistinguishable–he was, after all, Dancer being Dancer. Those were his best months: spring's planting, summer's watering and tending, and fall's cleanup.

Dancer reveled in being outside. All the time he worked on his simple landscaping tasks, he watched birds fly in lofty circles and squirrels climb trees and chatter, and insects swarm in clouds, and brightly colored flowers bend in gentle breezes. When the leaves turned yellow and red and fell and winter approached, his nature clouded over, his radiated shine of energy dimming in anticipation of months spent indoors. The names of the months on the calendar remained beyond his grasp, but he clearly understood the reality of changing seasons. For several weeks as the air chilled and the snows of winter approached, Dancer languished in his room or sat bleakly by the wired windows in the communal entertainment room watching other patients play checkers or sit in groups listening to the radio or watching TV programs like *Queen for a Day*. That was a gem where the contestant with the worst, most tragic life won a new washing machine or refrigerator. Then, finally, on winter's snowy days, happiness returned as he rode with Roscoe Perkins, pointing the way through the drifts and holding the doughnuts.

Anticipating the first heavy snows of December, Dancer knew Roscoe would come to wake him in the predawn darkness, handing him his uniform shirt and pants from his dresser. Dressing quickly, Dancer ran through the kitchen gathering three doughnuts wrapped in a napkin, one for him and two for his mentor, and rushed to the vehicle garage. Mr. Perkins would have the giant dump truck with its snow plow and salt spreader running and ready to go. Together they plied the intricate pattern of service roads and parking lots checker-boarding the huge facility. Like years before as a little boy in Miss Flossie's long dark Buick on the road to Athens, Dancer leaned forward across the dashboard. This time, instead of the twisting country roads of southern Ohio, he studied Michigan's drifted snow, carefully protecting Roscoe's remaining doughnut. Later in the day, he shadowed Roscoe and the men as they hand-shoveled the accumulated snow from sidewalks and entrance stairs leading to each of the buildings. They always gave Dancer his own snow shovel, and as he followed them, his gait made even more awkward by heavy galoshes, he meticulously straightened edges and removed stray clumps of snow left behind as the crew moved rapidly through their well-rehearsed chores.

Over the years, the things that made Dancer happy included being outdoors, working, caring for others, and being in the company of friendly people, especially children. Unfortunately, all too soon the rituals he came to enjoy at Ypsilanti State Hospital were lost to change and Dancer again was compelled to adapt to a new environment. Unbeknownst to Dad or anyone close to Dancer, the coming months would bring notoriety. What happened, and the widespread publication of articles about the event, vastly enlarged the circle of mystery surrounding the quiet, peaceful young man who had become a part of our lives. Dancer's silent bravery and love for others contributed to what many called a miracle, but the lives affected included his own.

Ten

The firemen stared at the smoldering wreckage, their attempts at extinguishing the fireball too little and too late. The fire's story ended before their arrival, at least the event ended; the story continued to grow, gaining a life of its own.

Over fifty gallons of gasoline melted the asphalt, consumed in a nearly instantaneous, towering sheet of flame and smoke visible for miles. Shoppers in downtown Ann Arbor swarmed to corner sidewalks with a westward view, astonished by the rising pillar of oily black smoke. Gruesome anecdotes continued to be told for years.

Flames and intense heat engulfed both vehicles, leaving only charred, twisted metal. The trunk lid and rear fenders of the automobile were recognizable by shape, its blackened license plate by its raised numbers. Its round plastic taillights melted into two small reddish puddles. Mangled and misshapen, the vehicle's front end pierced the dump truck's side fuel tank directly behind its right front wheel, setting off the initial, massive explosion, the speed of impact crumpling the smaller auto underneath the truck. The first fireball rose vertically, claiming the truck's cab and driver in the opening cataclysmic seconds. The driver, from the nearby village of Dexter, was in his late fifties with many years of experience operating large trucks. But, by all accounts of friends and relatives, he was in ill health despite his muscular build and lifelong strength. Heart attack or incredibly poor judgment or a few seconds of inattention; everyone debated the possible cause, the reason he may have turned in front of the oncoming car. Perhaps he underestimated the speed with which they approached each other or overestimated his ability to complete the turn quickly. Could the huge dump truck's engine have faltered or its gears failed to mesh in a frantic downshift?

The total destruction of the two vehicles culminated with the smaller, secondary, but still deadly explosion of the car's fuel tank. The deaths of both drivers denied a curious public and an obsessive newspaper reporter the answers they wanted. Four other witnesses existed; three survivors and one brave Good Samaritan. Three; a baby, a toddler, and a five-almost-six-year-old boy, were much too young to be able to describe the accident dirtying the clear mid-morning sky with its question-mark-shaped black cloud hundreds of feet high. One, our Dancer, lacked the vocabulary to respond.

The blue spruce trees lining the western edge of Mercywood's immaculately manicured front lawn on Jackson Road, placed more for purpose than aesthetics, were planted as a windbreak to protect its circular entrance drive from winter's drifting snows. The year the accident happened they were about twenty feet tall. It was easy to estimate their height from the newspaper photos of the scene with the police cars and a fire truck parked in the forefront. Running parallel to the busy three-lane highway with its treacherous center left-turn lane, a long, arrow-straight row of carefully tended waist-high hedges created a front boundary delineating the private hospital's property. Scattered about the grounds, several maple trees struggled in their adolescent years, each with a small helmet of silvery leaves in the early stages of fall's dramatic color show.

An orderly assigned to keep an eye on Dancer stepped out the front entrance doors and stood at the top of the steep steps scanning the lawn. The grating shriek of skidding tires made him look to the highway. Time stopped as a flashy black '56 Ford Crown Victoria hardtop, heading east, its distinctive band of chrome trim clearly visible across its top, struck the side of the westbound dump truck turning left into a construction site directly across the road. Hearing the deep, solid boom and feeling the concussion of the collision at the moment he spotted Dancer standing by the hedge with his wooden-handled clippers in his hand, the young orderly turned and ran back inside hollering for help and telling the woman at the front desk to call the police and the fire department. According to depositions taken for the resulting civil suit, the orderly, totally shaken by what he *had* seen, hadn't witnessed Dancer's actions since he'd been back inside the sanitarium's lobby spreading the alarm.

Dancer would be called to testify but, of course, couldn't. I have the photo of Dad standing with Dancer on the courthouse steps, there as his legal guardian. When the judge called Dancer's name, formally acknowledging that his testimony would not be forthcoming, he rose from his seat at the witness table and stood with Dad at his side. The entire courtroom leapt up from their seats and gave Dancer a standing ovation ended only by the judge's gavel as he restored order. Relatives of the three children who'd survived wept. To them it was about joy in the midst of tragedy and not about unanswerable questions of how anyone, especially a retarded young man, could have done what he did. It was about three little lives.

Some newspaper reporters spoke of Dancer's courage, unable to fathom the sequence of events and the incidentals of his actions, but recognizing the miraculous results of his intervention. The first policeman to arrive at the scene was a Washtenaw County sheriff's deputy. Receiving the radio call and proceeding there at high speed, the officer found Dancer sitting cross-legged on Mercywood's front lawn, his back to the road and the fiery crash, cradling two small children in his burned and blistered arms. A third child, a thin little boy with black hair, lay curled at Dancer's feet, sobbing, his face and one arm blood-soaked and his small hands clutching Dancer's ankle. Inconsolable, he refused to release his grip on his rescuer.

No one saw Dancer cross the highway, go into the car to retrieve the children, or carry them away from the flames. The passenger-side door of the hardtop Ford was wide open, jammed past the limits of its hinges. Whether it had been forcibly ripped open or sprung to that position by the collision remained a mystery. There was no mystery about the flames which quickly engulfed the truck's cab and the front of the car and, moments later, the rear of the car. Having struck the side of the dump truck at an angle depicted by the skid marks left beyond the radius of the scorched pavement, it was assumed the children's mother died instantly, her body pinned beneath the large steering wheel by the impact. Apparently pulling left into the center lane to avoid the truck as it turned in front of her, then either fearful of oncoming traffic or panicking and losing control, she drifted, skidding to the right, hitting the truck directly behind its front wheel.

During the 1950s, before the introduction of modern diesel engines, construction trucks were still powered by gasoline engines using their much more volatile fuel. Depending on configuration and vehicle size, rectangular side-mounted gas tanks often included built-in steps, making it easier to climb up into a truck's high-mounted cab. Struck from the front, massive steel bumpers shielded the side tanks. When T-boned, however, the results were disastrous.

After the accident, a wonderful article in the *Detroit News* spoke almost exclusively of Dancer's courage, noting only once that he was a patient at Mercywood, the private sanitarium, and never mentioning, let alone questioning, his intelligence or what he was doing out by the side of Jackson Road working as a caretaker on the hospital's grounds.

A city desk writer with the *Ann Arbor News*, Audie Beard, however, took the opposite tack, perhaps sensing in Dancer a local news phenomenon worth exploiting. Perhaps he envisioned his name on the byline of articles reprinted in the larger Detroit, Chicago, and New York papers. People intent on fame often lack any concern for the collateral damage they cause achieving their goals.

The week of the accident, I found it curious to hear everyone at home and at school speaking of Dancer's courage. The quality seemed to stand in contrast to everything I understood about someone so gentle, kind, and caring. I only knew the Dancer who loved being out in the sunshine working in the yard, and who sat quietly at family dinners taking in every word and movement around him as if he couldn't get enough of it all. I knew the Dancer who pushed Julie's wheelchair when she was sick and smiled confidently at her, sharing with her his own quiet determination. Maybe that was courage. It was difficult to imagine him pulling babies from a burning vehicle, but to those of us who knew and loved him, the enigmas which made him unique didn't require analysis, and by their very nature, made anything possible. I listened intently, learning more about my friend and about life. Only years later did I understand we really aren't supposed to comprehend all the answers to life's mysteries, and that the difficulty in knowing our own complexities can rival understanding the motivations of complete strangers. But, yes, Dancer was courageous and I'm sure my pride in his accomplishment showed.

Courage is, after all, more in the domain of the individual, and not found occurring naturally in groups. And, Dancer, well, he was about as individual as anyone could get. Plus, my belief he could act courageously was reinforced because I knew him and often witnessed his determination.

The more I thought about it, courage must also be part and parcel of goodness, another trait Dancer constantly displayed. Groups, by contrast, gain courage from the act of banding together, kindling their combined bravado through numbers while camouflaging small differences and dissent in the sense of force and presence they create.

Dancer's injuries were minor, so minor they created consternation among those studying the particulars of the violent accident. The burns and blisters on his hands and forearms required only cleaning and the application of salves and dressings in the emergency room at St. Joseph Mercy Hospital near downtown Ann Arbor. Dad brought him home that afternoon to stay with us for a couple days. All wrapped in bandages, Dancer looked like the Egyptian mummy in my school book. His eyebrows were almost non-existent, only tiny curled stubs remained, and the fluff of sandy-brown hair above his forehead was severely singed. Emitting a pinkish-brown cast, the skin on his face glowed. He looked unnatural and his burns must have hurt like the dickens, but he never complained. I would find illustrations of spacemen and Martians in my comic books that carried that same hairless, reddened, flash-burned look.

Of the three children, a little boy, the oldest, suffered the most severe injuries, including several deep lacerations and substantial bruising. Neither the baby, a boy, nor the toddler, a two-year-old girl, was injured–not at all, not a mark. Their total lack of trauma inspired many technically based theories about where the kids had been inside the vehicle. Inadvertently, the absence of injuries fostered bigger, inexplicable questions. Those less interested in facts came to see the mystery of the children's welfare as proof of a small-scale, local miracle.

Officials at Mercywood called Dad within twenty minutes after the accident, alerting him to Dancer's involvement and that he was being transported to the hospital in an ambulance with one of the children. Rushing across campus to the emergency room, Dad found Dancer sitting quietly in an examining room, oblivious of the extent of his burns. He was calm and looked up at my dad as if it were just another quiet day and it was perfectly natural for him to see my father walking through the door.

Years later when I was in college, Dad told me that, with one exception, the police agencies, the fire marshal, the doctors and everyone seeking information about the incident were polite and professional and respectful of Dancer's well-being. The one exception, of course, was Audie Beard. I once overheard Dad using Dr. Isaiah O'Connor's original first name, Thatsonovabitch, to describe the tenacious reporter from the *Ann Arbor News*. Dancer's welfare didn't even register with Audie Beard. It would be almost a year before Dad discovered the links to his own career and to Dancer causing Mr. Beard's animosity. As it turned out, the reporter's quest for fame was also tied to several politicians with their own agendas.

*   *   *   *   *

Maybe Dancer was supposed to move from Ypsilanti State Hospital, a state-run institution, to Mercywood late that summer. The *Detroit News* used the terms fate and destiny to describe the apparent coincidence of Dancer's transfer less than sixty days before the awful car-truck accident. The newspaper never discovered one other factor that put Dancer in the right place at the right time–Roscoe Perkins and the grounds crew at Ypsi State.

When Roscoe and the guys heard the scuttlebutt that Dancer might be moved to Ann Arbor, they brought a camera to work and took photographs of Dancer working on the flowers and trimming the hedges and riding on the back of the tractor. In one of the photos, he grinned and held onto his straw hat on a beautiful summer day in a pretty good wind. Somehow Dad ended up with a print of that picture and Mom framed it. That little black-and-white photograph with its sculpted edges still sits on a shelf by her fireplace. Sometimes, when he comes to visit, Dancer will take it down from the shelf and hold it, tilting it to clear away reflections across the glass, and gaze at his past. Watching him, we can only wonder at his thoughts, although he will occasionally softly say the name of someone in a photo as he studies it.

Two weeks after Dancer was moved, Roscoe and three other men from the Ypsi State grounds crew drove to Mercywood in Ann Arbor one afternoon and asked to see its administrator. They gave him the photos and explained everything they knew about Dancer and his talents and how much he needed to be outdoors to be happy. Roscoe even managed to take home Dancer's uniform shirts on the pretext his wife was going to mend them. He presented them along with the photographs and pointed to Dancer wearing them in the pictures.

The administrator, a bit incredulous, asked whether anyone ever voiced concerns about Dancer walking away or getting lost. Roscoe just laughed and nodded toward his co-workers. "No, sir," he said, "I'd be more worried about one of these guys doing that." They shook their heads in agreement, smiling at Roscoe and chuckling. "No, sir, he may not have both oars in the water, but he sure seems to have more than his share of common sense."

So, with a little help from his friends and confirmation from my father, Dancer was once again allowed to walk the grounds on sunny days doing small landscaping chores. Three children owed their lives to his need to be outdoors and, more importantly, his love for others; a level of caring that overshadowed any fear of the flames and heat of a burning automobile.

Unlike the writer at the *Detroit News*, my father knew Dancer's move from Ypsilanti State Hospital to Mercywood had more to do with politics and cost than fate or destiny. Dad accepted his position teaching psychology at the University of Michigan the year before and his successor at Ypsi State grew increasingly uncomfortable with Dancer's "privileges." The medical and psychiatric staffers clearly understood how unique Dancer was and readily accepted Dad signing him out to bring him home on Saturday or Sunday. Less than a year later, although no justification was offered or given, they were instructed that these visitations created a liability concern for the institution. Dad sensed the new concern was more likely rooted in professional jealousy, or simply an attempt to avoid a potential issue based on a fear someone might be criticized for allowing preferential treatment.

Eventually, Dr. O'Connor confirmed Dad's suspicions. He'd overheard his superior, the head of psychiatry at the State of Michigan's central office in Lansing, speaking with Dad's successor. A year after being promoted to administrator, Dad left the hospital to accept a teaching position at the university. The politically connected department head interpreted Dad's decision to leave as tantamount to a soldier abandoning his post. To him it was an insult to the state mental health system and mandated tightening up on any perceived irregularities in the way Dancer was treated, especially if it sent a message to Dad.

There was also a question of cost. The 1960s brought with them new ideas about responsibility for patient-care costs. The decade also brought tremendous growth—new cars, new houses, new every-thing after 1959's recession rocked the heavily industrialized state of Michigan. Given tight state budgets caused by the explosion of infra-structure expenses for schools and new highways created by popula-tion growth and the maturing baby-boomer generation in the '60s, mental health costs came under scrutiny.

Still closely connected with his former colleagues, Dad reacted to the early warning signals of change and purchased health insurance for Dancer. The policy, one of the first of its kind, was expensive with no exclusions for pre-existing conditions and covered institutionaliza-tion if required. This made it possible to move Dancer to Mercywood when the issues became insurmountable at Ypsilanti State Hospital.

In his relentless investigation, Audie Beard, the local city desk reporter, managed to gain access to the basic information in Dancer's file at the state hospital. That data connected Dancer to Dad and formed the apparent catalyst for future articles. Eventually Dad dis-covered one of Michigan's state senators, his focus on reducing the state's health care budget, used intimidation to get a copy of Dancer's complete file from Mercywood's offices and provided the information to Mr. Beard.

The first two articles in the *Ann Arbor News* didn't make much sense, especially when compared with coverage of the incident in the *Detroit News*. While showing only cursory sorrow for the deaths of the drivers and almost no relief that the three children survived, Audie Beard's words hinted of wrongdoing. His first story questioned why Thomas Daniel Higgins, a Mercywood patient, wore a work shirt with his nickname on the pocket and carried hedge clippers. Promising to get to the bottom of the situation, Mr. Beard insinuated Dancer was working illegally and taking employment away from Ann Arbor residents in need of work. His initial articles sounded as if he had an axe to grind with the private hospital. Dad was neither alarmed nor concerned, only bemused our local newspaper would choose to cover the story from an inquisitor's perspective rather than factually reporting the event and its aftermath.

A week passed before a follow-up article caused Dad to sit up and take notice. The attack suddenly focused on Dad and Dancer. Under a sixty-point, inch-tall caption, "U of M Professor Implicated in Health Care Scheme," Audie Beard, on page one of the section devoted to local news items, accused Dad, as Dancer's legal guardian, of fraudulently committing Dancer to Mercywood. He went on to state that "the young, mentally retarded patient" was removed from Ypsilanti State Hospital, a state-funded facility, because he was not a Michigan resident. Elaborating, Mr. Beard described Dancer's years as a patient at Ypsi State as a misuse of "precious health care monies" orchestrated by Assistant Professor Conway while he was employed by the state hospital, noting Dad frequently checked Dancer, Tommy Higgins, out of the facility to spend weekends with the Conway family in Ann Arbor.

Before he could get any answers from Dr. Isaiah O'Connor, another article hit the press. This time Audie Beard zeroed in on Dancer's role as an unpaid landscape worker at Ypsilanti State Hospital, questioning the legality of allowing a patient to work alongside state employees. In closure, Beard demanded answers from both Ypsilanti State Hospital, although he noted that the new administrator there had acted to correct the prior irregularity, and Mercywood officials who, in his words, "appeared to condone the use of patient labor."

He received one answer from Roscoe Perkins. In the letter to the editor he wrote, Roscoe tersely stated that Mr. Audie Beard didn't know anything about the "state employees" or the "mentally retarded man" he was writing about and, although implied in less direct words, should put his typewriter where the sun doesn't shine. Roscoe's letter included his signature and those of his fellow workers at Ypsilanti State Hospital.

Although each newspaper article invited "explanations from Dr. Conway," Dad held his fire, considering the articles to be the ramblings of an angry man looking for a fight, choosing not to reward or dignify the man's viciousness by replying. Two weeks later, that changed, when, under the startling banner, "Insurance Fraud Indicated," Audie Beard lashed out at Dad again. This time a response would be forthcoming, but from a source Audie Beard could never have anticipated and would never forget.

On the crisp Thursday morning in November when a bright-red Jaguar convertible with a tan soft top pulled to the curb adjacent to the cement-like rectangular office of *The Ann Arbor News* at the corner of S. Division and E. Huron, Audie Beard and his managing editor, Mr. Whitten, were seated in the newspaper's conference room readying for the meeting. A short, portly man emerged from the tiny door of the exotic-looking sports car with its long, low, sloping fenders and stood by the curb feeding nickels and dimes to the parking meter. He turned and smiled when Dad and Dancer walked up to join him.

"That is a mischievous smile, Mr. Hammit," Dad said, shaking the elderly attorney's hand. "You're looking forward to this, aren't you?"

"Please, call me Ziggie," he replied, smiling at Dad and carefully studying Dancer's face before turning to walk up the sidewalk, addressing his next words exclusively to my father.

"I was blessed with wonderful professors when I studied law at the same university where you now teach, Paul. They taught me to never start a fight unless the other guy had it coming and to settle frivolous attacks quickly and decisively when they were directed at those I represented. You and Dancer deserve better than to be libeled in this manner. And, yes, this will be fun." The latter was delivered with the drawn-out, emphatic tone of someone rubbing their hands together in anticipation.

Dancer's attorney, Lawrence Ziegfield Hammit, Esq., of Adrian, Michigan, was a Wolverine and a loyal alumnus of the University of Michigan. Dad hadn't known that before, probably because the old attorney's credentials were of no concern given his ebullient personality and steadfast dedication to Dancer's welfare. He was appointed by Dancer's mother, Emma, upon the recommendation of her late mentor, Miss Flossie Duncan. Ageless, the old attorney's short stature balanced well with the round yet precisely tailored cut of his gray pin-striped suit. White hair trimmed in a short, stubbly crew cut and a matching pencil mustache worked together to take emphasis away from the intensity of small, bright-green eyes. His clients, once under his purview, were advised to address him as Ziggie, his life-long, informal adaptation of the stuffy-sounding family middle name his mother burdened him with at birth. "Besides, 'Hammit' always comes out sounding like 'damn it' and makes me think I did something wrong."

Ziggie, always the poster child for eccentricity with his penchant for beautiful sports cars, responded immediately to Dad's call, and, after reading the newspaper articles Dad mailed him, readily agreed to drive up from Adrian to educate Mr. Beard in certain aspects of the law. At his instruction, Dad arranged for this meeting and put nothing in writing. Lawrence Ziegfield Hammit, Esq., promised a complete retraction by Mr. Beard and a prominently displayed apology from the *Ann Arbor News*. He delivered both.

After the first few minutes, Dad almost felt sorry for Audie Beard. Almost.

"Now, Mr. Beard, you do understand that the articles you authored about my clients were presented as news stories, not opinion or editorial pieces?"

"I . . . I approve of all the stories we put in the . . ." Mr. Whitten attempted to interject.

"Mr. Whitten, I was addressing Mr. Beard. I will address your newspaper's complicity in publishing his articles in a moment."

"But I'm managing editor here," he again began to explain.

"I'm sure the court will be impressed, Mr. Whitten, but I'm addressing Mr. Beard, who requires edification in our state's statutes covering libel."

Dad tried to remain expressionless, the good poker player, concentrating on Mr. Hammit's words. Dancer, clearly focusing on the intensity with which his counselor spoke to the newspaper reporter, stared at Audie Beard as if also awaiting his response.

"Mr. Hammit, my articles are truthful and based on documents relating to the patient, Mr. Higgins, and Dr. Conway, his legal guardian."

"Documents you obtained illegally, Mr. Beard, and documents which do not in any way support your libelous statements. The issues of patient confidentiality will be addressed separately with both hospitals. Those supplying you with that information will answer for their actions. You, sir, will answer for libel. You have made rash and damaging statements about my clients saying they committed insurance fraud and other crimes. For your information, Mr. Higgins's mother, a Michigan resident since 1938, appointed me to represent her son several years ago. She was instrumental in moving her son to Ypsilanti State Hospital from Athens State Hospital in Ohio, and in making Dr. Conway his legal guardian. With their testimony, I will prove conclusively in a court of law that all their actions were legal and above board and that no crimes were intended or committed. I sincerely hope you understand the gravity of your blatantly false statements."

"But Mr. Hammit," Mr. Whitten said, forcing his way into the conversation exactly when Ziggie hoped he would, "I'm sure we can discuss these matters without resorting to any legal actions."

"There will be no discussions, Mr. Whitten. Mr. Beard's articles have, unfortunately, by their ongoing campaign of falsehoods, moved the matter well past the point where discussions could be productive," Lawrence Ziegfield Hammit said, reclining in his chair, prepared to deliver his ultimatum. "For there to be anything other than a lawsuit naming Mr. Beard, you, and your newspaper, there will be an immediate retraction and an apology. The retraction will be carried on the front page under, at a minimum, the same size headline used for Mr. Beard's articles. It will not be hidden in small print on a back page. In addition, under your signature and those of the owners of your newspaper, a full apology to Dr. Conway and Mr. Higgins will express your genuine contrition at having published Mr. Beard's false accusations. Whether you continue to employ Mr. Beard is entirely at your discretion. We will, however, be watching for any further libeling of my clients and no further terms such as this retraction and apology will be proffered. Am I making myself clear?"

After a long thoughtful minute, his eyes downcast, Mr. Whitten straightened in his chair. "Of course, Mr. Hammit," he said, turning to stare at Audie Beard. "I accept and I believe my newspaper's owners will find your terms more than generous."

"I'm not agreeing to do that," Audie Beard began, only to be silenced by a fierce look from his managing editor.

"You have a lot to learn, Audie, but I won't have you learning it at the expense of this fine newspaper," Mr. Whitten said. He stood and offered his hand to Ziggie. "Thank you for being candid and reasonable, Mr. Hammit."

"Thank you, Mr. Whitten. I was certain that once you understood the seriousness of the situation you would act according to the long history of integrity shown by the *Ann Arbor News*."

Dad and Dancer followed Ziggie Hammit out of the conference room without a backward glance. Behind them, Audie Beard could be heard stammering defiantly. His words were cut off when the conference room door closed, swung shut by the force of its pneumatic cylinder. Message delivered. Message understood. Case closed.

The elderly lawyer walked to his car with his arm around Dancer in a grandfatherly embrace. "This young man is lucky to have you, Paul. I'm getting pretty old and I sleep well knowing you'll be there for him. But we do have to sit down soon and talk about his finances; there are some things you need to know. All good things, I assure you."

At the side of the red Jaguar, Mr. Hammit turned to face Dad and Dancer. He reached out to pat Dancer's shoulder affectionately then shook Dad's hand firmly, leaning toward him conspiratorially. "And I don't think that dumb son of a bitch will ever bother either of you again. But keep your ears open. Someone put him up to all that and I'd love to know who."

The stubby, round, yet impeccably attired shape of Ziggie Hammit magically disappeared through the tiny horizontal door of the sports car and the side window rolled down. "I'll call ahead and set a date to bring Dancer to see you and Emma," Dad said.

"Do that, Paul. And please make it soon. She's a great lady, but she's having some health problems. Seeing Dancer would be good for her."

Twin exhaust pipes chortled briskly and Pirelli racing tires on shining chrome wire wheels surged forward on the edge of squealing. The little car leapt from the curb and swung sharply left at the stoplight, a small hand coming out the side window in a quick wave goodbye. Dad saw the corner of a smile beneath a white mustache as Ziggie Hammit's Jaguar disappeared, slipping effortlessly into heavy traffic on Huron Street.

"That was an interesting meeting, Dancer," Dad said, not expecting a reply. His declarative statement elicited a smile from his companion; a smile holding a great deal of recognition, so much more than Dad expected to see, he stopped to look directly into Dancer's eyes. "I think you've got a great friend for an attorney and I think you know you do."

Lawrence Ziegfield Hammit, Esq., was indeed a great friend, and, as Dad would soon understand, the eccentric white-haired, sports-car-driving counselor at law, with the shrewd assistance of a spinster named Flossie, had changed Dancer's life forever.

Eleven

Several weeks passed before Dad arranged to meet with Ziggie Hammit and Dancer's mom on a Saturday. November's calendar page was ripped aside and December's snows arrived, speaking of the immediacy of Christmas.

What I understood of acceptance and responsibility were about to change. Julie and I were included, invited along, and Mom joined us, making it a family trip. Dancer rode in the front passenger seat of our new, four-door Oldsmobile Eighty-Eight, his gaze intent on the road before us, his excitement impossible to conceal.

The trip south from Ann Arbor was no longer the childhood road trip I remembered. It no longer took us through the main streets of the small towns that segmented the length of the gentle two-lane road into ten- and fifteen-mile sections. Traveling on the new interstate, US-23, we went past Ypsilanti State Hospital and Dad studied its long red-brick buildings in the distance. Then we bypassed Milan and the intersection on Dexter Avenue where the Indian tree grew at a corner gas station. More than a century earlier, indigenous Native Americans bent and tied its trunk to the ground causing it to mature into a permanent marker on the pathways of their times. I never knew what it pointed to; only that it clearly indicated the direction its observers were to follow. What must it have been like to walk through the forests and along the streams with them before towns, before streets and roads?

Downtown Dundee's business district, a testimonial to the area's strong agrarian economy, no longer caused us to slow down or pause on our journey. The massive parallel concrete roadways of the new expressway went past, too intent on their destination and our speed of passage to regret the loss. Eventually we left the new, modern highway and took a narrow two-lane road west to Blissfield, moving comfortably into an unchanged, slower-paced rural backdrop.

Flat and monotonous, farmland stretched to the horizon. The county road's rough surface hummed beneath our tires, the sound accentuated by the steady, stinging spray of snowy slush under our front fenders. Its crowned shape tilted each passing vehicle but guaranteed adequate drainage during spring's heavy rains and summer's thunderstorms.

We were south and east of Adrian, the nearest city. Mr. Hammit lived in Adrian and kept his office there in an old building downtown. Farmhouses and barns loomed as ghostly marks on distant fields, each winter-sheltered by an oasis of pine trees and summer-shaded by huge oak and maple trees. Rather than falling, new snow blew sideways across open ground, hanging low in fine pellets, catching at the edges of the roadway, glazing its surface, sticking to and highlighting the stubs of corn stalks in fields harvested months earlier.

Mr. Hammit was at the farmhouse when we arrived. I couldn't tell which car in the drive was his and didn't know if it would be proper to ask. I was now of the age where cars and their engines and equipment monopolized my interests and I reveled in every teenage boy's obsession; their stylish features of preeminent importance. The margins of my daily classwork at school held small, pencil-drawn amateur attempts at automotive design, tires always too large and elliptical, all silhouettes more influenced by jet planes than Henry Ford. The red Jaguar convertible Dad described was nowhere in sight; no doubt carefully garaged, maybe even covered, waiting for the sunny days of spring.

Dancer's mother, Emma, and her husband lived on a picture-book farm a mile outside Blissfield. A long, rutted drive led off the highway and Dad slowed, cautiously moving up the grade toward the huge, rectangular two-story farmhouse through an inch or two of fresh snow. A porch light with a yellow bulb was on beside a side door, a glowing spot of brightness on a day already cast in shadow and grayness even though it was only three o'clock. Darkness lurks in cloudy Michigan winter days, ready to chase the hands on the clock to evening, impatient for night.

Inside, in the warmth of their large kitchen, the table was set with plates of cookies and sweets. A Christmas tree decorated with strings of popcorn and simple round glass ornaments and white ribbons fashioned into bows dominated the corner of the sitting room. Two short strings of lights provided minimal illumination. A tapered-cone-shaped gold angel with silver tin-foil wings crowned the top. The hand-painted features of its small, round-ball face calmly surveyed the room from its high perch.

Entranced, Dancer stood by the tree. His mother took his arm and led him to the sofa where he sat quietly at her side occasionally turning to study her face. Thin and aging prematurely, her coloring spoke of deeper maladies. Although the room was toasty warm, she wore a sweater with a shawl over her shoulders. Julie and I sat on straight-backed oak kitchen chairs Dad carried in and arranged between the sofa and the doorway.

Mr. Hammit, seated in a worn upholstered chair in the room's center, addressed us casually. "If only Miss Flossie Duncan could be here today," he said. "She made what I'm about to tell you possible, and I wish I could thank her in person. Would you like to tell the Conways what she did, Emma?"

Dancer's mom squeezed her son's hand and began. "Well, she was an amazing lady. She believed in the ability of a well-run business to prosper and provide a future for its owners and their heirs." A quiet cough interrupted her words but not her thoughts. "When she brought me here from Cincinnati, she bought a farm and hired its acres out to surrounding farmers; a farm was just as much of a business as a brick and building supply company, she said."

Emma's husband, Mills, leaned forward in his chair and continued for her. "Flossie knew about more than how to run a business. She knew a whole lot about life and its good parts and bad parts. My missus had died the year before and I was trying to raise my little girls and keep my farm going–those were tough times. Then, suddenly, there was Miss Flossie Duncan down the road with this beautiful young woman living with her and my life started over again. I'll always think she sort of directed our meeting and courting, she knew what it took for people to be happy."

"That's been a number of years hasn't it, Mills?" Emma said, looking across at her husband affectionately. "The girls are grown and married and it's just the two of us in this big old house. I'll always thank Miss Flossie for pointing me in the right direction; it's been a good life here with you." Her eyes glistened. "And then there's Tommy Daniel. He's always been part of my life although I couldn't be with him. Miss Flossie loved him and thought about his future too."

"Yes, she did," put in Ziggie Hammit. "Miss Duncan came to me with a plan. I'll never forget our first meeting. She insisted on going to lunch so we could talk informally. I was being studied and sized up. She asked good questions and carefully judged my experience. She knew exactly what she wanted to accomplish and engaged my services to ensure it happened."

Mr. Hammit reached across to a nearby table and picked up a large manila envelope and handed it to my father. "These are the fundamentals of the trust Miss Duncan directed me to start for Thomas Daniel Higgins's benefit. She appointed me her executor and ordered me, at her death, to use the proceeds from the sale of her farm to guarantee Dancer's future. I hope it's all right if I call him Dancer, Flossie told me it was okay to call him that–she always smiled at the name, there must have been something special, a story, behind it."

"There was, Ziggie," Emma said. "It all started with a young conscientious objector, Paul Conway, and a wonderful old nurse, Mattie Bigelow."

At the time, I was stunned by the term conscientious objector, squirming in my seat wondering about it. I meant to ask Dad about it on the ride home, but fell asleep, full of Emma's cookies and lulled by the hum and vibration of the slow trip through the accumulated fresh snow. Two months later, in a high school history class, the term came up and I startled my teacher with the intensity of my interest, bombarding him with questions.

"The papers in this envelope, am I supposed to hold on to them?" Dad asked.

"Those are copies of his trust documents and they're yours now, Paul. I'm sorry I couldn't tell you about them before. Emma and I were waiting to see how your relationship with him worked out here in Michigan. Making you his legal guardian was a big step and helped make it possible to move him to Michigan, but you've become a lot more than his legal representative. You've become his protector and his family. I watched the way you handled the situation with the newspaper reporter and the administrators at the two hospitals. You did a great job. And, before, when you called me to ask about purchasing health insurance for Dancer, I knew you were planning for his future and it was time for you to be involved in his finances."

"When you agreed to pay for his health insurance in full, I was only asking if his mother would help me. You know, to share in the cost. I didn't expect you to pay the entire premium, Ziggie."

"Dancer can afford to pay for his own health insurance. Miss Duncan believed in good, well-run businesses. After her death, I invested the inheritance she bequeathed to him in the three stocks she selected. One of the companies is IBM, International Business Machines, the other two are airplane manufacturers, Boeing and McDonnell-Douglas. Both have advanced substantially. Young Mr. Higgins is well on his way to becoming very wealthy."

Dad stared at the large envelope, speechless.

"Miss Duncan also took good care of her nieces and Emma," Mr. Hammit continued, "passing on to them the remainder, a substantial portion, of the equity of her own inheritance, her sister's husband's companies in Cincinnati. She left the brick and building supply business in its entirety to Mr. Stimson and her Blissfield farm to Dancer. As her attorney, I studied her plans and advised her they were well formed. As executor of her will, I followed her instructions and am pleased to say all her desires were achieved as she wished. She truly was a remarkable woman."

"Can these financial arrangements be kept confidential?" Dad asked.

"They have been and should continue to be kept confidential, Paul. It was just time for you to be aware of his financial status so you can make informed decisions about his care."

"Thank you, Mr. Hammit . . . Ziggie," Dad said, reacting quickly to the old lawyer's smile at being called "mister." "I'm relieved to know Dancer's future is secure. The entire field of mental health care is in a state of flux. This way, I'm sure you can make sound decisions based on any unforeseen expenses involved in his long-term care."

"It won't be just me, Paul. I want you to begin considering those factors. Emma and I would like to provide you with a financial power of attorney so you can handle his expenses."

"I'd be honored, but shouldn't those decisions remain with you and his mother?"

"I'm getting pretty long in the tooth and I've got to consider retiring someday. The choice of my successor as Dancer's attorney should be made by a family member."

"Of course, I'm sure you can recommend someone to his mother when the time comes."

"It may not be that simple," Emma interrupted. "Paul, I'm facing some serious health problems and the 'family' left to make those decisions for Dancer may be you. That's a reality every parent of a retarded adult child faces. I've chosen to make those decisions now. Mr. Hammit said it's important, you understand, in case something happens which limits my ability to do so. You've meant so much to him already; I hope you'll accept this new level of responsibility."

"It really would be a privilege to act on Dancer's behalf. And you're right; your son's become a part of our family, too. I promise you we'll be there for him. Not just me. All of us," Dad said, looking to Mom and Julie and me in turn. "I believe I speak for my whole family." We all nodded our concurrence.

Dad made a promise on a snowy December day and kept it. I'm proud to say Mom and Julie have also been true to Dad's pledge.

*   *   *   *   *

"Mills, it's all right. Go to town. You can't be hovering over me. Do you realize you haven't been to breakfast with your friends in two weeks? Stop and visit Ernie or Mike. Make the grocery run before you come back, that's all. I'll be okay. I'm going to sit here and read this book and watch the rain that's coming. I can't have you pacing around here all day."

He left reluctantly, chastised into leaving by her insistence and loving words. From the padded rocker on the three-season porch, she watched him pull out of the garage and swing around. Its exhaust puttering, the small vertical taillights of his old light-blue pickup melted away into the new gray rain, descending the long drive, and she felt a strange pang of parting. Storm-laden summer air moved the slack screening in an open window sheltered by the big maple overhanging the west end of the house. The heavier plops and spatters of large raindrops began striking nearby south-facing windowpanes, dropped by swirling winds. July's heat had dissipated, its intensity now reflected only in the fields of corn surrounding the house and outbuildings on three sides, the sun's energy transformed by God, time, and good soil into tall, thick stalks. Tassels over seven feet high shuddered, rustling as they anticipated the approaching storm's hot breath.

Emma closed her eyes and put her head back on the flower-patterned cushion of the tall rocker, her book clutched in her lap. As she dozed, thunder crept north and east, rumbling ominously. Forming in northern Ohio, it encroached stealthily across miles of cornfields, pushing darker and darker clouds forward, obliterating the midday sun. Twenty minutes later, lightning flashed horizontally, streaking past their farm, seeking earth's contact two counts of Mississippi away. Awakened by the storm's ferocity, she rose wearily from her chair and checked the end window. No rain had yet found its way through the screen. She pulled the double-hung window closed as the storm escalated.

She'd been reading *The Robe* by Lloyd C. Douglas. Setting it on a nearby table, Emma moved across the long, narrow three-season porch and stretched out on the old sofa facing its front windows. The rain commenced in earnest, hurled more and more savagely by the thunderstorm's winds.

She drifted off. Decades evaporated, swirling in the mist of sleep. A delightful sensation of youth and beauty enveloped her like a cold fog and she shivered involuntarily, released from the present. No longer sick or weak, she ran and laughed. Caught up in a dream of life's unrealized promises, yet sheltered in innocence, Emma stepped back easily into her childhood, to a time teetering on the edge of maturity. As rain pounded the porch roof, she imagined herself running home through a long-ago downpour. A boy, her magic Daniel, laughed by her side, his footfalls pounding up a narrow, hilly West Virginia dirt street in a wild cadence matched by her own running feet. Splashing water flew in every direction, flying upward only to be beaten down by the storm's fury. Then, sheltered from another storm in another time and place, she stood in a trance of tingling anticipation, moving across an old screened porch toward a daybed, curling up under a patchwork quilt to find love. Daniel was there and alive, a young boy so many years before war and the waves off a bloody beach on the coast of occupied France could reach out to claim the man he became.

Then Daniel's face changed, subtly turning to look away and turning back to her with a little boy's questioning eyes and a little boy's wordless expression. She gazed at her beautiful five-year-old son. This was love too, but with a stronger, more intense and lasting attachment–different and unique and endearing. The little boy would stay a child in her heart just as the images of Daniel, his lost father, would cling within sweet memories, the minutes of passion that forever marked the end of innocence and the beginning of life's difficulties. Content at journey's end, the beautiful girl from Ellenboro, West Virginia, set down her burden and went home.

Two hours later, a gentle rain falling, the storm abated, Mills came in from the kitchen carrying a bag of groceries, calling her name. He found her there on the sofa. It was the first week of August.

Dancer's mother's life was cut short by cancer. At her funeral, Dancer stood with her two step-daughters, Mills's daughters. They held his hands, seeking to comfort him, but Dancer's stoic presence soothed their grief instead as they wept uncontrollably. Dancer's face, devoid of tears, carried the look of a distant, deeper loss–the shadows of his past, those parts of his childhood retained as feelings rather than distinct memories, individual moments of his mother's love and embrace and care. As always, he kept his emotions inside, known only to him, secreted away in unexplainable calmness.

With his mother's passing, Dancer's wealth increased again. In her will, Emma left her inheritance from Miss Flossie Duncan in equal shares divided between her son and Mills's two daughters.

Dancer stared straight ahead. He was seated before his mother's coffin in the middle of the row of little wooden folding chairs beneath the sheltering tent in the small country churchyard. To his right, at the far end of the row, I tried to focus on the beautiful blanket of flowers adorning the oak coffin, but found it impossible not to turn and watch Dancer, wondering at his thoughts. Standing directly behind us, there to support Dancer, an eclectic group assembled: Lawrence Ziegfield Hammit; Roscoe Perkins and his wife; Alice Freeman, Emma's sister, and her husband, Joe; Dr. and Mrs. Isaiah O'Connor; and a tall man I didn't recognize. A dark-haired little boy, perhaps seven years old, stood to one side of the stranger staring at Dancer. A toddler, a boy, rested his head on the man's shoulder. The little girl at his other side gripped his hand, peering around his leg to watch us. Dad seemed to know who they were and went over to speak with the man after the minister completed the graveside ceremony and each of us, including Dancer, placed a rose on the simple casket.

When Dad brought the man over and introduced him and his children to Dancer and Emma's husband and his daughters, I made the connection. Three little lives spared from immolation in the twin fireballs that consumed a black '56 Ford Crown Victoria on Jackson Road. As Mills's daughters cried on an August afternoon, they, too, had wept at a mother's funeral. The survivors, now a shattered family, greeted Dancer warmly. They were, after all, a family unit, and the idea that family is defined in many ways struck me for the first time.

Life's turbulence may alter the groupings, like Emma, Dancer's mother, becoming a step-mom, moving on to raise and love Mills's daughters. But, however reconstituted, a family consists of those who care for and love each other. It's not only about birth certificates or marriage licenses; it's about the bond of love.

Twelve

eing a teenager is never easy. A peculiar period in everyone's life, adolescence evolves differently for boys and girls. Reasoning and maturity and sexuality swirl together in the kettle of youth, life's gumbo; we season to individual taste, then savor throughout decades of careers and marriages, children and grandchildren. During their teens both genders share a common link, their mutual, headlong rush to adulthood; often an awkward trip on a bumpy road marked by acne and heartbreak. Barring accident, puberty conquers preteen childhood foolishness, fourteen gets you fifteen, sixteen miraculously turns twenty, and we reach our intended destinations in life somehow grown and only slightly the worse for wear.

Reaching maturity, time temporarily speeds up. Weeks blink past, months are hiccups punctuated by book reports in English class, much-despised math homework, and weekend dates with nervous teen kisses. First cars replace worn bicycles and we drive to the prom wearing Dad's sport coat. Years blur together.

I remember my sister, Julie, changing. The tomboy I'd known quietly vanished. Suddenly, how her hair looked mattered. Little hints of make up appeared and clothing choices dominated her conversations with girlfriends. She tolerated me, never criticizing my dirty T-shirts and blue jeans. Trademarks of my concentrated efforts in advanced bicycle and amateur automobile mechanics, I wore a daily layer of fresh grease stains and ignored dirty fingernails. Julie, being kind, never told me to abandon my bristly crew-cut hair in favor of cooler styles. Years later, I noticed all my high school yearbook pictures looked like a skinny Drew Carey with a much-too-prominent proboscis and Dumbo's ears.

From September to June, Julie read constantly, spending incalculable hours poring over her textbooks. She was never happy to skate by, completing the minimum required for each day's homework, the benchmark of mediocrity to which I aspired. Instead, a young overachiever, she constantly studied beyond her assignments. Separated by interests and academics, our time together lessened. Busy with school and activities, we saw each other coming and going; young siblings passed at the dinner table and in hallways. Still close in our brotherly-sisterly concern for each other, life distanced us, mapping the direction of our futures. A single season of closeness remained.

Our summers brought us together in new family ventures. Mom and Dad both taught at the university, creating a work-play cycle governed by its calendar. June through August reigned as annual respites, freedom from classes, homework, term papers, and just about every other time-consuming ordeal. In calculated, frenetic leisure, we joined forces in summer's warm weeks to celebrate our strong sense of family and the magic, mysterious energy of those years. As if paroled, released from the grind of the school year, our summer journeys took us to new locales.

Small rented fishing cabins on the Platte River near Honor, Michigan, gave us an introduction to the state's great outdoors and what it meant to relax. Dad relished his hours fly fishing in the fast-moving, icy-cold, shallow water. I marveled at the smoothness of his casts and the way he handled the line. None of the pros on Mort Neff's *Michigan Outdoors* television show did as well.

The smooth, constantly extending horizontal S-shape of his fly line stretched out over the water, the invisible leader dropping his fly delicately in quiet, protected pools at the water's edge where monster trout rested. I attempted to emulate the artistry of man and fly rod, but merely achieved a boyish clumsiness. My casts moved jerkily by comparison, my line ripping the water's surface, my leader and fly intent on snagging low-hanging tree branches. Looking back, Dad's patience was exemplary. He displayed the trait when I managed to put out too much line, and, as line, leader, and fly zipped back, hooked the exact center of my forehead. The trip to the small town's doctor's office is still bookmarked as an embarrassing paragraph in the story of my youthful summers. The barb was pushed through, then clipped off and the hook backed out with needle-nose pliers. Mom said I was brave. Julie laughed and volunteered to change my bandage, curious about my fish-hook wound.

Mom surprised us with her willingness to embrace the simple cabin's lack of amenities. She deftly cleaned the rainbow trout Dad caught, frying silvery filets perfectly in an old black iron pan for amazing breakfasts.

The brilliance of summer mornings and the haze of its lazy, humid afternoons balanced the year's scales against nine months of books and classes. Yet Julie and I still grew up trapped in the shadow of our parents' scholarship. As kids, we worked our way through the arduous routines of junior high and high school, caught up in our place in the educational process and in obvious, direct comparison to our parents' achievements. The aura of wisdom created about them by their doctoral degrees and teaching careers stood as an unspoken goal. Julie met their standard. I didn't.

But there's more to learning than books. During those summers, the classroom of the great outdoors taught character. To see our bookish parents relaxing on wooden Adirondack chairs, drinking beer from cans opened with what Dad called his church key, and discussing the relative advantages of fishing flies and salmon eggs was perplexing. On long, wonderful evenings, we watched them play euchre with the couple who owned the cabins. They laughed, and after Julie and I were in our beds in the next room and they thought we were sleeping, told stories about us. Their pride in us was clear and we grew to appreciate the basic and unassuming essence of our parents. Over cards, beer, and fishing lore, never once did they mention their positions as professors; I only heard the phrase, "work at the university." Those evenings were about friendship, not status.

Mom and Dad listened and learned about northern Michigan. The places mentioned soon became stops along our way on summer journeys. Dancer and I jumped and slid down the dramatic, nearly vertical face of a giant sand dune and Julie held her breath as we crossed the five-mile-long Mackinac Bridge, refusing to look down from its high perch over blue water. Even as kids, we should have seen the pattern, the change coming, the boundaries of our world expanding.

Dancer came along on our trips north. He reacted to the woods and streams and scenery with undisguised fascination. Eyes wide, he never tired of seeing new places. Having grown up in institutional settings, he peered off into the distance seeking the next horizon, his joy in discovery silent, yet intense. Given a simple instruction by Mom or Dad, he sat and enjoyed the scene before him. He never showed any sign of boredom or uneasiness, and never strayed away from us on his own. Enraptured, he simply took it all in. On several occasions, we noticed how closely the birds would come to Dancer, totally unafraid of his presence in their world. The birds understood, Dancer simply made things calm and safe. On one of our return trips across the Mackinac Bridge from camping in the Upper Peninsula, Dancer coaxed Julie into looking out the car window. Holding her hand, he cured her fear of the bridge's height. His steadfast guidance replaced her trepidation with amazement over the beautiful, wide horizons stretched before her.

Although too young to understand, those few amazing years of family vacations, those pivotal growing-up years, vested me with a sense of family as community. I learned the value of closeness–even if destiny would take such wisdom away from me for several years. It would come back. Not even a horrible war in Southeast Asia could take it away forever. The really important values in life always come back.

Those summer vacations represented the happiest of episodes. Until they were gone, I never understood that life's totality is the sum of periods of coming together like we did each summer and periods of moving apart, being alone. Sometimes we create our own segments of loneliness; often misinterpreting them as times of self-reliance. Sometimes politics and war create those periods of loneliness for us.

Many of my friends waited for the simple form letter from the local draft board. "Greetings," those letters began. The strangely cheerful word told them to kiss their girlfriends goodbye, sell their cars, and put their futures on hold. Eighteen years old and a June 1969 high school graduate with no immediate plans for college, I'd known it was coming and enlisted instead. For a lot of reasons I couldn't articulate, I wanted to go. I wanted to get it over with. It wasn't about a sense of duty or any romantic, patriotic ideas about going to war. A dark cloud hung over my generation. I chose to face our Asian enemies rather than run from them.

Mom cried. Dad did his best to keep a stiff upper lip. To his credit, he never openly opposed my enlistment or mentioned his own experience as a conscientious objector during WWII. When we discussed Vietnam, he gave me the best advice he could: respect the chain of command, be vigilant, take whatever job they gave me seriously, and learn everything they taught me as if my life depended upon it, because it did. Then he shook my hand as a man. He might not have wanted me to go, but he respected my right to make my own decision.

The anticipation and quick days of preparation flew past. Then going to war meant nervous excitement, a long quiet family car ride to Ft. Knox, Kentucky, tears and hugs and goodbyes, boot camp and new uniforms. Suddenly bound up in a finite two-year enlistment, the limits of eternity rested within a measurable thirteen months of jungle warfare, death, and horror. Going to war was too easy. Coming home was a son of a bitch.

The reception for returning Vietnam vets–especially wounded survivors facing orthopedic challenges, was a national disgrace. We knew better than to expect ticker-tape parades, but we did think of ourselves as citizen soldiers who obeyed the law and did what our country demanded. Arriving back in our native land, we were spurned as baby killers. The eyes of passers-by noticed our missing limbs and burned faces and quickly looked away. Instead of soldiers home from war, we were diseased outcasts–guilty of an unjust, undeclared attack on "those poor Asian peasants."

Home from a jungle hell, we thought differently, haunted by images of vicious killers in filthy black pajamas and the screams of our dying friends. To us, the survivors, those innocent peasants were Charlie, sub-human devils hiding behind women and children in villages during the day and murdering us by night.

Beyond immediate family, our welcome home was anything but; the affront heaped emotional scars atop physical ones. Gratitude for our service in uniform? Not a chance. Politicians and schemers sent us over. Tens of thousands of long-haired hippie protestors and Hanoi Jane welcomed us home.

Vietnam's pervasive ugliness meant close friendships were transitory and rare. Seeing the long black vinyl bags and hearing the daily body count, we often found solace in staying distant, reserved; tough guys on our own. We knew the moment could come when the person next to us disappeared, gone in the hollow thud and instant mist of blood from a head shot or pleading for death's release from a sucking chest wound or an abdomen shredded by shrapnel. Knowing no helicopter evacuation came until dawn when reinforcements arrived, help hours away–the minutes of life's clock vanished, an interminable countdown to oblivion. Too many dying eyes brimmed with desperate tears, contemplating the night sky.

Back home, the war protesters never stepped up to these realities. Hanoi Jane's righteous indignation was two-dimensional, as transparently phony and shallow as the tight short shorts and high boots she wore on her Hollywood movie posters. Our world, those thirteen months in Vietnam–that was reality, a three-dimensional nightmare. Students chanting and carrying placards on America's streets or running to Canada and the future senator plotting to give false testimony to Congress prolonged the war for those of us fighting it. Their actions etched a few thousand extra precisely lettered names on a granite wall. Coming home to the reception we received, it was too easy to hate them more than Charlie in his pajamas. It was too easy to run away from the society that rejected us. Even if we were back in the United States, it was their United States; it didn't seem to be ours anymore.

Like every other war in history, as eighteen-year-old expendable bullets fired by the great gun of our government, we developed our own language, our own expressions for the minutia of each day's absurdity. Two of the common terms of our existence were "tagged" and "ticketed." The boys starting their journey home in body bags were tagged and oblivious to the means or duration of their transport. After thirteen months, those completing the duty cycle without getting wounded got ticketed, receiving their ticket home. That was the contract we signed. They were in the final stages of the process. First, they became short-timers, counting weeks and finally days, then, ultimately, FIGMO–F--- It, Got My Orders. Guys in the last days of FIGMO hid from any chance of seeing action and no one blamed them. Envious, we left them alone, awaiting our turn. Soldiers lucky enough to survive and get ticketed also included those whose wounds kept them from returning to the fight.

Being a short-timer and getting your orders meant going home, but, as one entry on our long list of superstitions, we never, ever spoke the word "home." Home was the real world. We weren't in it. Rather than saying home, the guys would ask questions about what was going on in the world. We knew they meant home, wherever it was stateside, out there beyond the shores of the shit hole we fought in every night and every day.

Julie was back in the world going to college. Mom and Dad were teaching at the University of Michigan. Dancer still lived at

Mercywood Sanitarium out on Jackson Road west of Ann Arbor. Mr. Hammit still drove his red Jaguar convertible, or did Dad's letter say he'd gotten a new little silver Mercedes? Their lives existed in the real world. Not that the real world was perfect or entirely safe. I'm sure there were still car accidents on Jackson Road, hopefully not as bad as the fiery crash where Dancer rescued the three little kids. It was, however, best not to dwell on thoughts of friends or family living back in the world, that could be too distracting and anyone distracted here could end up tagged.

I didn't get tagged, but I did get ticketed at a week less than seven months in-country. Looking back, the war didn't print my ticket. Being just-turned-nineteen and living a moment in time that mixed fear and death and bravery and laughter in equal portions printed my ticket.

Five of us had stretched out with our gear on the floor of a deuce and a half. The brilliant midday sun felt like an open oven door. Its radiance baked our normally wet uniforms beyond dry, caking the layers of dirt and sweat and smeared grime permeating them. When it rained in South Vietnam, it came in sheets, unrelenting daylong downpours. When the sun got its turn, it wasted no time in sucking all that moisture back up so the sky could throw it down again. It was not a land of moderation. Neither was it a place to let your guard down like we did that day.

The little guy, the tunnel rat, I think his name was Beetlie or Wheatley, something like that. Funny, I can see his face, but his name eludes me. He had his eyes closed tight and his sawed-off, double-barreled twelve-gauge across his lap. The sunlight was too strong for his eyes. He wore dark sunglasses or kept his eyes shut whenever out in bright sunshine; none of us faulted him for that. He worked the tunnels. Strangely proud of his prowess and possessive of his shotgun, he actually looked forward to killing Charlie's moles. Protecting his night vision was critical so he favored rainy days over sunny ones. He might be crawling back into an underground maze any time and needed to be ready. The twelve-gauge, a specialized tool of his trade, warranted the same respect and special consideration. In the enclosed confines of a tunnel, a load of buckshot filled the space, requiring neither the time nor accuracy of aiming.

He wasn't the only one with his eyes closed. The stupidity of the moment or the beautiful, warm sunshine lulled us all into a state of dangerous lethargy. The light-duty six-by-six truck bounced along the muddy tire-slashed lane through dense, sometimes overhanging jungle. Calling it a road would have been a misuse of the word; it was merely a lane cut by the passing of men and ordnance in a variety of M151s and cargo trucks and trailers. Our two-and-a-half ton, the army's grocery-getter, was light enough to move through these non-roads without bogging down but heavy enough to carry the rations, supplies, and ammunition mandatory to support our monotonous patrols, most of which were conducted under cover of darkness. Riding along in the midday sun implied a sense of security, a lessening of vigilance that helped print my ticket.

The little Vietnamese man in dirty black pajamas with his rifle slung across his chest rode out of the narrow foot path directly toward the side of our truck. The look of shock on his face changed to recognition in a heartbeat. He frantically jumped off his girl's-style English bicycle, grabbed his rifle, and reached around to level it at us. He never accomplished the task, but gained an eternity to think about the hatred of Americans that consumed him. I was leaning back against the opposite side of the truck's cargo box looking directly at him as he came right at us. Instinctively, I reached across and picked up the tunnel rat's shotgun. His eyes shot open at the sudden removal of its weight from his lap, blinking into the sun's glare and twisting sideways as I stood and aimed above his head. The unexpected blast of the shotgun brought the truck's three other passengers wide awake and scrambling for cover.

Just like in a tunnel, the effective cone of the sawed-off twelve gauge's pattern did its job well. Charlie never finished aiming his old rifle. The load of buckshot tore into his chest and face, knocking him backwards off his feet as we passed by, never stopping to determine his fate. If he lived, he didn't live for long.

"Jesus Christ, Conway, give me that gun. What the hell do you think you're doing?"

"Saving your dumb, sleeping ass, that's what I'm doing."

The other guys were looking back down the lane trying to get a parting glimpse of Charlie and his bicycle. Their nervous laughter mingled with smart-ass remarks about my shooting skills and the dangers of jungle roads and we all relaxed, again dropping our guard against the unexpected.

"Come on, Conway. I can't be without my sawed-off. Give it back, okay?"

"Let me just hold it awhile," I said, clowning as the adrenalin rush subsided. "I'll give it back. Besides, I might get another little bike rider."

Taking a human life, even that of a nasty little vermin intent on taking yours, leaves you rattled, but I should've passed the shotgun back when the tunnel rat asked for it; my mistake. Whether fate or foolishness, the next few careless moments marked the rest of my life. Not all of life's surprises are pleasant.

The unexpected jounce of the rumbling cargo truck's right wheels seconds later dropped me straight down. I remember the sensation of hanging in the air, weightless before the fall. The rebound of the truck's heavy rear axles slammed upward, smashing dual, square-tube, Rockwell axle housings into the frame, causing the second barrel of the shotgun to fire. It was, after all, a sawed-off shotgun, probably no more than two feet long.

Whatever possessed me to drape my left wrist casually across the end of its twin barrels fell hopelessly into the past, into time before the accident, never to be rectified. The reason no longer mattered. That's what I'd done as we rode through jungle sunshine. The blast of the gun firing straight up carried the same sound as when I'd fired it killing bike-riding Charlie, but this time a cloud of pink mist blew skyward.

There really wasn't any pain, only a sense of numb panic and vacant disbelief. Where my wrist had been seconds before, only a mass of ragged, stringy tissue and white bone remained. The hand formerly attached to that wrist flew away into the passing dense green foliage. The useful opposing thumb and the four fingers that tapped out Beach Boys songs on tables, picked my nose, fumbled with my girl's brassiere clasp, and held the can of Simonize when I waxed my car disappeared; a quick meal for a rodent or small scavenging animal; American cuisine Vietnamese style.

"Dumb bastard," someone said.

Another voice, dripping sarcasm, corrected, "Lucky bastard, that's his ticket."

I watched my own blood spurt for two or three seconds before realizing the glistening red liquid squirting in measured intervals was mine. Just before losing consciousness, I felt two of my buddies grab me and pull me back down to the truck's floor. Apparently, I'd stood up. The tourniquet they pulled tight around my forearm, a nylon cord ripped out of the end of a duffle bag, saved my life, keeping me from bleeding out, a dirty green T-shirt pressed against the wound.

I never got the chance to thank them for their triage skills. I like to think I'd have done the same for one of them if they'd been stupid enough to get their hand blown off by a shotgun. I don't remember much about the helicopter ride out either. I got ticketed. If Bicycle Charlie had arrived a minute earlier and heard our truck coming toward his path out of the thick leafy growth, I could have been tagged. A variation of inches in the path of a bullet or the split second timing of an enemy's response determined the difference between a ticket and a tag for thousands of young Americans.

* * * * *

That first year out, you tell yourself you're going to write to your buddies, to stay in touch. You don't. Life gets in the way. That's if you have a life. I didn't, but I had a ton of anger. I didn't need war buddies to help me relive those seven months out of the world, although I bet the story of the dumb ass balancing a sawed-off shotgun under his wrist got retold again and again. Colorful images based on stupidity and teaching good lessons bear repeating. I found I didn't belong in the world I'd returned to. A less-than-memorable year passed before I found myself back in my world, a world I created albeit sometimes in a blind, drunken rage against demons in black pajamas and hippie girls in airports.

Real consciousness returned in a crowded hospital ward at a base in the Philippines. Looking up and down the row of beds, comparing wounds and counting appendages, I got off easy. Next, after reconstructive surgery to create a solid stump, I was moved to Hawaii; not the tourist version, the army version of sterile hospital wards with good doctors and chunky, thirty-something nurses who were all business. On that visit to Hawaii, I never saw any wide sand beaches, surfers, or lithe, tanned girls in bikinis.

The first time I set foot back in the continental United States, CONUS to whoever wrote my separation orders, was at Los Angeles International Airport, LAX, and I'll never forget it. I walked up the angled length of the extendible jetway, attempting unsuccessfully to stuff the two *Hot Rod* magazines I'd purchased and read on the flight into my sling without bumping my heavily bandaged left forearm, and stepped through the door out into the gate area. A girl, at first I couldn't be sure it was a girl, leaned forward, yelled something close to my ear, and spit on my uniform. Pure reflex and a good remaining right hand made me throw the rolled magazines in her face. They hit pretty hard, I heard the smack. She jumped back screaming. Shocked, I turned toward her, bracing myself for what or who might come next. Nothing did, just more taunts and obscenities from the girl and the small group of protesters behind her. What that girl, probably my age and definitely lost in her vehement anti-war cause, will never know is that if I'd been armed she'd have died right there. No questions asked, I'd have dropped her as cold as Charlie bike-rider and every one of his countrymen I'd sent to communist heaven.

After my warm welcome to Los Angeles, I hid in the USO lounge in its huge airport terminal and the one in my next, smaller, connecting airport, drinking fruit punch in paper cups and eating stale cinnamon doughnuts. Suddenly I wanted to see uniforms, any uniforms. Heartened to sit and talk with sailors in their whites, I avoided civilians. Back then, our superiors instructed us to travel in uniform. Dad said the tradition went back to World War II when many of the states, probably because of gas rationing, passed laws making it a crime not to stop and pick up any serviceman hitch-hiking in uniform. Apparently their welcome home was better than ours; a grateful nation even made sure they got rides to and from their hometowns when home on leave. Things change. Nowadays personnel of any service branch are instructed to travel in civvies. Deemed too big a security risk, uniforms are rolled tight and packed in heavy canvas duffle bags, as if the haircuts aren't obvious.

At Detroit Metropolitan Airport, my folks and Julie stood waiting in a little row with Dancer to their left looking lost in the crowd. I remember lots of tears and hugs made awkward by my sling. The minute I got home, I tore off my uniform, balled it up, and threw it away. I've never worn anything olive drab since. May arrived in Michigan. The high school class of 1970 prepared for graduation, closing the turbulent decade of the sixties. More naive eighteen-year-olds prepared to enlist rather than wait for their letter from the draft board. Some came home ticketed and unscathed except for images that never faded or went away. Some, also ticketed, were wounded, many far worse than me. Too many, thousands, got tagged, making the trip home in austere military coffins.

After ten or twelve days at home, I started to assemble everything necessary for my escape. Although not a conscious decision, the idea just snuck up on me. Using some of the money I'd sent home, I first went car shopping.

Small realities surrounded me. Shaving in the morning was difficult and time consuming. One-handed drivers have trouble with stick-shift cars, an issue I discovered when trying to negotiate Ann Arbor's one-way streets in Mom's little yellow VW convertible. My dreams of a big-cubic-inch, V8 muscle car with a four-speed transmission vaporized in the realization that manipulating the curved chrome T-handle of a Hurst floor shifter left no hand to grip the steering wheel. I ended up finding a good deal on a two-year-old Chevy El Camino with the basic small-block V8 and a Hydramatic transmission. No race car, but better gas mileage and easy to drive. Part car and part truck, it suited my needs perfectly.

Old friends, after difficult, bumbling first reunions and hand shakes, quickly deserted me as if I had the plague–I guess they feared I carried some Vietnamese virus, so a two-seater El Camino sufficed. I didn't need to carry a lot of passengers. Girls I remembered from high school physically winced at the sight of the rolled and pinned cuff of my left sleeve. Compassion and understanding were scarce commodities. Without written plans, I found myself stocking up on gear needed to camp up north. The vinyl tonneau cover on the El Camino meant I could keep stuff dry and it offered just enough space. Anything valuable I could lock in the front, a cab identical to the bench seat and dashboard of a standard, mid-size Chevrolet Malibu.

Dad knew. Selling him on the idea took two minutes. Almost without discussion, he dropped what he was doing and began helping me get everything ready for the trip. His ability to understand my longing for distance and isolation came either from his skills in psychology or from watching his generation's wounded and maimed veterans come home. In spite of my efforts to hide it, he read the seething anger beneath the surface of an uncomfortable return.

The need was obvious; a change of venue and time to recover made perfect sense. Cedarville could work. At least it was an immediate, available alternative to living at home in Ann Arbor, and it provided a reasonable distance away from everyone who had problems accepting the permanently altered, one-handed me. Several months later, before the snows of the next winter descended on the Upper Peninsula, I realized Dad understood the other basic realities I needed to face. I don't know if I will ever be as perceptive as he was, but I eventually learned to thank him for his caring.

The prescription he wrote for me included fresh air, time alone, and lots of hard work. I didn't see the hard work coming, but, ultimately, it was my salvation. Dad recognized I needed time to forgive myself and gave me the means to get the job done. It wasn't easy for either of us.

Thirteen

I was younger, hadn't been to war, and still possessed two hands when I first saw the land along what became Bay Drive. At fifteen, almost sixteen, gangly, and more kid than adult, my perceptions still carried childhood's lack of definition. But I remembered the trees and rocks and big water, the overpowering, majestic sense of wilderness. The day before Dad, with Ziggie Hammit's legal advice, closed on the incredible lakeshore property east of Cedarville in the U.P., Dad's financial conservatism and concern about borrowing money contributed to a case of cold feet, almost jinxing the deal. On the drive north, Mr. Hammit reassured him, pointing out the long-term benefits of the land purchase, comparing the costs to the returns. Of course it was a big investment, but it wasn't about now, he said, it was about twenty or thirty years from now, and he was right. Grandpa Mike had told Dad the very same thing in different words. He compared the land purchase to the tuition expense of getting a college degree, the process he associated with a farmer borrowing for seed money in anticipation of a later return. That was always his favorite analogy for worthwhile ventures. It'll be worth it when you've platted the land and sold off the other lots, Grandpa said, and he was right, too.

We stayed in St. Ignace and spent the next day driving around the area. We drove out to the land twice and slowly made our way along the edge of the property. I stood where the woods touched the stony beach. The incredible big lake spanned the width of forever, and, without realizing it, I fell in love with how the horizon over open water meets the curvature of the earth. The view is humbling. When it speaks, it questions what's beyond, but answers back–why do we need to know, why even ask, we have here and now.

Dad and Mr. Hammit hardly spoke as we walked. They only studied the shoreline, stared into the dense woods, and occasionally pointed, said a word or two, and nodded in agreement. Their steady concentration without any real exchange of words made me think of Dancer. At dinner in town they talked continuously and sketched the outline of the land with a winding road down the middle and a row of parallel lot lines from the road to the water that looked like a child's drawing of a rope ladder. The following morning we went to a realtor's office in a little white house on the main road between Hessel and Cedarville. Folders full of papers were signed and exchanged and Mr. Hammit smiled a lot on the way home. Ziggie knew a good thing when he saw it.

Returning at nineteen with a scraggy new beard and only the fingernails on one hand to scratch the itchy growth on my face, I'd changed, Lake Huron hadn't. The drive north on a slowly warming Michigan spring day provided a sense of release.

I'd gone up US-27 through Lansing and stopped mid-morning to visit a friend going to Michigan State. As arranged by a phone call, I sat on a concrete bench outside his dorm watching passing students, my left forearm tucked in my jacket pocket, and caught him as he came back from an early class. He was changed, too. Animated about college and football games and girls and living away from home, within fifteen minutes my friend unloaded his fear of getting drafted and going to Vietnam. Sitting there minus a hand, I suppose I reinforced his concern. Grades, grades were his enemy; he had to maintain good grades to keep his deferment. The whole setting seemed surreal to me, an artificial sphere of daily life called college spun by learned magicians, a subset of society divided into semesters and requiring tuition payments. I'd never bought into its culture and still couldn't get excited about it. I asked what he was studying and he rattled off a list of basic courses and said he wouldn't begin his actual agri-business classes until the next year. High school all over again; I shook my head in bewilderment at the contrived environment.

A late lunch at the Doherty Hotel in Clare, a stop Mom and Dad highly recommended, was terrific. The first time I'd been there by myself, it proved to be a dividing line. Behind me, to the south, my childhood stood in tall stacks of memories. In front of me, in the north woods, a new life as a young adult awaited me, its photo album pages empty. I ate in the small formal dining room off the old lobby. Bypassing the buffet, I ordered a great cheeseburger with fries and a big glass of milk, the basic stuff every returning soldier can't get enough of. At the hospital in Hawaii a nurse taught me to cut burgers and sandwiches into sections to make them easier to pick up. If the waitress noticed my empty sleeve, she didn't flinch or say anything. I looked a sight, but no one seemed to notice. My chin bristled with several days of new beard and my former short military buzz cut had grown out into an unmanageable fuzzball no comb or oily Brylcreem hair tonic could tame. Fumbling for bills and change from my jeans pocket, dropping some and spilling the rest on the counter, the girl at the cash register only smiled and helped me. Walking to my El Camino parked at the curb, I looked up and down the little town street. It felt peaceful and normal, life going on as it should; I sensed that the anti-war protests in Ann Arbor on the steps of the Michigan Union didn't happen in Clare, Michigan. No hippie girl screamed in my ear and spit on me. The spring day welcomed me back.

Across the Mackinac Bridge and north to my turn east on M-134, I reached Cedarville in the early evening as dusk approached. Mom and Dad wanted me to stay in a motel in St. Ignace the first night, but I stopped for gas and pushed on. They couldn't conceive of the nights I'd spent catching sleep in quick half hours on my poncho on the ground in a Southeast Asian jungle, jolted awake by the snapping of a twig. By comparison, stretching out in a sleeping bag in the loft of a lakeside garage, listening to the steady murmur of waves finding a stony beach, beckoned like the quiet comfort of a five-star luxury hotel.

No sign or mailboxes yet marked the entrance to Bay Drive. The name existed only on the plats surveyed and recorded with the state. Cutting the single-lane road through the length of the pristine waterfront acreage two years earlier defined the dimensions of the property. A bulldozer followed the meandering curves of the land, bypassing giant boulders, moving through new growth, sparing the largest clumps of old cedar trees. A daunting task in Dad's realm of associate professors, textbooks, and dissertations, clearing the road was everyday business to the local contractor hired to complete the job. The wooded land between M-134 and the rocky beach of Lake Huron, as it stretched over the distance separating the Les Cheneaux Islands and Drummond Island, lay east and west, parallel to the highway. Past a relatively flat shelf, it sloped gradually toward the bay. The land adjacent to the water maintained twelve to fifteen feet of elevation until it met the waves in a final drop dotted with huge, glacier-stacked, volcanic stones and an uncountable covering of millions of smaller rocks, fist-sized to bushel-basket-sized, pushed up by tens of thousands of years of winter ice leaning against spring thaws.

Dusk met dappled, fading light in deep shadows cast by towering pines and cedars lining the two-thirds of a mile of gravel drive. Winding my way in, I carefully avoided large puddles accumulated in low spots. I stopped twice to drag fallen branches aside. Every three or four hundred feet, a wide spot in the gravel path split to the left or right side to allow cars or trucks to pass. Traffic, however, other than herds of deer moving to the water, wasn't a concern. No one was there, just me.

The road reached east through the woods to its termination at the four two-hundred-foot wide Conway lots, culminating in a small circle, a dead end, halfway into our parcels. At the dead end, a single, narrow driveway went right, turning toward the water and stopping at the only building on our land, a lapboard-sided, wooden storage building patterned off a three-car garage but with only one sixteen-foot-wide roll-up overhead door. Dad had the large garage built early the prior summer just before I left for boot camp. Arriving there nearly a year later as damaged goods, I felt I belonged at a dead end, real or symbolic, for a lot of reasons.

Three other two-hundred-foot frontages had been sold at the other end of the drive near the entrance where the gravel lane turned north and met the paved highway, but the new owners hadn't begun building yet. Over the coming years the lots lining the lake would be sold off, broken in half into hundred-foot lots and sold again. I've always been glad our lots were wider and more secluded at the farthest end of the drive.

The idea germinated from Dad and Ziggie Hammit's plans for Dancer's future. Both understood he would need his own place someday and they chose well. The original plan, building a group home for Dancer and four or five other adults with special needs, never happened, but eventually Dancer lived there alone; self-reliant, yet surrounded by Conways.

The next morning, after a long sit by the lake wrapped in a plaid wool stadium blanket against the cold wind of morning, yet basking in the tranquility of the view, I drove to town and ate a huge breakfast at its only tiny restaurant. Genuine welcomes greeted me at the local hardware store and around the corner at the lumber yard. Calling ahead, Dad set up accounts for me to use to procure supplies and materials. Like my lunch in Clare the prior afternoon, nothing about my appearance caused alarm or warranted undue curiosity; of course they noticed, but they didn't flinch and they didn't ask. If a place called Vietnam existed, its newsworthiness went unnoticed north of the bridge in Michigan's Upper Peninsula.

Back at Bay Drive, I pulled the El Camino off the gravel to pass utility trucks and stopped to talk with the crews setting poles and stringing new electric lines. After waiting for the snow to melt, the power company moved rapidly to complete the lines. The woven wire cord of civilization reached my home in the garage loft by week's end. With power on the property, I contracted for the installation of a well and found a local company to dig and place a septic tank and field. The latter, given the rock shelf along the shore, required trailering a small dozer out from town to create a clearing, cutting the fallen trees as firewood, a few dump-truck loads of sand, and moving some soil around. It was fascinating and I listened to everything they said about the project as they worked.

Living there and following Dad's written instructions, my role as general contractor kept me occupied. By the time Mom and Dad and Julie and Dancer began coming to stay for long weekends and an occasional week over the summer, my Yooper accommodations included indoor plumbing. The tiny bathroom with a shower stall under the stairs going to the loft worked well for one, but grew crowded and messy with the accumulated paraphernalia of a family; the towels, combs, toothbrushes, soaps, and shampoos of four or five residents.

Dad and Dancer and I removed ourselves to sleeping bags on air mattresses in tents along the sheltering tree line at the shore each night, relinquishing the loft to Mom and Julie. I'd never seen Dancer happier. He simply glowed, his bright eyes beaming as he studied the cedar trees and the wide expanse of blue water reaching to touch the horizon. Passing freighters far out from shore caught and held his concentration. He woke me one night to show me the lights of a freighter anchored out off the island chain waiting for morning to pull into the dolomite plant west of us. As if a small city rose from under the waves, its lights bounced and flickered across the wrinkled surface of Lake Huron. Dancer pointed and smiled.

Our discussions, long family meetings gathering inputs from four of us and nods from Dancer, revolved around planning the house to be built on the center of the next-to-last lot, the one just past the turn-around. The end lot, to which no driveway access was planned, was Dancer's.

Dancer stayed close by my side during their visits as if subliminally conscious of something different, something wrong. It reminded me of years before when he shadowed Julie as she recovered from polio. With wordless companionship, Dancer showed his concern.

My parents and Julie weren't wordless. At first, their less-than-subtle attempts at persuasion were light and cheerful; direct but tactful. Each in their way wished I'd come back to Ann Arbor and look for work or go to school. Incredulous, none of them could accept my reluctance to leave Cedarville. Without reaching open disagreement, our differing views lurked dangerously close to breaking the surface of conflict over what I wanted versus what they thought best for me. I tried hard to appreciate their good intentions, but shouldn't the decision be mine?

In the end, I declared my independence, defending my decision to stay and work, preparing the lot for next spring. What about winter, they asked; wouldn't I move home when winter came?

In rebuttal, I pointed out the garage's indoor plumbing, electricity, and new insulation. In summation, I pointed out the tiny kitchen and the wood stove Dad and I installed. Case closed, I'd be comfortable. It's where I wanted to be, doing what I wanted to do, I said. Send me good books to read, I told them. I'll come home for Thanksgiving and Christmas, but I'm staying here. Woven tightly throughout Conway DNA, stubbornness borders on defiance. They finally acquiesced.

Labor Day weekend came and went. The bells in Burton Tower off State Street tolled distantly as the September-to-June gravitational force of higher education pulled my parents and Julie back downstate to Ann Arbor. A period of coming together ended. A period of loneliness began. I loved my family, but still sought distance, a separation allowing me to hide in the isolation of my new surroundings. It was like needing to be alone with thoughts I didn't have, waiting to realize truth I couldn't find.

Days of Indian summer, tokens of consolation ahead of winter's wrath, mingled over weeks of beautiful autumn weather. I went to work shaping the land for the building project planned for spring. The work was long and strenuous and required me to adapt to my new physical limitations. Every morning at full light, I began moving rocks using a low, rubber-tired, steel-mesh wagon. I'd found the oversized, rusty conveyance, an antique relative of a Radio Flyer, at a local farm auction. With my four-wheeled wheelbarrow and a strong, six-foot-long steel-pipe pry bar with a flattened end the hardware store located for me, I moved rocks.

Hanging onto the steel bar and pulling the wagon offered complications at first. Taking a pair of thick leather construction gloves into a shoe repair shop in St. Ignace and explaining my predicament to its owner, I found the assistance I needed. He puzzled over the left glove for a moment, examining its stitching and asked to see the stump of my left forearm. Unaffected by its scars, as if fitting a shoe to a foot without toes, he measured once across and twice around its end with a cord and marked the lengths on a piece of light-tan sole leather in a butterfly-shaped pattern. Smiling through bad teeth, he kept the gloves and asked if I could come back in an hour. I could and I did after first sitting on a bench at the water's edge in a park by the car ferry launch to Mackinac Island, then wandering up and down the sidewalks of St. Ignace's main street. The display windows in the tourist stores held knick-knacks, walking sticks made from cedar branches, and beautiful Native American paintings of eagles and deer and trout. Everything was on sale. Fifty-percent-off signs abounded, mixed with "Closed until Spring" notices posted in darkened shops.

Returning, the shoe repairman motioned me over to a counter by his large sewing machine near the back of the store. "Stick that arm up here and let's see what we can do about making this leather end fit without being too tight."

I followed his instructions, curious about what he'd made for me. Pulling a stool up, I placed my elbow on the countertop with my arm sticking up like someone who wanted to arm wrestle but forgot the hand required to grip his opponent's. He brought over a leather cup fashioned to fit over the end of my arm. It was sewn on two sides with two opposite seams left unfinished. Pulling it down over my arm carefully, he leaned close to examine the fit. A thin smile emerged as he admired his own work.

"Not too bad, I think it'll work. I fashioned a thick leather shoe one time for a friend's horse with a cracked, tender hoof. Of course I used a thinner piece of leather for yours and I worked it to make it softer and more pliable," he said, marking the remaining seams for a perfect fit. "And I don't want you to think I'm treating you like an old horse, son, but it's the same idea. The leather should protect without hurting your arm."

The man bent over his sewing machine and, in a matter of seconds, finished stitching the open seams while talking to me with his back turned, "This goes under your work glove. Keep the cuff string on the glove pulled tight so dirt and wood chips can't get inside the cup and it should work fine. I think it'll last you for a while and the longer you wear it the better it'll form to your arm. Try not to get it too wet, okay, and let it dry slowly in the shade if it does."

"This is great," I told him, admiring my new protective leather arm cup. "How much do I owe you, sir?"

The shoe repairman came over to where I sat and put his large, calloused hands out flat, palms down, fingers splayed on the countertop. "Son, it's not my business to pry, but that wound isn't all that old and from your age, your hair growing out, and the way you say 'sir,' I'm figuring you lost that hand in Vietnam, not in an accident working with farm machinery or in a factory. I served four years in World War II and came home alive with both these old hands I've used to fix shoes ever since. A few of my friends weren't as lucky." Reaching out to shake my hand, he placed his left on top, gripping our joined right hands. "This leather cup can't begin to say the 'thank you' you're owed for everything you went through wearing a uniform. Army, right? And, if there's ever anything else I can do to help you, you come right back here. And, please, call me Herman, okay?"

I thanked him about seven times and left with the work gloves and fitted leather cup in the brown bag he'd put them in. He'd even snipped the four fingers and thumb off the left glove and, turning it inside out, sewn up the openings from the inside as if they'd never been there–a glove without fingers for an arm without a hand.

A week later, I manhandled my wire-mesh, rock-toting wagon into the back of the El Camino and went back to see Herman the shoe repairman. Parking in front of his store, I asked him to come out and look at the wagon. I'd been pulling the heavy loads by gripping its pull-handle with my gloved right hand, straining my right arm and hand and occasionally losing my grip and falling down. I asked him about fashioning a leather harness to go around my shoulders so I could pull it using my whole body instead of my hand.

"I'd really appreciate your help, but it'll take a couple good lengths of thick leather strapping. You were too generous before, so I hope you'll understand and let me pay for the harness."

Herman laughed. "Of course, son. And I don't have what you need anyway, but I think I know someone who does. Are you sure there's no way we could find a good mule for hauling those stones?"

We walked back into his shop.

"Oh," he said. "The other day I forgot to tell you about our local VFW." He pointed north. "It's at the edge of town, an old Sherman M4 out front. I figure you're new here, having never seen you before last week. You've got a lot of friends there, son."

I never did go to the VFW in St. Ignace, but I envisioned myself in a conversation there. Surrounded by veterans, I was trapped, attempting an explanation after five or six draft beers. "Well," I would say, "I had this twelve-gauge shotgun propped under my wrist like this, see, and our deuce-and-a-half hit this huge dip in the road and . . . "

"Dumb bastard," someone would say.

Another voice, dripping sarcasm, would correct, "Lucky bastard, that's his ticket."

The voices in my daydream faded, each an echo, a pain-shaded memory from a distant land, long-ago last words repeated in a potential embarrassing moment that never happened, precluded by avoidance. I learned later that in the worst days of WWII, a great many of the tickets home were self-inflicted. At least mine resulted from blatant carelessness; still dumb, but a ticket with a more virtuous cause.

Leafing through a Rolodex file whose cards showed heavy staining from years of use and dark shades of shoe polish, Herman came up with a name and phone number. "There's a man with a saddle shop back across the bridge, just outside Petoskey. If I call him and describe what you need, would you be able to drive down there so he can fix you up?"

With the rock wagon loaded up and ready to go, I left for Petoskey, met the saddle maker that afternoon, stayed the night in a little rental cabin north of town toward Harbor Springs, and returned the next day with my new harness. I could never be sure, but I think Herman called him back after I left and told him about me. The harness cost a lot less than I expected.

The rocks got moved. I even opened a walkway to the water's edge that we eventually widened into a boat slip, but it probably wasn't a pretty sight watching me struggle. Like a one-man wrecking crew, I fought against the weight and irregular shapes of the stones. Bent in awkward postures, I handled them between arm and hand, often on my knees pushing them across the ground, forcing them up an improvised plywood ramp into my little wagon. The leather strap harness wore welts across my shoulders. Reduced to my singular role by day and bored, often falling into bed in early evening before nightfall, I made the mistake of going to town and making a poor choice in friends.

Blended whiskey acts to soothe bruises and sore arms and knees and shoulders, but looking back on those months, it only caused me more pain. Taking my bottled companions back to my loft over the garage by the lake, I drank my evenings away. Perhaps they acted as anesthetics, blocking thoughts of life and responsibility beyond those acres of woods and the changing mood of the ever-moving water's surface.

Black volcanic stones came at me from the woods like little Vietnamese men on bicycles and I destroyed them and carted them away, building great heaps of my dead enemies. The wind carried the cool air of fall intent on impending winter and my sweat, almost lathering, soaked my clothes as I worked myself to limits I'd never known. Out of breath, whiskey ran from my pores and the stench of Pall Mall cigarettes fouled each panting exhalation. At day's end I collapsed in well-earned exhaustion. My physical labor penance for a soldier's sins–each evening's whiskey masked self-imposed loneliness, blurring the images of dead buddies sharing a humid purgatory with me as we guarded each other's backs. I got ticketed, they got tagged. Some wars never end. We go on fighting in imagined, internal conflicts; still-living soldiers surprised and angry to have survived war's real battles.

Victims of the calendar's march toward Christmas, Indian summer ran away and mild fall days disappeared. Hours of daylight diminished, recognizing the U.P.'s location north of the forty-fifth parallel, surrendering to the onslaught of winter's drastically falling temperatures. With my rock wagon and pry bar tucked away in the garage below, snow blanketed my loft by the shore.

Fourteen

It snowed in Ann Arbor, but never like this. An unseasonably frigid Canadian air mass descended upon Michigan's Upper Peninsula weeks ahead of normal. Carried on cold winds, the moisture of Lake Huron's relatively warm waters ascended, forming the astonishing weight of lake-effect snow. Winter arrived in all its icy glory. Not only did the snow accumulate faster and deeper, instead of melting away to be replaced the next week like it often does in Detroit, it stayed, building a permanent base for the winter. The snowmobile riders rejoiced and ice fishermen looked longingly across the still-open water. The animals of the northern woods, with neither the time nor inclination to celebrate, hunkered down for the duration or foraged nervously through growing drifts.

Failing to approach driving in the U. P.'s deep snow with the same seriousness I took serving in the army, old man winter reached out to smack me, correcting the error of my ways. In the army I took Dad's advice until one awful day when I lapsed, losing the edge Dad instructed me to keep at all times, forgetting life's future generalities depend on today's immediate details. Stupidly, I'd lost a hand. I've lived with and faced the consequences of that mistake every day since

169

that hot, sunny day in South Vietnam. I saw a bumper sticker on a road trip out west once that said, "Shit Happens." I laughed out loud and whispered a quiet, "Amen. It sure does."

Snow in Cedarville gave new residents like me little time to prepare for its arrival and an extremely short learning curve to gain the skills to negotiate roads made treacherous by its onslaught. One day dusty leaves blew by, scattered across Bay Drive in increasing winds from the northwest, swirling in little whirlwinds. The next morning, with no tire tracks to follow, the gravel lane lay disguised, buried beneath a thick layer of snow. I coaxed the El Camino gingerly out to M-134's cleared asphalt, found a spot well off to the side of the road where I could leave it parked, and hoofed it back to my garage loft. That afternoon it snowed again.

One-handed snow shoveling is an art. To the casual observer it's like watching a one-armed wallpaper hanger on top of a stepladder. A sick motto crossed my mind as I shoveled, "Hire the handicapped, they're fun to watch." The guy driving the Mackinac County road truck spotted me digging the Camino out of the plowed edge of snow he'd locked me in with, and, after the initial, reflexive laughter subsided, took pity on me. For the rest of the winter he slowed and pulled off onto the wide inlet to Bay Drive, spun around, and, angling his blade, cut me two or three parking spaces and a clear access lane to the paved highway. The first year-round resident on our little road, I learned to cope with the U.P.'s harsh winters, but, as with so many other skills, I insisted on learning the hard way.

Granted, a half-car, half-truck Chevy El Camino is out-gunned by winter snows capable of snagging four-wheel-drive pickups, tying their transfer cases in knots, and grinning icicle to icicle in an ice-encrusted smirk when they're mired down in drifts three feet deep. The real problems arose from the combination of my lack of experience driving in severe winter conditions and the two whiskeys with beer chasers I had tossed back watching television news of the war in a tavern in Hessel. I'd done that on several other evenings on the way home to my loft to toss back many more, but I wasn't prepared for my first blinding white-out.

Unable to see the snowy edge of the highway, I drifted right, encroaching too near the invisible tendrils of its snow-plow-mounded ridge. It reached out to pull me in. Lifting me up and over its triangular peak, the icy ridge paralleling M-134 spun my El Camino around, dropping it and me sideways across the ample, sloping ditch into a clump of pines forty feet off the road and four or five feet below its glazed surface. The motor ran for a while keeping the heater running, finally stalling, suffocated by snow forced up into the engine compartment. I wrapped up tight in my coat, collar up, breathing down into folded lapels, and continued sipping on the open pint of Kessler's I'd purchased in town, figuring I'd wait it out. I was wrong. Whiskey's warmth is an illusion. Hours passed and, moving insidiously, foot by knee by elbow, bone numbing cold crept through me. Miles out on the road in the kind of darkness a starless, moonless, hopeless winter night with heavy windblown snow falling can create, I curled up, teeth chattering, dreaming of sunny days in a warm jungle half a world away. I left the parking lights on, as if the light-green illumination of the dash lights somehow provided warmth. Instead, their neon-like soft glow mocked me, a tantalizing reminder of mobility; speaking not of the machine's fallibility, but the poor judgment of its operator.

The snow and wind tapered off and stopped shortly after one o'clock in the morning. An hour and a half later, getting an early start on his route plowing his customers' private roads and driveways before they needed to get out in the morning, Thompson Crow spotted my taillights. Rapping on my window and getting no response, he pulled my door open against the drift and reached in, shaking me awake.

"Hey, buddy, I've got to get you out of there or you'll freeze, okay?"

I suppose he spotted the near-empty pint bottle, added two and two in alcoholic algebra and got DUI. However he managed the considerable feat, he carried me back to the road and heaved me into the warm interior of his big three-quarter-ton pickup's cab. In the morning he laughed, telling me I'd slept like a baby while he worked, soundless and unmoving as he pushed aside the fresh covering of heavy, wet snow. I don't remember anything until I woke up to small giggles, one elbow across my face, stretched out on an old quilt-covered couch in the narrow living room of a trailer house, my miserable state under the intense scrutiny of three small children.

"There's coffee if you're ready," a man's voice spoke from the kitchen. "You know you could have died out there in the snow, don't you?"

Trying to coordinate brain and mouth through the last mists of a Kessler fog, words attempted over a bloodless, crud-coated, cardboard tongue fell together in sequence but without articulate pacing. "I . . . guess I slid off the highway. Did I hit those trees?" My mind hurt; the interrogative an Olympian effort.

"No, truck's okay, just stuck pretty deep. We can drag it out when my wife gets home and you feel up to it. You livin' down that new road?" the man asked rhetorically. "I remember seeing your truck parked by the highway."

Rising from the couch and moving to the kitchen following the wonderful scent of fresh coffee, I said, "Yeah, there's no house yet. We made the top of the garage into a little cabin."

The man rose from his kitchen chair, extended his hand, and introduced himself as Thompson Crow. It was the first time I noticed his strong Native American features. "My wife waits tables at the restaurant in town, so I baby sit through the breakfast and lunch shifts."

"I'm sorry," I said, "I guess I forgot my manners. I'm Troy Conway."

"Well, pull up a chair, Troy, and tell me what you're doing out in those woods."

He brought me a steaming plastic thermal mug of coffee, asking me if I took cream or sugar. Learning I didn't take either, he sat down again, content sipping his coffee, not demanding answers.

Two hours later, after three or four refills and the easiest conversation I'd had since the long ago, far-away hours with my buddies in Vietnam, Thompson Crow's wife came through the kitchen door. She was beautiful and greeted me so cheerfully I felt embarrassed at how I'd come into their home.

"Not much going on at the cafe this morning. Thought I'd come home and make sure our guest was all right."

"Nice to meet you, ma'am. I'm sure sorry I've imposed on you and your husband. I'm lousy at driving in the deep snow and got stuck."

Smiling and turning to check on the children who ran to her, grabbing her knees, all talking at once, she spoke over little voices. "You're not the first person to end up in a ditch and you won't be the last. Don't worry about it. Thompson's pulled me out of the snow a few times. Oh, and please, I'm Kathy." She joined us at the cramped kitchen table after filling her own coffee cup, putting fresh grounds and water in the twelve-cup percolator and plugging it in to brew again. The Kessler fog was lifting.

"Thanks, dear," Thompson said. "She makes the best coffee in the world and, after a night plowing snow, I need a few cups in the morning."

"It really is great coffee, ma'am . . . I mean, Kathy," I confirmed her husband's opinion, holding the thermal mug out in a half toast. "And I wouldn't be enjoying this coffee if your husband hadn't dragged me from a snow bank last night. I'm sure grateful."

"We take care of each other up here, Troy. I'm glad I saw your taillights; you'd been out there quite a while. And, not to be nosy, it's a small town, you know, and one of my friends heard you'd been over in Vietnam. Stuck out in a snowstorm in Cedarville, Michigan, must be about as different as anything can be from the weather over there."

"Yes, I served seven months in Vietnam, then they sent me home," I said, motioning with my left arm. It was the first time I'd ever done so without being self-conscious. "Everybody's really kind here. I mean, nobody bugs me or asks what happened. Maybe that's why I decided to stay here and clear the lot my parents are building on."

"It isn't anybody's business but yours. And we're glad you're here. Cedarville can use good new faces. Too many grow up and can't wait to run off to the big cities downstate–probably because they want a good job. That's never bothered me; I belong here, part of this place I guess."

An hour later, after a breakfast of scrambled eggs, bacon, and toast, Thompson Crow drove me back out to my El Camino and, as I steered it backwards out of the drifts, pulled me out onto the edge of the highway. He opened the hood and leaned in, knocking the caked snow out the bottom of the engine compartment. Then Thompson hooked jumper cables onto my battery. Little snow clumps flew as the fan spun and the motor rattled reluctantly back to life, missing and sputtering. I fed the gas peddle and, finally, the choke on the Carter AFB engaged, the little V8 smoothed out in a fast idle.

He followed me back to the entrance to Bay Drive, and after he cleared a space, I parked by the road and walked to his truck's lowered driver's window to thank him again. Thompson pointed to the other side and told me to climb in. To my amazement, he smiled and shifted the handle of his T-case controls into four-wheel low and took off hopping and swerving down Bay Drive toward the lake. Motor revving, and plow blade hard to the right, Thompson opened a new path all the way to my loft garage. "There's more snow coming," he said, "so I don't know if you want to bring your El Camino back here, but that'll make the walk a lot easier."

I wanted to pay him for his help and reached for my wallet, but he gave me a look that said doing so would insult a new friendship. "Put that away, Troy. Like I said, we take care of each other up here. You'd do the same for me. But there's one favor I'd like to ask you for if it's okay."

"Sure, though I can't think how I can do anything to repay your kindness."

"That pint bottle on the seat in your car–I've been there and it took Kathy a long time to get me to understand all the bad things those bottles did to me. You've heard the rotten jokes about drunken Indians; well, I was getting there quick. You deserve better than what those bottles will bring you and I'd hate to find you wrapped around a tree on a summer night. I'm probably being too nosy again, like knowing you'd been in Vietnam, but I wish you'd slow down on that stuff. I'm preaching and I too have sinned, but, like I said, been there and I'm glad I got past it."

* * * * *

Thanksgiving in Ann Arbor with my parents, Julie, and Dancer passed uneventfully; no one pushed me to move home. Perhaps their confidence in the ability of winter's cold and snow to roust me from my cozy garage loft convinced them to let nature take its course, literally. Julie thought I looked fit, but tired and thin, and asked a million questions about how I'd moved the rocks. She offered good ideas about using the stones to build walls by the garage. Over too much turkey, dressing, and all the trimmings, plans for the house dominated our discussions. As early Christmas presents, Dad loaded me up with books on home construction. He'd already studied them, inserting index card page markers in the sections on electrical, plumbing, and heating systems. Over pumpkin pie with whipped cream, we shared the pros and cons of propane versus oil.

A good visit with far less lingering tension than our late summer days together, Turkey Day passed and I drove north. Again I experienced a clear sense of relief after crossing my imaginary line of demarcation running from Clare to West Branch. Happily ensconced in my small loft by the bay, I pored over the books on construction techniques, filling tablets with notes and ideas to discuss with the local builder Dad had picked for the spring project. I paced the lot measuring the proposed location of the foundation with a fifty-foot clothesline knotted in five-foot intervals, packing the outline into the snow with my boots. I moved the rectangle thirty feet closer to the shore than in Dad's sketches. The east-west view opened up beyond the remaining large trees. The house needed to be closer to the rocky beach. Moving closer to the water and building the house nearer the incoming waves added to the sense of openness. One huge, immovable boulder rested just inside a corner of the rectangular outline I chose for our foundation walls. To spare the expense of drilling and dynamiting the giant stone to remove it, I suggested leaving it and building around and on top of it. We did. It's still there in the corner of Mom and Dad's basement providing a visible reminder of the power of the glaciers that formed our land, a testimony to our status as new, temporary interlopers in a place where God tells time in millennia.

Marking all the distances on a detailed scale drawing of the lot, I mailed the plan to Dad. A week later, his approval and praise for my effort arrived in a return letter with instructions for me to "take charge and work out the timing and details with the local builder."

Opening a post office box in Cedarville partially resolved Mom's concern about my isolation–no telephone, no mail service. Checking the box twice weekly established a channel of communication. Telephone calls made standing at the pay phone inside the entrance to the grocery store further remedied Mom's separation anxiety. Even as a grown-up, wounded veteran, she insisted on mothering me; sometimes maternal instincts prevent full realization that the umbilical cord was cut at birth. The clank and bong of numerous quarters dropping through the slot into the metal box base of the pay phone kept our conversations comfortably short. I enjoyed being alone in my new world.

Within short weeks after Thanksgiving, around ten days before Christmas, the heavy snow arrived. I ended up freezing my butt off in a ditch clutching a pint bottle and waking up on a couch in Thompson Crow's living room. As Santa Claus readied his sleigh and inspired his reindeer, regaling them with stories of snowy rooftops and sooty chimneys, I sat and worried about getting home for Christmas. If the weather decided to replay the first big snow, I wasn't going anywhere. As if listening to my thoughts, Frosty the Snowman dumped on me again three days before Christmas, stranding me at the far end of Bay Drive. With no telephone, I knew I'd have to go to town and call the folks to let them know I couldn't make it.

Completely snowed in, getting my nerve up to trudge out to the highway and drive into Cedarville, sure the call home would disappoint my parents; I waited until early in the morning on Christmas Eve Day. Then, out of the silence of the surrounding woods, I heard the whine of a substantial V8 motor, the grinding, scraping sound of a plow on frozen gravel, and a strident beep-beep-beep below my gable window. Thompson and Kathy Crow came to my rescue, delivering Christmas presents. My gift, three squarish packages wrapped in white butcher's paper, included two venison steaks and five pounds of Bambi burgers.

"Do you have freezer or refrigerator space?" Kathy Crow called out as they climbed the narrow stairway to the loft. "If you don't, we can show you how to pack them in the snow."

On my last swing through St. Ignace, I'd purchased three toys for their kids, Tonka trucks for each boy and a doll for their daughter, but they weren't wrapped. I was self-conscious as I gave them the gifts in the store's paper bag.

"Can you sneak these under your tree for the kids? Santa doesn't gift wrap, does he?"

"Not the Santa at our house," Kathy said, looking askance at Thompson. "He's all thumbs."

Before the words were out of her mouth, she looked at my left arm as I struggled to re-roll the top of the big paper bag from the farm implement store where I found the toys.

"Oh, Troy, I hope I didn't hurt your feelings." She reached out to touch my shoulder, real concern in her eyes.

At first, what she saw as a faux pas didn't even register with me. Only her quick apology and concern made me think about her words.

"Please . . . Kathy, don't even think that way," I responded with a laugh. "I'd love to be 'all thumbs' but I'm stuck the way I am." I wriggled my right thumb triumphantly. "At least I can still hitch-hike. Someday I'll tell you guys the whole story."

Over all the years since, I don't remember ever telling them the exact details of the accident on that sunny day in South Vietnam. And they've never asked.

Fifteen

Sneezing, an interesting and complex bodily function, should not, in and of itself, be life threatening. One magazine article I read, however, pointed out that each sneeze stops the heart momentarily. This doesn't bode well for the infirm. I also know from experience it's impossible to sneeze without closing your eyes. Try it; definitely not a good idea driving in heavy traffic.

One-handed sneezing presents certain additional nuisances and complications. The details of location and duration of such sneezing require special attention. The circumstances of extended and energetic sneezing, technically a paroxysm, but the phenomenon I've always called a "sneezing fit," is even more challenging when attempted using only one hand while driving. Reach for and grab the Kleenex, pull from box, hold it to your nose. Squeeze gently, blow, wipe, and discard in the unspeakably vile paper bag of soggy used tissues between your knees on the floor of the moving vehicle. Repeat these actions. The simple, automatic process, like the lather-rinse-repeat instructions on a shampoo bottle, sounds easy. It's not. Body shaking with forceful misting, spraying nasal expulsions, eyes watering until tears run in rivulets down your cheeks adding to the fluidity of flying mucus, eyes closing, heart stopping, snotty tissues accumulating in and around the paper bag–who's steering?

Attempting to quell an unstoppable bout with marathon sneezing while driving across one of the world's largest bridges, headed north in the company of my silent, unflappable, steadfast friend, Dancer, also tends to exacerbate the situation. In two days, the cold I suffered from worsened rapidly, helped along by a lack of sleep and my pigheaded reluctance to admit defeat to a common germ and see a doctor. I could have easily found a doctor in Ann Arbor when I picked up Dancer. Half the residents of Ann Arbor, Michigan, were medical doctors. The other half were completing doctorates of philosophy in something erudite and mind-numbingly esoteric. By comparison, a lone general practitioner acted as the medical provider in the sister villages of Hessel and Cedarville. An appointment with him meant picking a day when no penciled "Gone Hunting" or "Fishing–Back Tomorrow" notes hung on his door. Several old dining room chairs lined the walls of his tiny waiting room. His fly-tying vise held a place of honor, permanently clamped to a scarred oak table in the sunny front room, his untidy office overlooking the marina that filled with sailboats every summer.

Midway across the giant span of the Mackinac Bridge, avoiding the tire-humming, car-wiggling, steel-grid-surfaced left lane and trying desperately to stay in the center of the concrete right lane, my foot came off the accelerator gradually. The El Camino slowed to a crawl. Racked by a continuous sneezing fit whose onslaught began on the uphill slope of the southern approach, the problem escalated quickly beyond human control. With a little help steering, I finally pulled to the right edge of the lane and stopped.

What Dancer had done then, reaching across to help me steer, wasn't really a surprise. He still does such things now. In occasional, unanticipated actions, he remains unpredictable. Having grown up observing him, I knew to expect his impromptu responses; nothing violent, nothing too fast, rash, never anything mean-spirited or cruel, merely actions based on his vision of the world. Ideas born in Dancer's mind have always reflected Dancer's private reality. Dancer's Dancer.

As I fumbled with yet another Kleenex, he reached across and grasped the steering wheel, holding it steady to prevent us from moving any closer to the green-painted, waist-high railing or, in his unspoken, calm manner, tumbling off the bridge. Staring straight ahead, intent on the roadway before us, Dancer continued holding the wheel dutifully even after we stopped. He didn't even turn to face the voice of the Bridge Authority policeman who pulled up behind us, lights flashing, and came to my window seeking answers to why, after driving erratically, I'd stopped at the crest of the span. Adding irony, a large "No Stopping on Bridge" sign loomed just ahead of where I'd managed to come to a halt.

When a situation reaches a high level of absurdity, laughter's unavoidable. Another of life's challenges, laughing and sneezing at the same time happens, but not without instilling humility. Well, that's what happened; my reaction the result of reading the sign and of repeated, sporadic glimpses of the police car's revolving lights in my rearview mirror between uncontrollable head jerks caused by ballistic sneezes.

I reached and pulled my wallet out of the right back pocket of my jeans with a soaked, gruesome tissue still clutched firmly between fingers glistening with the residue of my affliction. Another guffaw, sneeze, hiccup erupted. Removing my driver's license took eight seconds less than forever. As I offered it to him, replete with two tiny, clear strings of dangling snot, the policeman drew back as if a dozen lepers had spit on the only cookie left in the jar.

He read my name on the license I held unsteadily and gazed past me, focusing on Dancer's grip on the steering wheel. "Are you all right, Mr. Conway?" he asked, taking in the details of the situation before him.

"Yes, sir," I stammered, trying to contain yet another multi-functional bodily convulsion.

"Was your friend steering the vehicle, Mr. Conway?"

"Oh, no, sir," I lied. "This is Tommy Higgins. He doesn't drive. He's mentally retarded and," an explosive sneeze sprayed the dashboard and, on the rebound, nearly bounced my forehead off the top of the black plastic-rimmed steering wheel. Recovering, I managed a half-speed whisper, "I'm taking care of him. I guess he's holding the wheel to help me."

I was unaware of the exact moment the young officer noticed my missing left hand, but doing so brought the realization my inability to stay in my lane came from the combination of a physical limitation and a series of unrelenting sneezes. "You did the correct thing stopping, Mr. Conway. The sign is to keep tourists from stopping to take pictures. I'll stay parked behind you to move the traffic past until you're ready to continue across the bridge. Just wave when you're ready and I'll follow you across. Mr. Higgins won't be helping you drive anymore, will he?"

"No, sir," I said.

Removing his hand from the steering wheel, I turned toward Dancer, deliberately nodding my head twice to assure him all was well. My laughing-sneezing fit subsided, perhaps eased by having stopped long enough to gain control of its effects, and I waved a handless, bony, set-to-go, forward-ho sign out the window. The patrol car followed us, rooftop light bar flashing, all the way across to the Upper Peninsula side to the toll booth where he spun in a tight, tire-squealing half-circle around the concrete barrier in the median to return back across the bridge. He no doubt remembers the spectacle of me sneezing my way across his bridge while Dancer, unblinking, steered from the passenger side; filing the encounter under a category called weird yet funny.

At the cafe in Cedarville, I left Dancer in a booth by the window and went to the restroom to wash up and splash water on my face, toweling off awkwardly on the revolving length of cloth towel looping out of the white, wall-mounted metal box. Its small, tarnished mirror confirmed my pallor. Wizened possum eyes stared back feverishly. Pulling out the next length of grayish linen towel, the box's mechanism strained, grinding like a cheap tin toy. I felt cleaner and fresher but probably left enough germs to infect the next two towel users.

Who knows, maybe that's how I caught the stupid cold.

The late afternoon sun of a mid-June day arched downward in the sky, throwing the front windows of the little restaurant into the shade of large adjacent trees. The air coming through the open screen door behind us cooled perceptibly. Dancer looked around the room, comfortable in its surroundings. He'd been there before on his trips north and sat up straight, recognizing the waitress when she came to ask for our orders, studying her face carefully with wide-open, child-like eyes. Thompson Crow's wife, Kathy, wasn't there for the dinner shift. Speaking for Dancer too, I ordered two meat loaf specials; one of my favorites and readily acceptable to my companion. Dancer rarely refused to eat any food, although he's shown consternation over things like jalapeno peppers or spicy chili; confused by the lingering, burning sensation they created.

It was good to know he was away from the bureaucrats of Washtenaw County, his inept persecutors. Treated as a statistic in a calloused mental health care system, society's safety net abandoned Dancer and many like him. It was good to see him happy again. He'd suffered through a very difficult month and I looked forward to having him with me, well away from the support system that failed him. The nearly completed house I'd spent three and a half months working on, not to mention the long weeks spent moving rocks last fall, offered Dancer a new and secure environment. The four bedrooms of my parents' new home on the shore of Lake Huron provided ample space and needed only minor trim and finish painting. Mackinac County, while strict on building codes and inspections, viewed our occupancy permit with a friendly degree of informality, especially since I'd lived in the garage loft for a year and a month already.

How the bureaucrats at the social services agency in Washtenaw County could have turned Dancer loose, unsupervised on the streets of Ann Arbor, defied comprehension. Julie said the paperwork in his grimy coat pocket when she found him contained a plastic identification card with the account number of the checking account they'd established for him and eight checks in an account-starter checkbook.

If he carried other clothing with him when released on his own on the streets, he'd lost it along the way, obviously wearing the clothes on his back day and night for many days. This was their answer to budget cutting and deinstitutionalizaton. Amazing. Who, I wondered, was supposed to read the information to Dancer or fill in the checks for him? Who was supposed to help him find shelter or launder his clothes or eat regularly and properly?

No telephone lines ran along Bay Drive yet, so my sister Julie called our builder, Oren Banks, asking him to please send someone out to the house to tell me to come home right away.

Swamped with an overloaded summer school schedule, there was no way she could care for Dancer. If Julie's friend hadn't recognized him walking aimlessly down the street in Ann Arbor carrying his belongings in a sweatshirt with the sleeves knotted, he might still be homeless, a street person in real trouble. Dancer's unsupervised stay outdoors, lost in plain sight in a seemingly uncaring world, lasted seventeen days. Surviving on basic instincts, he'd been smart enough to find shelter sleeping in cardboard boxes underneath the I-94 overpass at Jackson Road west of Stadium Boulevard. Still upset by his treatment, Julie thought perhaps he'd recognized the area and attempted finding his way back to Mercywood. Six or eight city blocks away in the other direction, the group home he'd stayed in since January may also have attracted him.

Store owners along Stadium Blvd. said they'd seen him passing by each day as if looking for something. Caring employees of two local diners interrupted his sojourns to give him food and soft drinks. Dancer never ran from them when they asked if they could help him, but neither could he respond to their questions. Thank heaven for kind-hearted people; they represented society's safety net, not limited in compassion like a social service agency intent on categorizing their charges and controlling expenditures.

*   *   *   *   *

When pissed, Dad paced. Mom and Dad returned home early from a long-planned summer seminar, and, hearing Julie's story about finding Dancer homeless on the streets of Ann Arbor, drove straight north. Concern for his welfare overshadowed any curiosity or excitement about the progress made on their summer home in recent weeks. Dancer, serene and happy, sat on an empty five-gallon metal paint bucket in the corner of the unfinished kitchen watching Dad walk back and forth, following his movements like a devoted fan at Wimbledon tracking a tennis champion. Kitchen cabinets still in their tall rectangular cardboard boxes stood stacked in rows in the central living room, partially blocking its expanse of windows facing the lake. The triangular paper labels from the window manufacturer adorned the upper corners of each section of the most efficient thermal glass available.

"Look at Dancer," I said. "This is where he belongs, not at a big hospital or a sanitarium like Mercywood or in a tiny group home."

"It's not that simple, Troy. He should have been better off at the group home than he'd been at Mercywood, but something went very wrong."

"He *was* better off there," Mom interjected to amplify Dad's statement, turning away from the kitchen window's view westward across the bay. "I can't imagine what made that woman turn him over to Social Services without notifying us or Brian."

Dad had selected Brian Humphries, a young Ann Arbor attorney, to take over Ziggie Hammit's role as Dancer's counselor when the delightful, sports-car-driving eccentric from Adrian retired several months earlier.

"That's true, I hadn't thought about Brian being listed as a contact if they couldn't reach us. Somebody sure dropped the ball. Anyway, we'll find out what happened, but the immediate question is what's best for Dancer. And you may have a point, he may be much better off right here."

"Mom, Dad, it sounds like someone must have pressured the group home into calling Social Services, getting them to act in a hurry instead of waiting for you to get home. But why would anyone do that?"

"It was the police, Troy. Then Social Services apparently over-reacted. Call it fear, but it's really intolerance and the inability to understand people can be different and still be harmless," Dad explained. "All I know so far is that the neighbors behind the group home called the police because Dancer, doing what he likes best, stood outside for hours looking across the yards, studying the neighborhood. We know when he stares at children it's just his normal, loving fixation; he wouldn't hurt a fly. What he did for those children at that awful car accident proved his credentials, he loves kids. The neighbors just didn't know Dancer, so they were afraid."

"The good news is it's summer," I reassured my father. "I can take care of Dancer. The house is nearly ready and there'll be plenty of room."

"Son, your loyalty's admirable. I'm proud of you for offering, but you've accepted a good job offer from Mr. Banks and I want to see you pursue your own opportunities. You do know more people here than we do. You've been living here for a year already, so you can put the word out we need a caregiver. Someone will be happy to have the opportunity; we just have to pick the best person for Dancer."

We eventually compromised. Dancer stayed with me while I searched for someone to look after him. As usual, Dad's calm and all-encompassing vision of a potential problem quickly focused on a solution based on answers benefiting all involved. Dancer rode along with me during the first weeks of my new job with Mr. Banks. He followed me around each worksite and never got in the way. The men working on the houses readily accepted Dancer, never questioning his presence. Dancer sat on the El Camino's lowered tailgate, gently scissoring his feet back and forth, waiting for me as I delivered necessary supplies and materials and checked on progress being made at each project.

It was a unique time for Oren Banks too. He'd come to Cedarville three years before after selling out his successful, growing construction business in the northern suburbs of Detroit. I asked him once what made him relocate. The frenetic pace of doing business in the

Motor City, he said, every day another struggle through the perpetual rat race and snarled traffic. Before moving north he lacked time to enjoy his accomplishments; gaining no sense of satisfaction, he only encountered more demands, endless paperwork, and impatient, rude clients. People can run away from different kinds of wars.

His family had vacationed in the Upper Peninsula for years and the beauty of the place called him. The prior summer, he'd built three summer homes in the Cedarville and Hessel area, two of them waterfront, and was comfortable with his life there. Since I'd been constantly underfoot as he built my parents' new house on Bay Drive, asking a million questions and attempting to help whenever I could, he took notice of my interest. When approached in early May to build a house for Mr. and Mrs. Harold Burnette right there on Bay Drive where the lane turns north to meet the highway, he came to me and asked if I'd work for him. Without the extra help, he said, he didn't think he could take on another house. Before June was over, he'd taken on two more. It was a busy summer. He'd been watching me, he said, and thought I had a natural talent for construction. Never once did he express any concern over my physical handicap. I took great pride in the fact he wanted to hire me for what I could do, unconcerned about what I couldn't. As Oren Banks eventually taught me, there's more to building a home than pounding in sixteen-penny galvanized nails with a framing hammer.

Mr. Banks displayed trust in me. He wasn't alone. Dancer's reliance on me through those summer months the year after I returned from Vietnam still clings to me as a lasting memory, a warm shadow of those times; his constancy bringing meaning to my changing life. His strength and innocence blend together in vivid memories. I gained from the opportunity to share in the subtlety of Dancer's gifts, his silent charisma, and the unique level of attachment that comes with being his closest friend and caregiver.

Dancer doesn't ask for anyone's help or assistance, yet, unsolicited, he offers his own brand of caring, even holding the steering wheel when needed. His unfailing willingness to follow simple instructions creates a lasting impression of his eagerness to please, his unspoken acceptance of his role in the endeavors of others. With a quick look and a tilt of the head, Dancer can be directed to follow along, and, usually without spoken direction, he grasps the idea of what he can do to help. When I spread blueprints across the hood of the El Camino to discuss the construction details of the houses with the crews, he automatically stood by, holding down the far corners of the large sheet of paper so it couldn't roll up or slide down the sloping hood. On countless trips to pick up an unending list of supplies and hardware, Dancer always helped carry boxes, placing them carefully in the back of the truck.

As with his prior responsibilities as a messenger at Athens State Hospital and a groundskeeper at Ypsilanti State Hospital and, to a lesser degree, at Mercywood, he thrived on being of assistance. Unafraid of work, he often displayed his own form of initiative by beginning a simple project on his own. Every room of Mom and Dad's new summer home warranted his attention as he picked up loose nails and scraps of cardboard and, using his favorite broom, painstakingly swept up sawdust and every trace of drywall debris. Oren Banks marveled at Dancer's diligence and bought him a Detroit Tigers baseball cap to thank him for his efforts. Those were great years to be a Tigers fan.

A steady flow of family, new friends, and fellow workers from the construction crews brought life and laughter to the new Conway summer home, stretching busy afternoons into the waning, twilight hours of evening. Cars and pickups were parked along the road and across the yard all the time. Thompson and Kathy and their kids stopped by often and Mr. and Mrs. Burnette showed up every Saturday, bringing doughnuts or sweet rolls, to check on the week's progress on their home. The new, higher level of activity pleased Dancer, as did the doughnuts and rolls. He responded to each new face with a quiet smile and his undivided attention. Thompson's boys and little girl followed Dancer around in rapt amazement, constantly ready to take part in his ingenious schemes for their amusement—hide and seek amongst the cedar trees, skipping stones across the bay, gathering branches and stacking them precisely to fuel an evening bonfire on the rocky beach. The foursome walked down Bay Drive, two little boys flanking a gentle man living his entire life in the quiet happiness of perpetual boyhood, a dark-haired little girl skipping ahead. Thompson told me later on it was Dancer's affinity for children that motivated him to speak to Kathy's little sister, Marie.

Marie survived the early years of a difficult marriage to her handsome but less-than-responsible high school sweetheart in Sault Ste. Marie, an hour's drive further north. One day she found herself without a job or support. Her young husband, unconvinced of the illegality of joyriding in nice automobiles not belonging to him, fell astray of the law. Along with her little son, she'd been living with friends in a crowded apartment, undecided about what to do next, abandoned by circumstance but afraid of being on her own. When Thompson asked her to consider becoming Dancer's caregiver, filling the void Dad recognized, the mix of possibilities changed, old doors swung shut, new doors opened.

After over a year of moving away from happiness, living on the lonely, downward slide of separation in the cycle of moving apart and coming together, I reached a plateau. Aware of impending change yet unaware of its direction, aware of the human need to seek companionship and purpose, I remained blind to the future. As usual, Dad understood. With uncanny skill, he foresaw the positive influences of opportunity, the utilization of youth and energy and their worth in achieving happiness and success. My year and several months of self-pity drew to an anticlimactic close. From the single millisecond of a shotgun's excruciating roar to the crisp slap and quiet slam of a wooden screen door swinging closed behind the rushing footsteps of Marie's happy little boy running outside, time and place moved the gears of life's clock forward. The tick wasn't audible, but the perceptible motion of its click reverberated through my psyche, hinting of things to come.

Mr. Banks gave me an unusual assignment one day in mid-August.

He sent me downstate to pick up last-minute, special-ordered ceramic tile to finish two bathrooms. It wasn't so much that he tricked me; he just made certain the errand served a larger purpose. Leaving early in the morning I got to Traverse City and picked up the tile. With my primary mission accomplished, I drove across town to meet Stanley Harrington at Northwestern Michigan College. Mr. Banks had given me the address.

The classroom buildings of the beautiful little community college lined both sides of narrow streets, nestled in acres of tall, mature pines. Empty parking lots in the last weeks of summer break contributed to the park-like tranquility of the place. The construction trades building took me completely off guard. Several pickup trucks and delivery vans sat helter-skelter about the lot. Two flatbed stake trucks loaded with lumber waited by an open overhead door to be unloaded.

I wandered in through the delivery entrance. Two young men loitering by an employee break area nodded. No one questioned my presence, my age making me a likely student or summer employee. The open, friendly environment of the campus spoke of acceptance, a casual yet carefully organized and purposeful non-pretentious educational setting. By the time I located Mr. Harrington's office, small yet persistent bells jingled, crisp wake-up calls signaling the need to organize my thoughts. Curiosity or the seeds of future plans, this place hummed with contagious anticipation.

A girl with brown hair pulled back to a long ponytail leaned across a desk covered with piles of multi-colored papers, obviously digging for a missing form or memo, looking occasionally over her shoulder toward the open glass-windowed office door behind her. A strong voice called from within the office, booming through the open door on a cloud of cigarette smoke.

"Jesus Christ, Maureen, we can't have lost the September supplies schedule, we just finished it last week."

"Jesus isn't here, Mr. Harrington, but I could use His help with this mess. Maybe we should pray for a filing system, you know, a real file cabinet with drawers and those manila folders with tags."

"That *is* my filing system. Everything we need is right there on the table. It works every year, why would it fail us now?"

"There's someone here to see you, Mr. Harrington. Can I send him in?"

From around the corner, I learned he was expecting me. "That's gotta be Mr. Troy Conway. Oren Banks sent him in. What do you think, Maureen? You know Oren. Should we take a chance on a guy he recommends?"

"I guess Mr. Banks is a good guy," the girl said, continuing to address the open office door while reaching out to shake my hand. "Troy looks pretty smart. Since divine intervention's unlikely, maybe he can figure out your 'filing system.'" Turning back to her task in exasperation, she motioned me toward the voice asking her opinion of me.

Stanley Harrington came out of his office, stopped, and scanned me up and down over pursed lips. "Yup, Oren's right. I think Mr. Conway's come to the right place." He walked past me, reaching back to shake my hand and turn me toward the delivery bay. "We're going for a walk, Maureen. It's too damn smoky in here, I need some fresh air."

"I don't smoke, Mr. Harrington. That smoke's your doing. Pollution, that's what it is, nasty, rotten pollution. How can you make me work in a cloud of tobacco fumes like this?" the girl said, feigning concern, never looking up.

"Campus tour if anyone calls, okay, especially the dean."

"I'll tell them you took a long lunch again, okay, especially the dean."

"Tell 'em campus tour, Maureen. Remember, you get to work here with real men, not those eggheads over in the math department."

"Yes, Mr. Harrington. Real men build houses and stuff, right?"

The thin, middle-aged, balding teacher walked briskly for a small man. He waved at the two young men I'd seen in the break area. They were unloading a flatbed stake truck with a forklift. His idea of fresh air included two more cigarettes smoked as we walked and he talked and pointed out buildings.

"Oren Banks is a friend of mine, Troy. He's hired several of my students. Bet some of the guys you're working with told you about our program, didn't they? This isn't a typical college, so I guess my students aren't typical college boys."

"Two of the guys said they'd taken classes here. They liked it a lot."

"I'm really proud of this school. We turn out more than paper diplomas. Our students work hard and earn the credentials to open doors to good careers. That means a lot to me. Oren thinks you belong here, what do you say?"

The tour complete, we returned to his office and talked for another forty minutes. Maureen came in waving the September supplies schedule.

"Made an extra copy this time, didn't you?"

"Yes, sir, two or three," she said, smiling and fanning a fresh cloud of cigarette smoke away from her nose.

The conversation was comfortable–a good teacher has a way of putting you at ease. Sitting in his office being treated as an adult, answering questions about my interests and ambitions left a peculiar sensation, an aftertaste of potential meaning and a disconnected feeling of intertwined challenge and assessment. If it was a test, I passed.

I'd heard the term "watershed moment," but I'd never experienced one, except maybe a painful, negative one in the back of a deuce-and-a-half on a sunny day in Vietnam. Driving home with a Northwestern Michigan College catalog, two copies of their application form, paperwork for a physical exam, financial assistance brochures including veteran's benefits, on- and off-campus housing lists, and a request for transcript to send to my high school, I felt different. The first step down a new path began with an unexpected and unusual campus tour on an August afternoon. Even without knowing where I would ultimately end up, looking forward felt a lot better than looking back.

Sixteen

Marie kept vigil from a comfortable chair in the massive, sunny living room, her pencil poised over an incomplete grocery list on a small lined pad of notebook paper. Debating whether to add chocolate chips to make their favorite cookies, she watched Dancer and her son, Michael, roam the beach in search of another perfect, baseball-sized black volcanic stone. Her son's current passion revolved around constructing a two-foot-tall rock fortress wall between the trunks of two cedar trees. Dancer provided encouragement and engineering expertise and assisted in materials selection.

Continuous change spun throughout her thoughts of the last two months in a whirlwind of new things and responsibilities and pleasant days. Denim jackets replaced late summer's T-shirts. Her initial apprehensions about caring for an adult with special needs dissolved, disappearing in their early weeks together. Dancer's kindness reassured her. His sweet mannerisms and constant concern for her and her son convinced her she'd made the correct decision. And Thompson had been right about everything he'd told her about Dancer and the Conway family; they were all special in their own ways.

Initially, Dancer startled her on a regular basis. It was never intentional, but his lack of conversation, diminutive height, and soft, shuffling steps invariably placed him underfoot, right around the corner, sitting or standing in the next room. Marie usually walked in, barely avoiding bumping into him, interrupting his peaceful contemplation of whatever captured his gaze. Nothing ever startled Dancer–he only looked up, glad to have company, eager to watch someone else, sharing vicariously in their efforts.

Most people, when asked if they're accustomed to the presence of a mentally retarded adult, respond with a story: "Of course it's okay, I worked with kids like him at school," or, "Sure, my cousin's little boy is just like Dancer." Trust me, no one is "just like Dancer."

It isn't that Dancer lacks the ability to converse: he speaks with his eyes, an occasional word or name, and, in most cases, his heart. If love were words, Dancer would be a great orator, perhaps a philosopher; astonishing in technique, incomparable in the mute delivery of his messages. Dancer speaks carefully, not in a condescending way, but meekly, presenting wisdom in a shy smile or a mischievous glance.

At first Marie's son, Michael, while fascinated by his new companion, remained reticent. He chose not to speak to Dancer because Dancer rarely responded and then, when he did, called him Mickey instead of Michael.

Dancer quickly learned to work his way around the name "Marie," but he pronounced it in a childlike, two-syllable, sing-song manner. Any concise pronunciation of "Michael" eluded him. Neither the boy nor his mom worked to correct him. Dad toiled diligently when teaching Dancer how to say Mom's name so many years before when they visited him at Athens State Hospital on their honeymoon. He still says her name correctly.

Perhaps Marie's name felt comfortable, a quiet variation of Amy. Dancer learns, but, inexplicably, once he latches on to a name, it's permanent and there's no changing his often-unique way of saying it.

My sister, Julie, put forth a theory about Dancer's insistence on calling Michael "Mickey," certain the problem rested somewhere in

Dancer's memories of another Mickey. Although Dancer no longer watched much television, for several years he was especially enamored with every afternoon's repeat broadcast gathering of the *Mickey Mouse Club*. Jimmie and Roy, the grown-up Mouseketeers, and the kids, Bobby, Cubby, Doreen, Lonnie, and Sharon were okay, but Julie noticed Dancer thought the sun rose and set on Annette Funicello's smile. Besides the one pretty teenage girl engaging his rapt attention, the Mouseketeers' music and songs drew Dancer like Winnie the Pooh to the honey jar, infrequently standing to dance along but often head-bobbing and swaying from side to side in his chair.

Dancer still greets Michael exuberantly as Mickey when he visits. A grown man now, Michael never complains. His arm around Dancer's shoulder, he hugs his childhood friend and they walk the path along the beach or Bay Drive in wordless companionship unchanged by time.

On a long-ago fall day, planning to bake cookies, Marie watched her then four-year-old son walk side by side in an involved conspiracy with Dancer, big and little children studying the stones they carried toward the fort-in-progress. Dancer radiated contentment and held sway as the central joy in their lives, spending his days watching over them as Marie cared for him. Constantly at Michael's side, a silent, positive influence, he guided his young charge, turning him away from dangerous temptations like jumping between giant, rain-slicked boulders by the water's edge or climbing too far out on low-hanging tree branches. Dancer functioned as a little boy's best friend, mentor, and an unusual but extraordinary teacher. As a very special but unconventional teacher, the door to Dancer's classroom opened to everyone who grew to know and love him. Over the years he has had many, many students.

Since Dancer never attended school, he missed out on what Julie and I and our friends experienced. We learned that good teachers rock, but the manner in which we view them changes as we mature. During our elementary years, we stood in awe of our teachers, showing them absolute respect. Hanging on every word, we were caught between a duality of fears: not pleasing them and disappointing our parents. Then, in our early teen years, we unfurled and flexed our wings of independence, testing, unsure of how to face our individual needs to achieve acceptance by our peers.

Ultimately, as adolescents, many of us, caught up in ourselves, made a regrettable mistake, mutating into know-it-alls, our short-term transformation obvious to everyone but ourselves. More grievously changed, our parents and teachers got stupid. They completely lost all reasoning power for three or four years, irrelevant in our world of girls and boys and boys and girls and cars and parties.

Eyes watering, coughing as we inhaled but stifling the gag to stay cool holding our first cigarettes, we took time out to invent beer. Fun at any cost reigned supreme, an adolescent's highest priority. Somehow, and just in time to relieve consternation over our actions, our transition from teenagers to young adults miraculously reconstituted the brains of our parents and teachers, returning them to working order.

Many great teachers help us grow up–although we may only recognize their contributions in retrospect. Starting a new segment of life as a student at Northwestern Michigan College, stabilizing a life rudely interrupted by war, optimism reformed what guns and killing and living in fear obfuscated for a time. The concern and patience shown by teachers gives us something else, too, something equally important–respect. The magic of maturity provides a glimpse of one ultimate truth: respect is earned. No one passes it out with a diploma or a school book or even a uniform and an M16. And, like respect, self-esteem comes from accomplishment. It can't be bestowed. Regrettably, too many members of the Vietnam generation failed to make that connection.

Many veterans clung to those early years, drinking both to remember and forget. Some lived in small communities of warrior-victims, their own self-styled communes, letting the chaos and mindless destruction of war linger.

With a great family and Dancer's silent tutelage and wonderful teachers, I moved forward, leaving those long months behind me. I walked out of the jungle. Too many young Vietnam veterans either refused or were unable to shake off its clinging malaise. For them, life was a cruel teacher, and, by their culpability, they failed as students, becoming stagnant and complacent, neglecting to listen, missing life's next lesson.

Getting older and looking back, it gets clearer. Understanding what happened becomes easier, but we must wait until our perspective allows us to smile at life's outcomes and not despair or wonder over its what-ifs–to relish contentment, knowing we've done our best. Sneaky years unravel the mysteries of adolescent unknowns, revealing our futures one day at a time. Then our twenties and thirties and forties, the central years of our lives, peel away the layers of decaying linen encasing the mummy of ancient wisdom we aren't supposed to look upon in our youth.

Mom and Dad lived through it; been there, done that. Julie's bout with polio surely brought them face to face with life's outcomes and uncertainties. Grandpa Mike and Grandma Rebecca lost their only son, Bryant, Mom's brother, to Hitler's psychotic megalomania. Each couple lived and loved, cried and laughed, raised families and worked and prospered, overcoming obstacles, celebrating achievements, putting failures behind them. They survived the entire process and reached the point when age provides twenty-twenty hindsight to those who persevere, growing wise. Based on all my memories, I believe they relished the trip, even given the heartbreaks they endured. They're all gone now, except Mom, who provides a loving connection to the past, the years that shaped our present; and Dancer, who defies the effects of aging, his dual sparks of childhood wonder and happiness still vibrant.

Years pass, but no cosmic Monday-morning quarterbacks wait to tell us how we did, to critique our form. We have to find out for ourselves. There's no alternative. Suit up, run cheering out onto the field, play each game and hope to win. Two generations of family coaches guided me; victory meant happiness.

What family couldn't teach, we stumbled through as teenagers and young adults, sometimes painfully. The winds of fate and good old-fashioned luck blessed most of us.

Recounting those early years in Cedarville confirms the value of happiness and the many ways we struggle to achieve it.

On a personal level, the story underscores how much Dancer and my family and Thompson Crow and Oren Banks and Stanley Harrington and others contributed to my life. With no immediate, tangible way to repay their mentorship and kindness, it took the next thirty years to thank them properly. And, as it turned out, doing so ended up providing me with the calling I now cherish.

Marie remarried, finally divorcing her first husband when he added recidivism to his list of youthful mistakes, jumping back into trouble and an orange jumpsuit before the inked signatures on his parole dried. Later on, she said it was her years caring for Dancer that changed her, compelling her to grow up and face the realities of a doomed marriage. She met a great guy, a friend of her brother-in-law, Thompson Crow, and started over. Michael gained a full-time dad who loved him and, eventually, a little sister who looks so much like his mom we think she was cloned. Before her second marriage, we shared the beginnings of a friendship that's lasted for three decades; some thought it was more.

Marie was incredibly beautiful, but in a different way than her older sister. Kathy radiated confidence through timeless, strong Native American features, soft dark eyes deep as oceans, and a flawless complexion. The self-assured mother of three, totally in love with Thompson and the life they possessed, her happiness showed. Marie, a younger, more fragile version painted with the same brush, held back, unsure of the future, her temerity caused by difficult times. Past the corners of her smiles, the harsh edge of reality's touch left a constant hint of self-doubt and assumed inadequacy. True joy came infrequently and uneasily. Today, too many people would assume we were an item. It was more like two young people, both walking wounded, comfortable in each other's company, no strings attached.

Marie's compassion, like her love for her little boy and her growing affection for Dancer, easily encompassed an awkward, one-handed guy going to building trades school and starting a life in her native Upper Peninsula. Some credit for steering my path toward a lasting career also belongs to Marie; she showed me how, although sometimes unclear, the best things in life can be right in front of us. We just have to be smart enough to open our eyes to the obvious.

"Troy," she said one Saturday evening in my second year of community college, after dinner across the cleared table strewn with textbooks. "Does Dancer understand money?"

I stopped, not struck by her question so much as her intent, her direction.

"He has a car, but can't drive it, I drive it for him, and I know you want to build him his own house here in the woods, but he may never be self-sufficient."

"That's part of his trust fund. His attorney handles most of that stuff. But, you're right, the concept of money means nothing to him."

Silent minutes passed as I returned to my homework.

"Troy, do you want to be rich or happy?"

"Both, I guess."

"What if it were one or the other?"

"Happy, I guess; rich and miserable sounds like an ugly combination."

"Dancer's happy, isn't he?"

I pushed the books aside. "I've always thought of him as happy. He seems to do it by osmosis, making others happy then absorbing their happiness. That's his gift–it's a two-way process, like breathing out and in, creating joy then taking it in and giving it back over and over."

"What's your idea of happiness?"

"Doing something that makes me feel good about myself, I suppose. Everything I'm studying about construction is great, I love everything about it, but I'm still not sure exactly how I fit in. I've got to face up to an obvious little physical problem I created for myself and a lack of the funds required if I want to start my own business. It took Mr. Banks years to get where he is today. I've learned a lot working for him the past two summers, including what it takes to open your own business."

She listened too intently, almost frowning, so I continued, steering the conversation away from negatives. "Typing presents a problem, too. I did well in typing class in high school, even met a couple cute girls, except now my home row is limited to the J, K, L, and semi colon."

"Okay," Marie brightened, suppressing a chuckle. "So being a secretary is out of the question. But what about being a teacher?"

"I beg your pardon?"

"A teacher, you know, a regular teacher-teacher, a high school teacher; they teach shop classes and woodworking and all kinds of things about building trades, don't they? My girlfriend transferred from a community college to a four-year college to get a teaching degree. Couldn't you do the same thing?"

"And you think a school would hire a one-handed teacher?"

"Why not?" Marie's tone tightened across the drumhead of total honesty. "You've got to quit thinking of your missing hand as a handicap, a limitation. When you think that way, you make it one. If you work hard enough, you can make it into a real excuse, a way to keep from doing anything you think might be too difficult, a way to tie your good hand behind your back."

It takes a real friend to dish out tough advice. Marie qualified. She held her ground, adamant, as if the disappointments she'd encountered increased her determination to make sure I made the best choices. A loyal, lifelong friend, she succeeded.

* * * * *

Like circles within circles, so many lives are interconnected in small communities, and yes, our little town on the shores of Lake Huron was and is small. The sidewalks and beaches of July and August overflowed with laughing, running children, but when the chill and first frost of autumn turned to look, it found them gone. They'd returned to lives and homes far south of our seasonal world of islands and cottages and little sailboats in sheltered bays. In college towns where the population was divided between students and townies, the end of each school year brought an exodus followed by quiet summer months. In our realm of vacation homes, Kodak moments, and summer memories, the opposite migration occurred.

The transitory illusion of a busy, thriving community bloomed between Memorial Day and Labor Day; a recurring, annual phenomenon. Winter months brought scarcity as unique as summer's plenty. Silent days and nights displaced the din of children's voices, picnic lunches, and evening bonfires at the water's edge with softly building drifts of white snow.

From September to May, the breadth of our community shrank. It atrophied naturally, pulling in on itself as summer's tired, sunburned revelers drove away in overloaded station wagons. Year-round residents of Hessel-Cedarville's bays and inlets remained; not left behind, but preferring to be there in the woods along the shores. The blasts of the winter winds of prior years hardened us, leaving us prepared, unafraid of their successors.

Everyone knew everyone, and as the years passed, everyone knew and loved Dancer. Eventually he gained a form of notoriety threatening his solitude as the hordes of seasonal sun and fun seekers sought a glimpse of the little man called Fawn Talker. In response, the permanent cadre of locals began to quietly protect their unique neighbor, shielding him and guarding his privacy from unwanted intrusions. When asked, their answers were nebulous and evasive. "Oh, he's around here somewhere," they'd say. "Out there in the woods," they'd offer, pointing eastward. No one was quite sure where.

During the winters, a tight core of the year-round populace coalesced, of necessity both individually self-reliant and supportive of each other when anyone needed assistance. No one asked for help, it just came, preserving individual dignity. During those years, I read of supposed poverty in Detroit and shook my head. In their world of food stamps and welfare checks, spoiled kids still watched color televisions in homes and apartments with central heat. Too many families around me survived the winter on powdered milk, venison, homemade bread, and vegetables diligently preserved in mason jars months ahead of winter snowstorms.

The children of the Upper Peninsula dressed each morning close to a newly set fire in a wood stove and spent their evenings huddled within the circumference of its glow. At night in tiny bedrooms, ice coated the insides of windows. No one thought of themselves as poor and hand-me-down clothes brought no shame.

I became part of our U.P. community, building a life for myself with the help and advice of good friends and teachers. It took a little time and I couldn't have predicted the future awaiting me. It happened in stages. One thing led to another. Marie saw where I belonged when I couldn't. I'm eternally grateful for her vision.

* * * * *

During four semesters at Northwestern Michigan College, I spent long days working in the Building Trades Center, many times returning after a quick dinner to help Mr. Harrington and his staff with their adult evening classes rather than going back to my little rented room a block off Front Street. More than a student, it meant I was part of something.

Traverse City continued to amaze me, even on gloomy, overcast, or rainy days. In bad weather, low clouds swirled malevolently and the wind blew out of the north, channeling down the length of Grand Traverse Bay. Gusts and gales intensified as the natural contours of the surrounding hills funneled them into the central business district, tugging at the big paper bags carried by hurrying shoppers, turning umbrellas inside-out.

On calm, beautiful sunny days, regardless of the ambient temperature, I fabricated excuses and errands, going downtown to walk along the shoreline. Like Lake Huron in Cedarville, I felt drawn to the magnificence of the open water.

After two years of school in Traverse City gaining self-confidence and learning skills in tradecrafts, I transferred to Central Michigan University in Mount Pleasant and completed a bachelor's degree in education. I'd been there a year before my tedious world of classes and part-time jobs changed completely. I met Laurie.

In Mount Pleasant the overwhelming grip of dry land captured and depressed me. Surrounded by miles and miles of flat nothing, the horizon obliterated by too many buildings, blunted by city block after city block of homogenous streets in rectangular grids, fast-food restaurants, and mini-malls, I longed for the openness and clear air of the northland. To obscure the stifling oppression of Central Michigan's campus, I poured myself into academics, taking overload class schedules. Immersed in required courses, rushing toward a degree, I created a near obsession with homework, not only finishing every assignment on time but stretching forward in my texts, preparing for future classes.

Too many miles of US-27 and I-75 separated me from the Mackinac Bridge and Cedarville to make the drive every weekend as I had from Traverse City, but every three-day weekend and school holiday found me heading north, savoring the open highway, returning to Dancer and Marie and Michael. Then, on an early September day in my second year everything changed and Mount Pleasant seemed pretty nice after all. It all started in a class called Great Religions of the World. Although interesting, the subject matter posed no real challenges, and the professor did his job with wit and thorough attention to detail, but neither created a real spark of interest until Laurie played with the loose curl of hair over her ear.

From my desk's place in the row behind her, I sat entranced every Monday, Wednesday, and Friday morning by the repetitive circular motion of Laurie's index finger as it grasped and twirled a long, loose strand of hair, a strawberry-blonde feather above her ear. Attempting to pull my attention back to the lecture and the endless lists of facts covering the chalkboards, her profile drew me back again and again. Worried she might sense my stare, actually perceive its intensity, I forced myself to lean forward over my spiral binder of notes, often writing meaningless nonsense and doodling in the margins. She never turned, never acknowledged my interest, although I saw our professor catch on and smile in my direction.

Over coffee and a mediocre cheeseburger in the student union, focusing on an editorial about the war in the campus newspaper, I never heard the plastic chair across from me as it slid back. She carefully arranged her books and papers on the table, her presence nudging my consciousness.

"Reading about the war?" she asked over the top of the folded page.

"Yes," I answered, looking up, my thoughts moving from the words on the page to the lilt of the familiar voice I'd heard in Great Religions.

"That's what happened to your hand, isn't it? Are you okay with that now? You seem to do pretty well."

Wow! She asked the tough, direct questions up front, pulling no punches.

"Yes, my contribution to the war effort." I smiled, taking in the soft gracefulness of her beautiful face, the lines and shape of her long strawberry-blonde hair pulled back in a simple ponytail. Up close, she took my breath away, pulling me into the sparkle of green eyes, assaulting my senses with the dusting of tiny freckles across the tops of her cheeks. "And you're right, it seems like a thousand years ago."

"My brother went," she said. "He talks about it all the time and runs around wearing his army jacket like he's showing off."

"My olive-drab stuff went in the garbage the day I got home, that's behind me. I'm not making a statement either way, no protesting against the war, no patriotic speeches. One empty sleeve's not the end of the world; it's an inconvenience, in a way it's a daily reminder I'm lucky to be alive."

I thought of explaining the difference between a ticket and a tag but didn't. She radiated everything beautiful and American, every-thing Southeast Asia never represented and never would. I refused to sully the moment.

She sighed and glanced at the student newspaper. "I wish you'd write an editorial; I think a lot of people need to hear your version, you know what I mean, the real story from someone who's been there."

"Thank you, but no," I said. "I lived through it, but anything I say could be used or misused by someone with a cause to champion." A silence ensued until common courtesy shook my shoulder and I offered to get her a coffee or a Coca-Cola. She chose coffee.

"I'm Laurie Pittman," she said when I returned. "And I know your name's Troy."

"Troy Conway," I said, my response automatic.

"I wanted to meet you. You don't know Shelley, do you? She's one of my roommates; four of us share an apartment just off campus. She sits right behind you in Great Religions."

My heart flip-flopped in my chest, skipping a beat or two. Her roommate must have seen my obvious interest in Laurie and told her.

"Shelley said we needed to meet each other. I thought you might get around to introducing yourself. I hope I'm not too forward–that's not very ladylike is it?"

"No, please, I'm glad you're here. I really wanted to meet you. I guess I'm not too good at social things, maybe I've never been. And, you may have guessed, since I came home with this empty cuff on my sleeve, the girls haven't looked my way."

"If they couldn't see the person wearing the shirt with that sleeve, I'd say those girls suffered from limited vision, wouldn't you?"

My God, I thought, this girl's amazing!

"Where's home, Troy Conway?" she said.

"Ann Arbor originally, but I lived in Cedarville for a year, if you know where that is in the Upper Peninsula, and Traverse City for two years before coming here last year."

"You were in Traverse City? That's where I'm from, small world, my dad's Coast Guard. What were you doing in Traverse City?"

"School. I finished up at Northwestern Michigan, building trades, and then transferred here. I'm working on a teaching degree."

"Teaching? Me too, I'm majoring in elementary education. I love the reading classes; the look on the faces of the little kids when they react, you know, first connecting the words to their meanings, it's like a light turning on."

"A reading teacher, that's pretty nice. Are you sure you want to associate with a lowly shop teacher?"

And that's how it started, easy conversation and coffee in the student union. She unconsciously twirled a loose strand of hair by her ear as she talked. Its tendrils spun around my heart making tomorrow something to dream about and forever seem too soon. We walked the long way around campus to her apartment and said goodnight on its front steps.

Back in my dorm room in Barnes Hall, two of my three roommates busily plotted another weekend's entertainment, anxious to invite me to a beer party at one's fraternity. By their standards, my propensity to study and my odd jobs for pocket money cast me as too serious. Two years older than two of them, a year older than the other, I considered their college-boy escapades too juvenile.

They repeatedly told me I was missing out on the fun of college, as if their greatest achievement hinged on getting their roomie, the one-handed Vietnam vet, to party hearty. Their constant questions about my experiences in the army, their curiosity about my wound, grew annoying as the months passed. Extremely high lottery numbers isolated two of them from the draft. The third, puny and constantly sick, nearly crippled by asthma and chronic allergies, couldn't have passed the physical if he'd wanted to.

Just below the surface of feigned friendship, a trace of ghoulish morbidity permeated their interest in me as if, through my stories, they could somehow identify with the thousands of returning veterans, sharing the trauma of war without its risks and hardships. I would neither deny nor confirm having killed enemy soldiers, probably exacerbating their prurient interests in what I'd seen and done during my seven months in Vietnam.

In the coming weeks and months, I saw very little of my three roommates; instead I spent long, precious hours with Laurie. We studied in the library wing of Ronan Hall, CMU's teacher education building, its plain, two-story red-brick facade the focal point of our existence. We met each morning under the almost mockingly modern, white-painted concrete frame jutting outward in front of its row of glass and aluminum entrance doors.

My current employment, clerking in a local hardware store, became a burden, monopolizing the hours of two evenings a week and my Saturdays. Stocking shelves and waiting on customers grew tedious; time slowed, the hours crawling by until I could clock out and meet Laurie for a late coffee, a pizza, or a fast-food dinner.

Two months after we met, she took me to Traverse City. Arriving there late on a Friday afternoon, we stopped by the Building Trades Center. I wanted to introduce her to Stanley Harrington. He smiled and fawned over Laurie, telling her what a great student I'd been. Finally, uncomfortable in the glare of his praise, I was glad to leave, looking at my watch and apologizing, telling him we were late for dinner with Laurie's parents, which we were.

Her parents were incredible. Before the dinner dishes were cleared and dessert served, they'd made me comfortable, both telling stories about Laurie, each enjoying the opportunity to tease her. They never asked about Vietnam and only inquired about classes and future plans. I told them about my family; how proud I was of my parents and my sister, Julie. I described my work in Cedarville on their summer home. Laurie wanted me to tell them about Dancer, but I purposefully abbreviated my stories about him, telling Laurie she'd have to meet him herself and tell her parents about him. Two weeks later she did. We joined my family in their new tradition, celebrating Thanksgiving in Cedarville.

Crossing the Mackinac Bridge and driving through Hessel and Cedarville, Laurie snuggled next to me on the seat of the El Camino, taking in the scenery. In those years Lake Huron was at the peak of its twenty-year cycle of high water. In several locations, waves broke dangerously close to the edge of M-134. Rust now perforated the quarter panels of the El Camino, and its small-block V8, conscious of its odometer, wheezed lethargically and spewed a minor but steady cloud of blue exhaust.

I'd been apprehensive, afraid of awkward moments of introduction. They never materialized. It was all too easy. Within an hour Laurie and Julie were girl-talking and laughing, their asides no doubt at my expense. My mom just hugged Laurie and welcomed her, immediately enlisting her help in the considerable effort involved in pulling together a Thanksgiving dinner. Dad held back, at first the formal host, maintaining a professorial air, then as the afternoon developed, warming to Laurie's presence as he observed her rapid assimilation into our family dynamic. Dancer's instantaneous acceptance is a clear memory in my mind; his evaluation and response unforgettable. One moment he shyly studied her face as I introduced him and the next he stood next to Laurie in the kitchen like he'd known her all his life, helping with the preparation and placement of bowls of potatoes and squash and plates of cold veggies and warm rolls. She spoke softly to Dancer, lovingly directing his actions, undisturbed by his lack of verbal response. Laurie belonged, unquestioningly a part of the scene and its activities. Dancer's judgments, quiet and sure, are absolute; like an infallible barometer, I've never seen him misjudge. I had reason to give thanks that Thanksgiving.

We spent Christmas apart, each with our own family, our last separate holiday season. The next months passed too rapidly, spinning schoolwork and hours together in hurried, finite, individual moments blended together by time. Looking back, I can't specify a unique event when, in life's synergy, one and one became more than two, where together became more natural than apart. Like so many transitions, it just happened, the change unheralded but obvious. For Mom and Dad, the combination of their lives evolved during the turmoil of World War II, transpiring across great distances from Germany to Michigan. For us, the campus of Central Michigan University, its academic buildings and sidewalks, Laurie's apartment, the library in Ronan Hall, the student union and the restaurants we frequented became the backdrops of the daily scenes of our growing relationship.

Love is a scary thought until it happens; an unknown, intimidating tightness gripping each breath. Then suddenly it's there in a look or a whispered word or a meaningful embrace and it's not frightening anymore. It's as natural as sunshine and the sweet smell of rain-cleansed air after a storm.

In February and again in April, we made trips to Cedarville to spend long weekends with Marie, Michael, and Dancer. Our first trip there without my parents or Julie in the house, we fell into a comfortable camaraderie with Marie. She was watching us, weighing the situation and its possible permanence. Her sideways glances and knowing smiles told me she approved, sharing in our happiness. Dancer stayed constantly at our side, never quizzical, always comfortable with Laurie's presence, totally at ease. Michael ran to Laurie with coloring books and crayons and toys, confirming the attraction I knew children felt for her, foreshadowing decades as a second grade reading teacher and wonderful years raising our own kids.

The unexpected snowstorm in early April when we visited during spring break marked a turning point, and yes, a commitment. Arriving Saturday, we planned to stay in Cedarville until the middle of the next week before making the trek to see her parents and mine. The weekend offered a quiet respite from school and we enjoyed special days with Marie, her little boy, and Dancer. Then, on Tuesday night, it snowed and changed our plans and, in a sweet, fascinating, unforgettable way, our lives.

At the end of the evening, we yawned and fought sleep, and begrudgingly, decided to call it a day. I said my goodnights and prepared to retire to the loft over the garage. Laurie slept in a guest bedroom in the house. She gave me a simple but affectionate kiss as I pulled on boots, donned my coat, and headed out to my bachelor quarters; the distance across the yard and driveway precluded any semblance of impropriety.

Snow which began softly just before dinner intensified as the evening wore on, creating a moving, directional show we watched in the floodlights across the deck. By eleven o'clock, the accumulation already placed a question mark beside any idea of leaving for Michigan's lower peninsula in the morning.

I'd warmed the loft with its wood stove earlier in the evening in preparation for sleeping there overnight, but let the fire die down when I came in. Drowsy and content, I stood at the gable window and looked across at the house. The lights in its windows went off one after another like heavy eyelids closing to sleep. With thoughts of school and Laurie and the future revolving, commingled in my mind, so many what-ifs and unanswered questions, I went to bed, cozy under thick covers as snow fell about the eaves.

I slept soundly, wrapped in a winter night intent on defying spring's advance. The door at the bottom of the stairs made no sound, no footfalls or creaky treads woke me. Sometime between one and three a soft voice at the edge of a dream spoke my name. She came to me beneath the covers, her face and hands and knees chilled by the snow, everything else very warm.

By morning's first light, the snow let up and the sun broke through thinning clouds sending shining spears across the angle of dawn to bounce off newly formed drifts. Nearly a foot of fresh, crystalline covering blanketed everything, obscuring the distinct edges of the road and driveway and the trodden pathway linking the house and the garage. The tall pines beyond the loft's windows bowed to the mass of their thick coating, snow-laden branches exhausted arms drooping from rounded shoulders. Shrubs and boulders stood still, impatient for the day, marshmallow sentinels bordering the yard.

Curled against me in silky, long-legged nakedness, Laurie moved slowly, blinking and stretching in the pure light, looking out the window at the remnants of the snowstorm. She'd come quietly across the distance from the house in the middle of the night, her winter coat over a short pajama top and matching boxer briefs, both discarded where she'd dropped them on the floor by the bed. Blue jeans and a bulky sweater sat atop the tiny kitchen table, neatly folded, a corner of feminine underthings peeking out from beneath the pile.

"Are you sure this is what you want?" I whispered, knowing she was awake. "I'm not sure I deserve you or that I ever will; you're too amazing."

"Yes," she said, the word spoken with a loving finality which startled me.

The woodstove pinged and creaked as thick, soot-coated cast iron expanded. The new fire I set came to life and we talked in low voices as if the cozy, low-ceilinged room might recount our secrets. The loft warmed, displacing the chill that mandated quilts and covers. Pulling them back, I marveled at the beautiful creature beside me. After making unhurried, uninhibited love again in the white glare of a winter morning reflected through frosty windowpanes, we dozed wrapped in each other's arms, secure in a new beginning. As Laurie drifted back to sleep, she unconsciously twirled a strand of strawberry blonde hair by her ear. I reached to hold that hand, moving it aside to lightly kiss her ear and brush that glorious strand of hair backward toward the quilt I pulled up over her shoulder. It's true, cats aren't the only animals that purr.

When we finally dressed and made our way through the snow to the main house, Marie, to her credit, only smiled and welcomed us, never acknowledging our changed relationship. We stomped snow off our boots on the porch, came in, and hung our coats on wall hooks in the mudroom. As I set the table, I watched the two young women in my life prepare waffles and bacon. I thought I witnessed one or two conspiratorial smiles; non-verbal communication unique to the female of our species.

Dancer and Michael finished a project of boyish importance in the living room and came to sit with us at the table, watching us devour our late breakfast and sip mugs of steaming coffee. Life changed completely, but it didn't change at all. A future together began wrapped in the constancy of friendly faces and a place and things already known. We relished and absorbed the blessing and approval of extended family. Before the week of spring break ended, we broke the news of future plans to our immediate families in Traverse City and Ann Arbor. No one seemed shocked or surprised. They'd anticipated our announcement, waiting to apply hugs and handshakes, parental seals of approval, confirming what they'd known before we did. Julie and Grandma Rebecca cried.

Married in Traverse City in mid-August, we honeymooned in Washington, D.C.; Laurie wanted to see our nation's capital. We walked everywhere, oblivious to distance and the heat and humidity, staying in a small hotel on New Hampshire short blocks from Dupont Circle, its traffic a continuous, swirling cacophony of honking horns and near misses. Typical tourists, we photographed monuments and statues. In the early evening, we wandered up and down the gradual slopes and long curves of Connecticut Avenue, holding hands and gazing in the windows of small shops. Taking cabs to Georgetown, comfortable in its crowds of young people, we ate our dinners in tiny restaurants on M Street, watching people, guessing their roles as government employees or students. After four days, sunburned and exhausted and very much in love, we drove home on the sharply twisting, hilly roller coaster ride of the Pennsylvania Turnpike. Its exits and toll booths flew past, punctuated by stone-sided Howard Johnson restaurants with orange tile roofs. Countless little white posts supported an endless guardrail dividing the turnpike's opposing lanes. Following its hypnotic, flashing ribbon, we journeyed into the start of our life together.

*   *   *   *   *

Teacher's certificate in hand, Oren Banks and Stanley Harrington and my two favorite professors at Central Michigan wrote letters of recommendation for me. During my interview with Cedarville's superintendent and acting kindergarten-through-twelfth-grade principal, he carefully studied their letters and my application and, without looking up, asked a single question: "Did you ever play ball, son?"

Taken aback, I stammered, "Yes, sir, football and basketball."

"Good," he said, reaching to shake my hand. And that was how it all started. Of course the Cedarville Trojans didn't have a football field yet, that would come a year later, and the cafeteria-gymnasium-auditorium was half-court sized with low hanging wire-caged lights that took a beating from errant basketballs those first years.

Every journey's got to start somewhere; mine was inauspicious. Faded photographs of our first sports teams still line my office walls. I taught wood shop and eventually begged and borrowed enough equipment to put together a respectable metal-working shop which, with a lot of student inspiration and too many broken-down old cars, evolved into an auto shop class.

After years of those classes, they call me Coach, my role on their grassy field, dusty baseball diamond, and scarred wooden court taking precedence over chalkboards and shop tools. Dancer doesn't have an official title, but two generations of kids and their parents have grown accustomed to seeing him sitting in the bleachers by our football field or in the gym, a familiar, grinning face applauding our accomplishments when we cheered and, head bowed, sharing our defeats when we were glum. He had his own student desk in my classroom. Two wood shop students proudly crafted and attached his name plaque, Mr. Higgins, across his desk's front edge. Darkened by handling and time, it's there three decades later and so am I and Dancer still visits my classes occasionally, providing a white-haired, grandfatherly presence my students find irresistible.

He loves to sit in on science classes when they have live animals like guinea pigs or even big snakes, but they have to be live animals. One day, years ago, he walked in and saw several partially dissected frogs left out on the countertop, pinned spread-eagled to cardboard. His eyes went wide and his jaw dropped open. After that he always peered carefully around the doorframe into the lab before entering, making sure no cut-open, formaldehyde-tainted, dead frog specimens were laying about.

Dancer often brought in orphaned baby raccoons and rabbits he raised. One spring spellbound classes watched as Dancer fed a newborn fawn whose mother had died, hit by a truck on M-134. One hand cradling its slender neck, he guided it softly as it stood on trembling, spindly legs reaching to take milk from the baby bottle he held. Across the classroom you could hear heartbeats, the emotion palpable.

Fawn Talker, the name Thompson Crow gave Dancer, respecting his mysterious ability to reach beyond man's assumed boundaries and communicate with the animals surrounding him, became known. To their credit, the high school kids kept up their prior formality, addressing Dancer as Mr. Higgins. Perhaps it was their way of honoring a unique human being who obviously cared deeply for them; returning, in a small way, the smiles and sparkling eyes he brought them.

High school kids are funny about names. I've always told my students it's all right to call me Troy after they've graduated and grown up, that the Mister in Mr. Conway is part of going to school. None of them ever do. I see them in town years later with wives and children and, usually shouted from halfway across the grocery or hardware store, I'm greeted with a resounding, "Hey, Coach," or "Hi ya, Mr. Conway, how ya doing?" I'm grateful they think of me fondly, that's a nice feeling. I do my best to remember their names, but I'm not always successful.

Seventeen

Eventually, three generations of Conways and Dancer lived in Cedarville in Michigan's Upper Peninsula, relishing the scenic enclave we'd built on Bay Drive in the woods on the shore of Lake Huron.

Mom retired from teaching at the U of M but didn't abandon her Troll past and become a full-time Yooper until after Dad passed away. Finally, when the time came, she announced with great determination that their large old house three blocks from the U of M's quadrangle was too lonely, sold their home in Ann Arbor, and moved north to be with her grandsons year round.

Dad, either unwilling or unable to completely break away, had held on to his teaching position and continued publishing. Even with a reduced number of classes, his devotion to the University of Michigan meant they spent nine months a year commuting on holidays and every weekend they could manage to drive up. He did love Cedarville, though. In his last years as a professor of psychology, his graduate assistants worked lots of Fridays and Mondays; a fringe benefit of his years of service and great training for them.

As always, Dancer's presence was central to all our lives. Our sons, Tommy and Danny, spent long hours with him as they grew up. Whenever Mom and Dad came to stay, Dancer immediately gravitated to their home. The boys followed, spending extra time with their grandparents. I'll always believe that was Dancer's intention; he understood joy comes from shared lives, especially the happiness that skips a generation.

Life fell into a natural, seasonal cycle; Dad's sailing lessons, the boys bicycling up and down Bay Drive and camping out overnight in tents by the shore, it reminded me of summer vacations long ago. It was a time of coming together.

My sister, Julie, built her story-and-a-half, Cape-Cod-styled summer home on the last remaining, fourth lot. Its three levels of decks reach down a steep slope to the jagged rip-rap rock protecting the shore from erosion. She did an incredible job decorating and furnishing its rooms. I've always thought it should be presented in *Better Homes and Gardens* with great color photographs showing the results of her labor of love. And, yes, she found love too; maybe, in part, because of the view from her living room and enclosed sun porch.

Perhaps apropos for a noted heart surgeon, she held her love's heart in her hands before he captured hers. She literally found her future husband on an operating table when she received a call to assist in a delicate surgery being performed on an amazing man, Sam Church. A man without a permanent home, he'd served our nation for over twenty years, first as a soldier, then a citizen of the world, and, as I would eventually learn, a clandestine representative of one of our government's intelligence services. Listening to Sam and Mom discuss world events in subsequent years, I came to understand that the line between diplomacy and spying is a fuzzy demarcation determined by political circumstance, the imminence of approaching hostilities, and the need for clear and current intelligence data.

Sam, one of Mom's star students when he completed his master's degree in political science, took her advice and went to the U of M hospital when he needed surgery to repair complications from the internal scars of old wounds. When asked for the name of a cardiologist to assist, he carried Mom's recommendation one step further and unhesitatingly specified Dr. Julie Conway. As a young warrant officer on his second tour flying a helicopter gunship in Vietnam, he'd been shot down. The primary blood vessels carrying life in and out of his heart were compromised by their proximity to heavy scarring from prior surgeries; Julie's expertise helped guarantee his long-term prognosis remained optimistic.

Only a few years older than Julie and me, and still athletic in build, Sam's face bore the fine print of his background in a visage of lines and creases beyond his chronological age. Streaks of white highlighted his dark hair.

After the war he'd gone green to gold and attended the University of Virginia on an army scholarship for his undergraduate degree in engineering. As a newly commissioned officer, he pursued a career in the army's Air Cavalry and rose to the rank of major before, facing the reality of his health issues, he accepted a job with the state department. His service there led to other assignments. Sam, a reticent, private person by nature, never discussed details, offering only cryptic explanations of his career when queried by our neighbors and friends. We grew accustomed to his weeks of travel punctuated by sudden, unannounced returns and unexpected departures.

During Sam's recovery from his surgery, as one of his physicians, Dr. Julie Conway did something completely out of character with the prior pace and circumstances of her life. She invited him to Cedarville to spend several weeks with us on Bay Drive. On his first trip north, Julie drove him in her car. After he recuperated, Sam, an avid pilot, began flying to the Upper Peninsula and kept his plane, a been-there-and-back-looking but impeccably maintained twin-engine Beechcraft Bonanza, at the little paved airport north of Hessel. Nowadays, with its distinctive V-shaped tail, it's there every summer. In the winter, it's in a hangar at the wonderful regional airport in Pellston south of the bridge on US-31 toward Petoskey or back in Ann Arbor.

The year Sam and Julie met, he stayed in one of Mom and Dad's spare bedrooms and, early each morning, crossed the yard to have coffee and breakfast with Dancer. The soldier and world traveler found tranquility and instant friendship in Dancer's company; an oasis of genuineness away from the world's turmoil.

Julie came to stay on Bay Drive much more often that summer, extending her previously infrequent vacations. The frightened little girl Dancer coaxed into looking out the car window at the view from the top of the Mackinac Bridge now gladly flew in Sam's twin Beech. With a wide-eyed look and broad smile, Julie described the first time Sam let her take the controls and how he taught her to hold the plane true and level and on course. Caught up in the freedom and exhilaration flying offered, she eventually earned her own pilot's license.

She and Sam cooked their dinners together each evening and, weather permitting, dined on the deck off her comfortable kitchen, lost in the view across the waters, talking quietly. They were married the following spring in the same stone church on Washtenaw Avenue in Ann Arbor where our parents tied the knot in 1947.

Watching Sam and Dancer pulling weeds in Dancer's garden or silently drinking coffee at the breakfast table untroubled by any need for conversation, I've marveled at the disparity in their backgrounds, the gulf in the sea of life experience separating them. A global traveler, the scope and breadth of Sam's world dwarfed the childish limits of Dancer's, yet, as two men of essential goodness, they complemented one another.

Too many conflicts witnessed on too many trips to too many third-world countries tore at the edges of Sam's heart as much as any scarring from old shrapnel wounds. The conscious awareness of man's inhumanity to man, a reality most of us never see, let alone comprehend, burdened him, draining away vitality and joy; an unshakable albatross named duty. His love for Julie and Cedarville's beautiful shoreline and Dancer's simple ways stood in stark contrast to the misery and famine and cruelty he'd seen.

For the first time in decades, Sam truly possessed a home to return to, a sanctuary and haven on the leeward side of the world away from the gale winds of adversity he'd known. Within five years after they married, his long absences slowed and then stopped entirely, his odyssey over. He retired, and moving comfortably between Ann Arbor and Cedarville, devoted his energy to adoring Julie.

Mom continues to attempt to persuade him to write his autobiography, even under a pseudonym if he deems anonymity a necessity. Sam never says he won't, only that he's not ready yet. I believe he's content, glad the past is past, a soldier through and through who understands that to tell his story he must relive its experiences and stare once again into the snarling teeth of past monsters. Discussing world politics with Mom, his favorite poli-sci prof, keeps those specific monsters tucked away in interesting academic generalities. Putting them on paper might bring them back to life. He prefers them in their vanquished, long-buried state. Besides, it's a question of priorities. Enjoying Dancer's vegetable soup is way ahead of publishing a chronology of past accomplishments; what's done is done. Somewhere, a new, younger dragon slayer wields Excalibur. Julie's knight in shining armor, a good man, returned from his country's crusades to find love, family, and peace.

Although not as regular a visitor as Sam or Julie, Dr. Everett Marshall, Dad's fellow psychology professor and friend, came at least twice a year during the months of summer. He stayed in the caretaker suite in Dancer's home each time because he snored. Not a serene, gentle, old man's nightly melody, but a raucous, window-rattling nocturnal rendition unique to his deep, throaty voice. While not forcibly evicted from Mom and Dad's home, he chose to avoid their teasing by moving in with Dancer. Dancer, always accepting of others, didn't seem to mind and, of course, never complained.

Difficult to describe, the stillness of summer nights in the woods by the lake miles from the nearest small town is a natural corollary to the ability of sound to carry across open water. City dwellers find such extreme silence disconcerting, if not unbelievable. The distant resonance of thunderstorms crosses the lake almost before the flicker and spark of their visual approach can be perceived through dense clouds. With a soft breeze moving along the shore, I swear I've heard

Dr. Marshall's snore over a hundred yards away through the trees. Its deep vibration emanated from an open window at Dancer's and carried all the way to our bedroom window, a faint yet discernable, guttural geriatric growl.

* * * * *

Quiet nights and loud snoring by the lake aside, those years weren't totally without excitement. Although an incredibly beautiful place to live, the Upper Peninsula wasn't totally idyllic. Things happen, even in paradise, and Dancer was involved in the resolution of a crisis now and then. Never part of their instigation, he managed to contribute in his fascinating manner to touching the lives of our families and friends. One summer, Michael, Marie's son, by then a strapping running back on the high school football team, was once more the focus of Dancer's attention.

Michael went through a common stage of adolescence. People called him a troubled youth. Dr. Marshall, fully sixty-plus years past his childhood in New Jersey, speaking about Michael's brush with the law, pronounced youth as "yoot."

"These yoots today, Paul," Dr. Marshall said to my Dad in total seriousness. "These yoots face issues we never dreamed of at their age."

I struggled valiantly to cover my amusement, looking away, not wanting to offend him. And only days before, Dad and I sat at the same table and talked about Dancer's habit of hanging on to mispronunciations, his special way of adopting them in moments and hanging on to them forever, making them permanent. Whatever neurons and synapses in Dancer's mind caused him to do so, he shared with Dr. Marshall.

Easy to see but difficult to define, the "trouble" in "troubled youth" bubbles and festers on the surface, a visible manifestation of the hidden causes of antisocial behavior. Terms applied to negative teenage behavior patterns range from clinical to colloquial to downright resentful. The J.D.'s Officer Krupke rousted in the famous *West Side Story* song were juvenile delinquents. Punks, hoodlums, or hoods, whatever the label, the phenomenon boils down to the rebellion of youth, or yoot if it happens in New Jersey.

For my generation, rebellion reflected the process of self-realization, what it takes to declare oneself an individual, a person of your own making, not a puppet mimicking the values and goals of parents and teachers. Was I rebelling when I enlisted in the army knowing the rice paddies of Vietnam came next?

"Dumb bastard," someone said.

Another voice, dripping sarcasm, corrected, "Lucky bastard, that's his ticket."

Maybe that was what it took for me to proclaim I was my own person, my gauntlet to run. Circumstances vary and wars come and go, but that portion of the process of growing up, however configured, never really changes.

Some kids rebel, and, of those who do, many can never articulate the reasons behind their actions; they go to extremes but don't know why. Bent on making his rebellious years memorable, Michael pushed the envelope of creativity. The fear that he'd inherited his disregard of the law and of society's rules from his biological father haunted his mother.

Marie came to see me at the high school twice, at a loss, seeking a friend's advice and a teacher's insight; concerned Michael's stepfather's temper would overcome his restraint. A good man, Burt Tallman had adopted Michael years before. They'd shared a close relationship, but this time he couldn't reach Michael to convince him of the folly of his actions. Now a dozen years older than when he'd built stone fort walls between cedar trees along the beach with Dancer, Michael bounced between the gravitational pull of his upbringing, respecting his parents, and the forces of teenage curiosity and daring, the allure of disobedience. We're glad he survived unscathed and, with a little help from Sheriff Almstedt and Dancer, we're glad his life took a turn in the right direction. No one said being a teenager's easy.

* * * * *

A magnificent automobile when new, the effects of time and uncaring drivers showed on the gigantic, slab-sided, late-1970s Mercury Marquis two-door. Its deep-blue metallic paint sun-faded and dull, the stitching at the edges of its once-proud black vinyl top frayed, "rode hard and put away wet" best described its condition, but the aging car still packed the muscle to go fast.

Pitching at a wild angle, its tires screamed in agony as it slid sideways out onto M-134 carrying with it a dust-choked shower of gravel from the side road. The secondary throttle plates of the Holley four-barrel carburetor opened up, feeding the huge four-hundred-sixty cubic-inch V8. Enough high-test fuel poured in to launch a space shuttle.

Still exhibiting the torque and horsepower inherent to its displacement, the massive motor pushed the speedometer's orange needle steadily higher past eighty, cresting ninety, and touching a hundred miles per hour whenever the two-lane highway straightened out permitting higher speeds. Sure, Stephen King's *Christine* embodied pure evil, but this monster reigned supreme in size, the heavyweight archangel of sheer mass, the poster child of brute force.

Nearly five thousand pounds of vintage Detroit iron surged, wallowing and swaying, toward the villages of Hessel and Cedarville. The six-year-old car rose skyward as it floated across rises, then, nearly bottoming out, crushed tired springs at each sharp dip in the road.

Sometimes blatant exhibitions of stupidity go beyond reason and mathematical calculation. Running the only stop sign in town at thirty miles per hour, the posted speed limit, is dangerous. Running it at eighty miles per hour is more than just fifty miles per hour faster, it's lunacy. The difference is the level of shock and awe such a display of brazen lawlessness creates. The handful of citizens who witnessed the perpetrators setting Cedarville's land speed record actually ducked their heads; the same instinctive response a low-flying jet fighter generates.

Earl Frey, owner of the corner grocery, locking his front door at 10:10 p.m. after helping two stock boys replenish shelves for an hour after closing, cursed aloud, stepped back inside the door, and called Sheriff Gil Almstedt on the pay phone. Gil no longer did patrol duty on Saturday evenings. "Too many drunks and dumb asses," he once said, shaking his head at the nightly mayhem and carnage on the county's two-lane rural roads on summer weekends.

"Yep, thanks Earl, I heard it on the scanner radio a minute ago. Came down a side road outside Hessel and started flying eastbound; ran a couple cars right off the road. Must be going like hell if they passed your store already. Dumb kids, they're driving like they're being chased. Well, they are now. I'd say reckless driving for sure, possibly a DUI."

The sheriff paused to listen so Earl could repeat the description of the color and make of the big car, the speed of its flight through town making reading its license plate impossible.

"Yep, now they're in trouble. There's a trooper headed south on 129, lights and sirens on, should pass your location in a couple minutes."

The distant wail of the fast-approaching southbound Dodge police cruiser, now discernable, carried faintly over the phone line.

"Don't pull out on the road yet, okay Earl? Give him a chance to go by," Sheriff Almstedt warned. "He'll catch up with them eventually unless they find a place to hide."

He did, and they weren't hiding. The remains of the large Mercury two-door, its hood peeled back, grille and headlights disintegrated and radiator spewing steam, sat astride grisly clumps of venison and bone. Deer covered the highway. Puddles of blood accumulated where the asphalt met the gravel shoulder. When the trooper reached the scene, he administered first aid to the injured and radioed for an ambulance and a tow truck.

Moments before, the two lead deer had crossed the pavement cautiously. Stopping, their heads came up and pivoted slowly. Two pair of delicate ears poised tall, locked onto the sound of the approaching low hum. The Mercury Marquis hurtled toward them, its headlights turned off, the banshee howl of its engine a frightening crescendo beneath blaring music from its tape deck and the audible tearing sound of worn tires across asphalt at great speed.

The fading light of evening easily crests ten p.m. in the last days of June in Michigan's Upper Peninsula. Sitting in the back seat, leaning forward to watch the highway in the failing illumination of twilight, Michael saw the silhouettes of the two deer, and, reaching to shake the driver's shoulder, yelled a warning. A child of the U.P., he knew if there were two, more would follow.

Finally, with quick, agile kicks of their hind legs and the sharp, fragile scuttle of hoofs on pavement, the lead deer jumped toward the south shoulder. Misinterpreting their movement and caught up in the tangible fear in the air, nine deer hiding in the shadows of the tree line behind them ran out on the road.

His knowledge of bucks and does limited to Walt Disney cartoon characters, and slightly buzzed on marijuana, the driver actually accelerated; seeing the two lead deer move off, he laughed and ignored Michael. Accustomed to the traffic on Detroit's Woodward Avenue, he never touched the brake. He drove straight into the herd.

The subject of debate for weeks among diners and drinkers in our single restaurant and several taverns, most local residents attributed the survival of the two young teenage couples in the Mercury Marquis to the size of the car and the age of the deer. The consensus of opinion said the more mature, larger deer stayed hunkered down in the thick brush of the wetlands in the summer, finding water in the creeks north of the highway, leery of the sounds and smells of the seasonal human residents in the cottages along Lake Huron. Younger deer, they reasoned, moved to the lake, more nervous but less experienced.

An undercurrent of resentment spiced the comments of local residents. While concerned for the welfare of the kids in the car, many felt a degree of anger; the sanctity of their wildlife brutally violated. And the drugs and stolen guns, that really turned up the volume of discussion. How could that happen here? Sure there was marijuana; Upper

Peninsula kids probably smoked a little weed, but cocaine and guns, no way. That stuff only happened in the big cities downstate, not here.

In a normal deer hit, and they took place regularly along that stretch of highway, the impact bent the bumper on a pickup truck or broke one of its headlights. The hood and fender of a passenger car might be mangled, a windshield shattered. When the big Mercury struck the deer herd that night, it wasn't a normal accident, it was a massacre. A bloody mess coated the highway when the trooper reached the scene. Two boys and two girls, bruised from the impact and cut by flying glass, staggered from the totaled vehicle. Three of them, shocked from the crash, milled about in the cone of lights from the police cruiser as he stopped behind their crumpled vehicle. One of the girls stared at the dead deer, steadied herself with one hand, gripped the big Merc's fender, and threw up.

One of the boys, moving quickly yet erratically, opened the trunk, reached in, and tried desperately to throw some small plastic-wrapped packages out into the tall grass past the shoulder of the road. The pain of a broken arm hindered his efforts. In the distance, melting away into the night, the deputy saw a fifth passenger run into the trees south of the highway. The driver suffered two broken bones. Deep facial lacerations required immediate attention.

"What a waste," the tow truck driver said as the deputy methodically put down three severely injured but living animals with his service revolver, each shot crashing through the still night into the surrounding woods.

In the midst of the carnage, the ambulance pulled away and the tow truck driver and the trooper pulled deer carcasses off the highway.

Sheriff Almstedt, unable to sleep, stopped his patrol car alongside the road, leaving his rooftop lights rotating. Not doubting his deputy, but worried about the injured kids, he'd decided to come out to inspect the scene.

Listening patiently while his deputy filled him in, Gil Almstedt finally interrupted. He asked, "And you're sure you saw another kid running off into the woods?"

"Yes, sir, I'm positive; long black hair in a ponytail and running pretty well."

"It was a boy, right?"

Ready to answer, the deputy turned away momentarily.

"Good night, Bill. Thanks for your help," the deputy called to the tow truck driver as he finished attaching safety chains to the wrecked auto. The sheriff's half wave-half salute acknowledged the man's efforts.

The tow truck's engine bogged down and its front wheels bounced down then up from the cantilevered weight it towed as the driver up-shifted from first to second gear, pulling the immense burden of the dead Mercury.

"The kid who ran for the woods, he ran like a boy, Sheriff, too wide in the shoulders to be a girl. Even in the dim light, I've got to say it was a boy."

"Those kids will tell us who it was. I just hope he wasn't injured. I don't want some boy dying out in those woods trying to run away."

"I removed the handguns and the rest of the drugs from the trunk of their car and picked up two little plastic sandwich bags of stuff he'd tossed in the grass. First, I took pictures of the kids, the guns, the little packages of drugs, the front of the car, and a few of the deer on the road. Then I put the guns and drugs in a big evidence bag and locked them in my trunk. There was cocaine in there, Sheriff. This isn't like having two joints of north woods weed; this will go down pretty hard on those kids."

"No bout adoubt it," Sheriff Gil Almstedt punned. "Their folks will be calling lawyers and buying bail bonds. You radioed in to get someone up to the hospital tonight to charge them, right?"

"Yes, sir."

"You did a fine job out here tonight, son," the sheriff said, suppressing a yawn. "Well, I'm glad they all survived. Now all we've got to worry about is the runner." Thanking the deputy again, he sighed and walked to his car, already thinking about Bay Drive off in the distance.

As I watched so many of our young people grow up and face life's tough decisions, sometimes making unfortunate choices, I knew the parents of Mackinac County's teenagers, blessed with Sheriff Almstedt, needed to offer up a quiet prayer. It was good he lived nearby, maintaining a small family farm near the water outside Hessel, instead of in St. Ignace. Proximity meant he could be there for our kids when they needed him. That night, out in the woods south of M-134, scared and possibly hurt, one of them did.

✳   ✳   ✳   ✳   ✳

Our county sheriff, Gilbert "Gil" Almstedt, had separated Michael from older boys leading him astray and from situations on the edge of delinquency and delivered him home after curfew on several occasions. Marie and Burt thanked him profusely each time and did their best counseling Michael, their earnest attempts at parenting, at protecting him and steering his future, falling on deaf ears.

Pear-shaped and belly-over-belt heavyset with sagging jowls augmenting a sad, middle-fifties face, Gil Almstedt understood that enforcing the law, much like being a good high school teacher, required the wisdom to avoid a punitive approach. Running stubby fingers through a fringe of dirty gray hair combed across a balding pate, he preferred a fatherly discussion to pressing charges for disorderly behavior and minor incidents of underage drinking. Beer and mischief, teenagers' normal aberrations, their anticipated youthful digressions, those the sheriff chose to tolerate if they ceased under his supervision, although he gave no quarter to any drug use. Our first lady, Mrs. Reagan, may have said, "Just say no," but Sheriff Almstedt said, "Hell no, not in my county," and he meant it.

It didn't matter whether Sheriff Almstedt or one of his deputies picked up one of our kids with a pocket full of Mary Jane, the problem wouldn't disappear with a warning, no matter how stern. They'd be arrested and booked. Then the downward spiral commenced; the deputy's initial paperwork the start of a long, expensive downhill journey replete with lawyers, courtrooms and judges, county jails and state prisons. A drug offense on a police record changed lives and limited futures. If Michael hadn't remembered his years with Dancer when he ran into the woods headed to our home that night, his fate could have followed that tragic pattern.

* * * * *

Being cool is difficult, especially when meeting an adult who meant a lot to you when you were little. Michael encountered Dancer twice at the tribal community center in the short weeks after school got out for summer vacation. Each time, he briefly endured Dancer's bright greeting. He brushed off the embarrassment as his childhood friend called him Mickey in front of his friends. Their bond still ran deep and his teenage friends knew Michael's mom had been Dancer's caregiver and Michael had lived with the mentally challenged, older man for several years. The mystery and legend of Dancer's ability to communicate with animals which inspired his nickname, Fawn Talker, carried over to Michael because of their long ago relationship. But, as an adolescent, Michael needed to maintain his new image as the leader of his peer group, a hell-raising, rebellious teenager, not a blubbering chump getting nostalgic over a childhood buddy, especially one as unusual as Dancer. So each time he ran into Dancer he remained aloof, quickly acknowledged his old friend, and returned to his current tough-guy status and role. Turning away from his past, he swaggered away with his pals. After his second exuberant greeting from Dancer, he leaned toward one of them and rolled his eyes as he glanced back at Dancer.

"He's not so cool, he's just an old retard," Michael said, disparaging the simple, childish man who would always love the little boy he called Mickey no matter what.

Michael suffered from a temporary condition, the teenage, solipsistic delusion that the world spun exclusively around him. He didn't know he was headed down the wrong path, but, as it turned out, Dancer recognized the danger and acted to protect the little boy he'd known, even if that boy now stood six feet tall and carried a pack of Lucky Strikes and a Zippo lighter in one pocket of his blue jeans and a switchblade in the other.

*   *   *   *   *

A few minutes past eleven, Sheriff Almstedt pulled slowly into the end of our driveway and toggled the switch on his rooftop lights once, throwing their eerie moving beams of blue across our windows. Still awake, I went out the back door. Laurie woke up, telling our son, Danny, everything was all right, sending him back to bed before she joined me on the porch in her robe.

"Is something wrong, Sheriff?" I asked as Gil Almstedt lumbered up the sidewalk, stopping to put his foot up on our first step.

"Troy, you taught my youngest boy in school, if you're going to call me Sheriff I'll have to call you Mr. Conway—and, to answer your question, no, I think everything's okay. Sorry to bother you this late, but I'm worried about one of our local kids, Burt and Marie's son, Michael Tallman."

"Is he in some kind of trouble, Gil?"

"I don't know yet. It may not even be him, but he fits my deputy's description. There was an accident out on M-134 about an hour ago; a big, old Mercury drove headlong into eight or nine deer, hit 'em going pretty fast. That many deer may be a record. Four kids, two boys and two girls from the Detroit area, came out of the car with cuts and bruises. I guess the driver was hurt the worst, the crash cut up his face and broke his arm. They'll be okay, but the deputy saw one boy hightailing it off into the woods northeast of here. Good runner, big shoulders and a long black ponytail; sound familiar, like maybe your football team's best running back?"

"Could be," I said. "But if it's Michael, he hasn't shown up here yet."

"Too soon, I think. I didn't even run my spotlight through the trees looking for him and I hope I didn't scare him off just now with my blue lights. Troy, I'm worried he might've been hurt in the crash."

"There's some really thick brush and low tree branches between here and the highway—Brer Rabbit's back in the briar patch. How far east of us was it?" I asked.

"A good piece down the road, I'd guess at least three-quarters of a mile cross-country."

"That puts it by the wetlands where the creeks swell and run off to the lake in the spring melts. It's low ground, unbuildable. Anyone would have trouble coming through there in the dark. Whoever it is, he'll probably have to hold up until first light."

"Will you call me if he does show up tonight? If it's Michael, he's headed here. I'd appreciate your help. It's getting late but I think I'd better call his parents, you know, to see if he's home and let them know what's happened if he's not."

"Of course, Gil, and you'll let us know if anything changes, right?"

"Sure will, Troy. Good night, now. Good night Laurie," the sheriff said, turning back toward his patrol car. Carrying the weight of the world, he trudged away into the night.

Drawn by the sheriff's blue lights, Dancer had stood silently beside the bushes in the impenetrable darkness. He'd listened as Gil talked about Michael lost in the woods. Looking back on that June, what Dancer did next delivered a very important message in a quiet manner we'll never forget and gave us the central idea that will help many of our young people find their futures.

*   *   *   *   *

Sitting wide awake in a straight-backed chair at his kitchen table the rest of the night, one small lamp lit in his living room, Dancer saw the first tinge of light permeate the shadows of night across the tree-tops. He waited patiently until the new day's sky bounced off the lake's surface, then tightened the laces on his work boots and went outside, making sure the screen door closed soundlessly. Crossing his yard in the near dawn, Dancer skirted the edges of his garden and stepped off into the woods beyond the rear boundary of his yard, the last lot at the end of Bay Drive.

The densely spaced tree trunks and gnarly branches of the untouched northern forest, pristine state-owned land, surrounded and accepted him. Cold, damp air soon enveloped him, sending a chill through his light sweater. Within two hundred yards of careful, small steps through tangled branches and over uneven ground and fallen logs, the eyes of several deer turned, studying his movement. None of them bolted. One, a mature doe, rose from her matted bed in the thick grass, stretched slowly, and stepped out to follow her friend.

A thousand yards from Bay Drive, Michael slept, sheltered beneath the low-hanging bottom branches of a massive spruce growing at the edge of a rocky clearing he'd visited as a child. Protected from the night air yet unaware of the impending dawn, the sensation of being watched caused him to stir.

Dancer sat near his feet, leaning back against a huge, black, pock-marked volcanic rock, not disturbing the teenager's slumber. Bruised from the accident and scratched from moving cross-country through dense tree branches in the darkness, Michael woke to the pale cast of daylight seeping down through the branches, rolled over, and sat up, brushing pine needles from his pants legs. He looked up to see the statue of a deer standing beside Dancer. His childhood friend sat cross-legged, Indian style, waiting. The statue's eyes opened. Dancer smiled. For the first time in years, Michael sobbed softly.

Whether the doe remembered the scent of the man who carried her, a frightened fawn, into a high school classroom and fed her from a baby bottle is a curious question for a whimsical God to answer. Some connections swirl in the thoughts of humans and animals, inseparable from instinct, stronger in ways than mere conscious memories.

There's no doubt Michael remembered his days walking these woods with Dancer as his guide. For the second time in his life, he realized the power of unspoken friendship. He walked slowly, fol-lowing Dancer, often crouching to go underneath low tree limbs. The doe stayed close behind, untroubled by the presence of the teenage boy, stopping occasionally but always keeping the small, white-haired man in sight.

Dancer brought Michael into our kitchen shortly after seven a.m. They sat quietly at the kitchen table as Laurie gathered a shallow pan of hot water and wash cloths to clean the abrasions on Michael's face and arms. The iodine she applied to the deeper scratches with the bottle's little glass dauber stung, but the boy never flinched. There was little conversation until after he'd eaten and his nervousness subsided.

"I've got to call Sheriff Almstedt, you know that don't you, Michael?"

"Yes, sir," he responded, "I should call my parents, too."

"Everything will be all right," Laurie said. "The sheriff came here late last night. He was worried that you'd been hurt in the wreck. He's a good man, Michael. You can trust him to help you."

Gil must have been up and around because he showed up on our back porch between twenty and thirty minutes after I called his home. Surprised he wore a plaid shirt and blue jeans, I looked out the window to see his pickup in the turnaround, not his patrol car.

"That was a pretty rough crowd you were running with last night, son. Do you know much about them?" Sheriff Almstedt began questioning Michael.

"No, sir," he answered respectfully. "They just started coming by the community center a few days ago."

"Can you tell me what they were looking for, Michael? That kind's always looking for something."

"Marijuana, they wanted to score a lot of pot to take back to Detroit."

"Are you involved in drugs, son?" Gil asked, lowering his gaze to watch the boy's reaction.

"No, sir, but some guys I know are; I took them out to their place."

"What made them drive so fast? Did they think the police were chasing them?"

"Not the police, but those guys ran them off, you know, threatened them. They didn't want to have anything to do with them. It got rough. The guys yelled at each other and the girls cried; they were scared. Then the guy who drove made us all jump back in the car. He said he was going to get his cousins, older guys camping by Drummond Island, you know, to come back and beat up my friends."

"They're not really your friends, are they, son?"

"No, sir. I just kind of know them; they're older than I am. When they started yelling, I wanted to get away from them. I think they're really mad at me for bringing those Detroit kids to their house, that's why I ran into the woods."

"Don't worry about them, okay?" the sheriff reassured Michael. "The biggest concern I've got is that they had some bad stuff in the trunk of their car. Did you know about any of that?"

Michael shook his head emphatically. No, he didn't.

"Were the kids in the car high on drugs, Michael?" Gil asked.

"The driver was smoking pot, sir. The smoke didn't smell like any cigarette I ever smelled."

"You mean like the ones in the pack sticking out of your back pocket?" The sheriff chuckled. Michael flinched. "Well, whatever he was smoking, he sure clobbered those deer last night, completely totaled that old Mercury. Didn't he see all those deer in the road?"

"I saw two and hollered, but it was too late. They jumped off the road and the rest came on across. Are those kids okay, Mr. Almstedt?"

"Banged up and the driver's arm's broken. It's a miracle no one got killed."

Turning to look at Dancer but addressing the sheriff, Michael said, "I know I'm in real trouble and I'll have to go to jail. So any time you're ready, we can go, Mr. Almstedt."

"Son, I didn't come out here to arrest you. I've known your parents for years, they're wonderful people. I count your uncle, Chief Crow, and your aunt, Mrs. Crow, as my friends. What we have here is a chance to make a situation that's been going bad, get better. I called your parents and told them you're all right. They know you're here and they'll come by late this afternoon to pick you up. It's okay if Michael stays here today, isn't it Laurie, Troy?"

Hearing "Michael" Dancer perked up, smiled, and said, "Mickey."

"Of course, Gil, he's always welcome in our home," I said. Laurie nodded her concurrence.

"There may be talk about a fifth teenager getting away, so it seemed like a good idea if Michael and his parents weren't seen coming or going from Bay Drive this morning. I wanted the dust to settle from the car wreck out on the highway. There's a steady stream of folks driving out from town to look at the place where that big car hit the deer. The county sent out a dump truck and a crew to clean up and it'll take a couple good rains to wash the road. Never been a deer hit like that before, so people are pretty curious. The car's all smashed up. It got towed to the police impound in St. Ignace. A few people have even gone in there to look at what's left of it."

"What about Michael? He's a witness. Doesn't he have to a least file some kind of a police report?"

"Michael? No. I'm not dragging him into this. My deputy saw someone run into the woods last night, but he can't say who it was; too dark, too far away. And a funny thing about those kids, Troy, they don't even know Michael's name. They're so scared right now, they're not doing much talking anyway–I heard their parents sent a lawyer to the jail this morning to tell them to keep their mouths shut. Imagine what it costs to get a lawyer out before eight on a Sunday morning."

Suddenly very serious, Sheriff Almstedt continued, "That boy driving, those girls or the other boy, even Michael here; any one of them could have died last night, and for what?"

Michael's eyes stared straight ahead as he attempted to understand what was happening.

"Then this is our secret, Gil?" I said.

"Yep, it's our secret because this young man's family and friends really care for him. And he's told us the truth. I can tell. I also know he's going to promise us nothing like last night will happen again, and that he'll stay away from those guys he knows who think growing marijuana is okay. It isn't, and I'll end up catching them." He stopped, staring at Michael. "You'll give us your word on those things, right Michael?"

"Yes, sir, I promise. You have my word," Michael said, his tone suddenly very grown up, his eyes locked with Sheriff Almstedt's.

"Your word is worth a lot, son, always remember that, and I'll hold you to it. I also want you to think about Mr. Higgins here. He came out into the woods this morning to find you, didn't he? That means he really cares. His quiet ways, his actions, did the talking. Those aren't words, but I want you to listen, understood?"

"Yes, sir," Michael said humbly, turning to study Dancer.

Gil Almstedt shook hands all around, gave Laurie a quick hug, and walked across the yard to his pickup. I noticed a certain spring in his step like the world was a better place.

Later that afternoon, after lunch at the big picnic table on the deck, Dancer disappeared. I thought he'd gone home to take a nap; he'd been taking more naps recently. Twenty minutes later, he returned, struggling up the outside stairs to our deck carrying a cardboard box. Setting the box down on the table, Dancer began handing its contents to Michael.

He'd gone into my parents' library and selected the row of my college textbooks I'd left on a bottom shelf years before. He even pulled out two of my basic carpentry books from Northwestern Michigan College and placed them in front of Michael.

"Mickey books," Dancer said, holding a book in both hands as if it were the Holy Grail.

Laurie turned away, wiping a tear from her eye. "He can't read but he knows your future came from those books. He watched you study them so he knew which ones to bring. That's incredible; he thinks they can do the same thing for Michael. Can you see what he's doing, Troy?"

"I sure can."

"Mickey books," Dancer repeated, his eyes now disconnected,

looking across Lake Huron.

"What are these books about, Mr. Conway?" Michael asked, staring at Dancer, sensing if not comprehending the seriousness behind his simple words.

"My life as a teacher came from studying these textbooks, Michael. Your mom steered me toward these books about teaching, did you know that? Dancer understands but he doesn't understand; he's telling you it's time to find what's right for you. It might not be in these particular books, but, if you'll let us, Mrs. Conway and I will be happy to help you find the one's for you."

"Yes, sir," Michael said. "I'd like that a lot."

Dancer again focused on the conversation. He watched our exchange and smiled. On this, as on many other occasions, we truly wondered how much of what we said Dancer actually comprehended.

* * * * *

When Dancer gathered up those old textbooks for Michael, a light bulb lit up for Laurie and me. We acted on his suggestion, helping Dancer do something for Michael Tallman and all of Thompson's kids, the children of the Chippewa community.

A week after the accident, Thompson Crow and his wife joined us for a family summer barbeque to discuss the idea.

Our friend, the Chief-Tribal Council President-casino operator set his half-empty beer aside and turned to me. "What you're doing in Dancer's name is very special, Troy. I hope someday our teenagers understand."

"Truth is, Thompson, it really was Dancer's idea. Right, Laurie?"

"It really was," she interjected. "Standing right here at this picnic table, he stacked textbooks in front of Michael and said, 'Mickey books.'" Unconscious of the similarity of her action, collecting her thoughts, Laurie looked up and stared off into the distance across the lake exactly mimicking Dancer's actions on Sunday afternoon the week before.

"It was a clear message. Dancer showed Troy and I what needed to be done. In his way he reminded us how important books can be to young people, the difference they can make helping them find their futures."

"Well, I appreciate his generosity, but can he really afford to do this, Troy?"

Dad and I laughed and reassured our friend, unknowingly adding to the mystery surrounding the man Thompson called Fawn Talker.

"Chief Crow," I said, adding a tone of respect to the occasion, "Mr. Thomas Daniel Higgins will be proud to sponsor the new additions to the library in the community center and the kids will respond. It's his idea; Dad and I just do the bookwork for him. Sometimes, Thompson, it's not the lesson, it's the teacher, especially when it's a very unique teacher offering a message that reaches out and grabs a student's attention. Dancer is that kind of a teacher, the kids will know."

Thompson, Kathy, Laurie, and Marie all worked together ordering books. I helped a little. Months later, when completed, the dedication ceremony made the front page of our small local weekly paper and even got covered in St. Ignace, Mackinaw City, and Sault Ste. Marie.

The week after the articles ran in the newspapers, a television news crew from Traverse City called and drove up to film the story at the Chippewa Community Center. Thompson stood in front of the incredible eight-by-ten photograph of Dancer framed on the wall by the door to the library addition.

Julie's husband, Sam, took the picture with a long lens. In it, Dancer sat cross-legged deep in the woods in a shaft of midday sunlight filtered by cedar branches. He held a days-old sleeping fawn in his lap. The doe stood close by, her head turned, eyes gazing directly and serenely at the distant camera. The inscription on the brass plaque below the photograph reads: Our friend, Mr. Thomas Daniel Higgins, Fawn Talker.

The television interview aired on a Sunday morning, proudly broadcast as a home-grown, northern Michigan news special. Chief Thompson Crow described the library's shelves full of biographies and autobiographies of famous Americans and Native Americans and the rows of books covering occupational skills and careers. Another shelf he pointed to held do-it-yourself books and illustrated volumes explaining how things work from power tools to washing machines to the Hubble telescope.

Within a year, two shelves filled up with catalogs received from community colleges, colleges, and universities. Marie Tallman, appointed librarian of the Fawn Talker collection, added volume after volume of self-help books and study guides for college entrance exams, many with sample questions and practice sessions. She also ordered college textbooks for the initial years of classes in science, math, history, general business, English, psychology (my dad's idea), and a long list of other subjects.

"One way to get kids to college," she said, "is to bring a little of it here so they can see what it's all about." She was right.

The summer the big Mercury hit the deer herd and Dancer went out at dawn to find Michael in the woods was a turning point. And when he carried that box of books up the stairs to our deck and gave them, one by one, to his friend, Mickey, Dancer reached out to touch Michael's life and the lives of the children of our community for years to come.

Eighteen

In the end, the privilege of telling Dancer's story fell to me, and rightly so, mine was one of the lives he touched. Neither Dancer nor Dad could tell it. Dancer may have the memories, but he lacks the words and Dad preceded us both on the trip *there*. The finality of Dad's oft-repeated phrase, "See ya when we get there," proven when he died, speaks to how much we miss him. I can still hear him, his voice as clear as sunlight. His message rang true, capturing the precarious nature of mortality's grip on each new day's dawn in its recurring contest with forever and what comes next.

As I finish telling this story, take a moment to imagine a slightly paunchy, middle-aged, one-handed, high school shop teacher and coach sitting on his deck by the shore of Lake Huron writing, slowly hunting and pecking loving memories into the new-fangled laptop computer his wife gave him for his birthday. Cool summer mornings are my best times for writing. A steaming coffee mug sits on the railing next to my lawn chair and, pulling another chair toward me, I prop my feet up so the laptop sits level and doesn't move about. The breeze off Lake Huron often dictates the need for a flannel shirt, even in early July. Tapping the Chiclet-shaped, round-cornered, rectangular keys, one after another, the pages accumulate and I'm able to share with you the story of two very unique human beings.

My words tell the story of Dancer and my dad and how their lives were intertwined. It's about a man who chose the path of a conscientious objector during the horrific world war of his generation, then spent his career teaching understanding. It's also about an amazing little man who never went to school and never learned to read or write; yet, untroubled by spelling or the rules of grammar, became a great communicator. It's about a man who found joy in creating simple pencil drawings of animals and trees and in gardening and making vegetable soup. Along the way he's shared his quiet wisdom with the rest of us, those not blessed with insights uncluttered by life's responsibilities.

Vegetable soup and little boys, building homes by the lakeshore and tackling endless lists of small projects, those and thousands of other daily events have occupied our family's years on the shore of Lake Huron.

Our two sons, Thomas and Daniel, came to us a little later in our marriage than Julie and I came to our parents. Before Tommy and Danny were born, Laurie and I spent several years on our own. We lived the glorious life of a young married couple, hoping for and anticipating children. Please don't take me wrong, those were incredible years full of love and laughter and good times and hard work, but they pale when compared to the feeling of fulfillment that came later watching our two sons grow up.

By the time they were born, we'd accomplished a lot in material terms. We completed the initial stage of our home on Bay Drive. Both teachers, we loved our jobs and, other than the usual, minor stuff young people purchase on credit like one or two kitchen appliances or a new car when necessary, no extreme financial burdens worried us. No reason to despair ever haunted us; we didn't lack anything that truly made a difference. Still, the laughter and quiet hugs and treasured moments children bring to your life, those things without price tags, go so far beyond all other measures of success. Plus, we had

Dancer. A permanent resident of Bay Drive, he played a primary role in all our lives.

Dancer's positive influence on our boys was phenomenal and lasting; those years were very special. The company that bakes Wonder Bread calls them the "wonder years," those fleeting times when small children, like our Tommy and Danny, grow up. Their claim to fame, that their nutritious bread "builds strong bodies twelve ways," represents some basic, physical truths about what children need to prosper. It's good bread and a good slogan, but Dancer has it all over them. He built strong lives in his mysterious, inexplicable ways; he built character and values just by being himself.

Until new acquaintances got to know him, his daily activities seemed strange or different to them, as if he were an ancillary responsibility at the edge of our busy days, some kind of a distant relative dumped on us, left under our supervision. They only needed to spend time with him and watch the way he stood quietly in the background, the way he grinned as first Tommy and then Danny joined us, how he held out his arms as they ran to him on unsteady little legs that had barely learned to walk. He comforted our boys when thunder shook our home by the lake. He taught them to snap green beans into bowls when they were five years old and wanted to help him with his gardening and cooking chores. For all the important early stages of their lives, Dancer was there for them. He'd been there for Julie after polio and for me after Vietnam and for Michael when he faced a difficult turning point of adolescence. He was there for all of us; Dancer, a shaper of lives. So much of his story revolves around how he affected others, what he gave to them.

In remarkable cases like Dancer's, what a person gives to others is composed of long lines of mirror images, reflections of the history of how other lives touched theirs; a reciprocal process, love and care received being returned. To understand Dancer from that perspective we need to step back and consider the people whose actions helped form and nurture his life. First and foremost, I credit my father. Dad gave Dancer a world outside an institution. Even if Dancer had lived a good, safe life, sheltered and protected and cared for; without my father's guidance, he never could have reached out beyond that asylum's walls, changing so many lives.

Emma, his beautiful mother, gave him life itself, and by doing so, drastically altered her destiny. She lives on in Dancer, as does the spirit of his biological father, Emma's beloved Daniel. Forever a fifteen-year-old boy, the son of a teacher in a tiny West Virginia village, he also lives in Dancer even if he never shared in the joy Dancer has brought to so many of us.

Less notable but still part of his past, what Tommy Higgins, Emma's first husband, did for Dancer rests in what he didn't do and what he never accomplished. Although cruel to Emma in her son's presence, his viciousness never drove Dancer's joy underground, locking it behind a closed door of permanent fear, and he never succeeded in instilling his bitterness in Emma, although I doubt he ever could have.

Miss Mattie Bigelow, the wonderful old nurse at Athens State Hospital, watched over Dancer, nurtured his sense of family as he regularly came to her home for dinner, and helped Dad locate his mother.

Miss Flossie Duncan, with the legal advice of Mr. Ziggie Hammit, gave Dancer wealth. Although fortune is a concept beyond his understanding or desire, it ensured his independence. Some, hearing the details of Dancer's life story, have reacted to Miss Duncan's part in having him institutionalized at the Athens Asylum for the Insane in the first place as a bad thing, a mean-spirited thing. From all I've learned, I disagree. Dad explained to me that she was a strong-willed spinster who possessed the backbone required to always look far forward into the future. That's a daunting task. She understood what it meant to do the right thing for Emma and for Dancer, what it took to direct their lives ahead, moving them each to where they needed to be, recognizing that, if left together, each would suffer.

Emma remarried and raised her widowed husband Mills's daughters on his farm outside Blissfield, Michigan. She lived a good life and she never forgot her little boy, Thomas Daniel. How could she? How could anyone forget Dancer?

Our neighbors on Bay Drive and the permanent members of the Hessel-Cedarville community grew to love Dancer. Thompson Crow accepted Dancer unquestioningly, bestowing the name Fawn Talker on him in recognition of his affinity for animals, the world of nature Thompson so deeply reveres.

A great friendship developed between Thompson and my father. The tribe elected Thompson their chief following the death of his predecessor, an honor which spoke of his lifelong dedication and the seriousness with which he addressed his people's problems. As always, in discussing Thompson's concerns, Dad spoke of patience, but the dreams Thompson Crow held for the children of his tribe couldn't wait; he knew they'd waited long enough. Chief Crow understood the mind of a Native American child encountering the world beyond tribal customs and beliefs; he'd lived through their apprehensions and learned the answers to the questions troubling them.

Dad brought to bear his years of experience in psychology, looking for the reasons behind change, offering the wisdom of someone who dedicated his life to understanding the enigmas caused by volatile social conditions. Dancer often sat with the two men as they talked; listening intently, his eyes alternating between their faces, seemingly recognizing the importance of their combined effort.

The afternoon Dancer carried my old textbooks up on our deck, gave them to Michael and said, "Mickey books," he joined Dad and Thompson in their effort to improve the futures of all of the area's children, helping to achieve rapid social change through the proven bootstrap method of self-determination.

Many of those lucky enough to have met Dancer and get to know his idiosyncrasies and baffling abilities shook their heads in disbelief. Some pitied him, seeing the loss. Doing the old "there but for the grace of God" comparison, they sensed what he's missed: going to school, learning to read and write, having a good job. Although not entirely wrong, they missed the point. They failed to adequately comprehend the beauty of what Dancer does possess and what he has accomplished.

Dancer's life on the rocky southern shore of the Upper Peninsula includes sunrises and sunsets over Lake Huron and the beautiful woods of the Les Cheneaux Islands, a unique community of family and friends who truly love him, a glorious garden to tend, his own home, independence equal to his abilities, and the devout companionship of every chipmunk, bird, gull, and deer within the sphere of his world on Bay Drive.

Reaching the level of self-sufficiency Dancer enjoyed in his later years required the efforts and trust of a series of live-in caregivers. Marie and Michael were the first of several. After Laurie and I built our home next to my parents' summer house, it was decided Dancer should finally have his own home on the end lot. By then, he could certainly afford it and he'd shown he was familiar with his surroundings, more than content to walk up and down Bay Drive visiting the neighbors he knew well. He often went into the woods alone to draw pictures of the animals and sat on boulders along the beach watching the out islands and the freighters crossing the horizon. Dancer was at home, as self-reliant and trustworthy as he'd been as a child running errands at Athens State Hospital. It was time.

Since my parents were spending more and more time on Bay Drive, it seemed natural to also complete their original plans for his protection. An extension of their driveway was opened up while his home was built and his garden put in. Both required clearing trees, grading the area, moving boulders, and bringing in many truckloads of sand and topsoil. A narrow walkway lined with trees and bushes replaced the access road. When finished, his safe haven adjoined their home, linked by a path winding through young pines and lilacs. The ferns and plants of the woods quickly reclaimed the landscaped spaces along the walkway. Dad and Dancer traversed that path side by side, back and forth between their homes, year after year, continuing their lifelong friendship, companions on a half-century odyssey.

Dancer's interest in gardening evolved from countless visits to the Burnette's house where Bay Drive turns to meet the highway. Watching Mrs. Burnette weed and water her flower and vegetable gardens, a daily, early-morning ritual, may have triggered memories of his years as a uniformed but unofficial grounds worker under Roscoe Perkins's guidance at Ypsilanti State Hospital. But vegetables, there was something about growing vegetables he found absolutely fascinating. Dancer not only helped weed the rows in her garden, he stood by, entranced, as Mrs. Burnette washed and prepared the vegetables from her garden for her own table. She sent home Tupperware bowls of her harvest with him and he always stopped by Mom and Dad's and our home to show them off. Dancer's first garden was a long rectangular area Dad and I roto-tilled for him out behind the loft garage. He had carefully tended it for several years, so it was decided he should have his own larger garden.

The idea of making vegetable soup came from Sam Church. No one ever told Sam what Dancer could or could not do, so he took it upon himself to help Dancer combine all his vegetables into one finished product. Sam's school of vegetable soup making took almost two weeks. Even after Dancer graduated with honors, Sam continued to supervise his efforts, making sure he was safe as he peeled and sliced his vegetables and worked around the boiling pots of soup. Displaying great patience, Sam stuck by his dedicated culinary pupil and Dancer's vegetable soup is still as consistently delicious as it was the first time he made it. In fact, he makes so much vegetable soup it's a staple of the diets of everyone along Bay Drive. Some neighbors bring excess zucchinis from their gardens, sharing bumper crops, some bring tomatoes ripening in paper lunch bags during the last days before fall's frost descends; with Dancer it's vegetable soup. It really is incredibly good soup.

*   *   *   *   *

Laurie still teaches summer reading classes at the Chippewa Community Center. The children and a stooped, fragile, little man named Dancer sit in a circle while she reads. His walk is much slower now and often unsteady, the foot-dragging clumsiness of his shuffle more pronounced. Saying Dancer is loved is a huge understatement. Watching the kids walk patiently beside him as they cross the playground together helps explain the phenomenon.

Sheriff Gil Almstedt died of a massive coronary the year after Dad passed away. He was working on his small farm trying to free his tractor when it mired down in a muddy field. Mackinac County's sheriff, a fair man who understood that being a teenager isn't easy, he made a strong impression on a rebellious young man Dancer called Mickey, and I know he was there for many, many others. He's greatly missed.

Michael Tallman, still Mickey to Dancer all these years later, graduated from Michigan State University with a Bachelor of Arts degree in criminal justice. He's now director of security for the six casinos owned by the Sault Ste. Marie Chippewa tribe. Before every election year, Thompson Crow asks Michael to run for sheriff. Michael's beginning to warm to the idea. Gil Almstedt would approve. What goes around comes around.

Mom is with Dancer most of the time now. Her arthritis bothers her on cold and damp days, both specialties of our shoreline homesteads, so Dancer comes to her home each morning. She brews the coffee while he makes the toast or fixes bowls of cereal. She thinks she's caring for him. They watch world news on television and Mom gives Dancer a running dialogue about what's going on in each faroff land. He nods his head and studies her face, concerned if she's too serious, relieved when she laughs. In the afternoon they sit in a sunny corner of her living room and she reads to him. Any book Mom reads is all right with Dancer. They've never missed a selection from Oprah's book club.

Laurie and I are still teaching; we wouldn't know what to do if we weren't at school every day. What we do has become what we are. Someday we'll have to retire, but we don't want to think about it now. Tommy graduated from Central Michigan University last June, an English major with a degree in secondary education. Now in his first year of teaching, he's living in Traverse City. Danny's bouncing in and out of school, working odd jobs in construction. The last time he was home he talked about joining the military. Sam Church, Julie's husband, created a lasting interest in airplanes and flying in our youngest son, an itch Danny may have to scratch. I'm very proud of both my boys and I know in my heart they'll be just fine.

Each time I walk through the worn footpath into Dancer's yard, I pass the spot where we stood as a family while Dancer sprinkled my father's ashes across the soft leaves of rain dampened low ferns. Dad's in the leaves and the soil, a part of this place. Sometimes I stop and talk with him–that sounds corny, I know, but I'm sure I'm not the only son who's stood at a gravesite and continued a long-ago conversation with his dad. Mine's *there* and he's a great listener. The breeze rustles low-hanging cedar branches as Dad's presence offers advice. The stems of fragile plants and grasses bend. Watching the leaves move, I know Dad's heard my words and answered my questions; that he's confident his children have done their best; that he believes in the natural progression of life from generation to generation.

A conscientious objector, he abhorred war and its killing, yet he accepted what I'd done in Vietnam, never dwelling on the injury I sustained, responding non-judgmentally. I believe he would trust in his grandson Danny's ability as a young man to make his own decision. He allowed me to find my own way there and back. So long ago when I went off to war, I know he loved me enough to let me learn life's lessons without forcing his ideals upon me. Given his principled stance against killing, it must have been difficult for him to watch his son march off to the rice paddies of Southeast Asia.

Dad and Dancer were there for Julie and me when we needed them most. We were lucky. And I'll always be thankful my sons had Dad's love for as many years as they did, and that they've grown up within the circle of Dancer's caring, touched by his selfless wisdom.

Looking back over the years, I know many have failed to understand Dancer. Incapable of appreciating the unique ways he provided love and guidance to those around him, they focused solely on the fact that he's different. Of course he is, but so what? After all, we're all different, aren't we? Each of us, every father's son and daughter, is inherently different; Dad recognized and understood it's those differences which bind us together in a cohesive chain called family. Dad knew each of us must live our lives our way, accepting the consequences of our choices, good or bad.

Dad's quiet sidekick, Dancer, has given us love in twinkling eyes and taught the beauty of compassion with his shy smiles. Over the decades encompassing three generations of our family, his devotion has transcended life's complications. Dancer has provided, in his soft, miraculous way, a testimonial to Dad's faith in God's inexplicable plans for us all.

* * * * *

Last week Dancer and I paused once again by the small brass letters–C O–atop the foot-tall metal rod beside the footpath. They were Laurie's idea, her way of honoring dad and of reminding us he's here in this spot on the path between my parents' home and Dancer's. I can study those brass letters, dad's only physical monument, and raise my eyes, looking through the trees to gaze across the open water of Lake Huron, to take in the subtle curve of the horizon, unable to see the far shore. The setting suits his spirit and his legacy.

I've been with Dancer many times over the years when he's stopped on the pathway through the woods and looked at the little brass letters, and I know he visits here regularly by himself. Together, we've passed by on cool, rainy spring mornings and dry, dusty, hot summer afternoons, shuffled through fall's crisp fallen leaves, and left our footprints in winter snows.

Dancer's age now mandates walks taken in small increments. On this trip across the pathway, I held his hand, the soft lapping of waves on the rocky shore the only sound. The air carried the scent of the thick layer of red and gold leaves covering the ground. Indian summer warmed the late-fall afternoon and disguised the imminent onslaught of winter days. The sun strong on my face, I closed my eyes and thought of the first weeks I spent here, an embittered young war veteran working to prepare his parents' lot, struggling with a heavy metal pry bar and moving hundreds of rocks in a rubber-tired, wire-mesh wagon.

Dancer, also reluctant to move on, swayed gently side to side, tiny movements that could have been the infirmity of age or a ray of child-hood memory cutting through time. Momentarily restless, it was as if there were some thought, some idea he needed to describe and communicate to Dad. His eyes stayed downcast, focused on the brass letters for the longest time. Finally, with a deep breath and a wistful sigh, he raised his head, turned to me, and smiled. It was the first time I've ever seen tears in his eyes.

I put my right arm around him, my hand gently squeezing his shoulder, and pulled him close to my side. We walked to his shel-tered home by the water's edge. Inside, I knelt and helped him untie his heavy white cotton laces and take his work boots off. He nodded approval as I set them in the shallow plastic tray on the floor in his laundry room. Whatever thoughts of my father, whatever memo-ries brought him the joy of love or the loss or regret of sadness as we stopped on the footpath dissipated in a warm breeze of now; the passing cloud from his past cleared away leaving blue skies.

I left him sitting in a big comfortable chair by his front window. He wiggled his toes in white socks as he stretched his thin legs out on the ottoman, resting, comfortable in the world Dad created for him. The dance of his life nearly completed, Dancer was content, smiling as he watched two gulls wheel and circle, floating effortlessly above the rocky beach.

From the apex of their flight, the two gulls, inseparable like Dad and Dancer, turned and dove downward, skimming the ripples of the water's surface, each driven by instinct to fulfill life's duties. Then, moving off into the distance out over open water, again banking heav-enward on wings held wide, they crested the wind, spiraling upward, floating on the simple joy of existence.

Book Club Discussion Questions

1. Which character's life do you believe was most influenced by Dancer's presence?

2. Dancer had an affinity for animals. Can animals instinctively know when a person likes them? If so, how are they able to know?

3. How would Dancer's life have been different if he'd been born in 1870 instead of 1930? In 1990 instead of 1930?

4. Do you believe wisdom can occur naturally in young children and in mentally challenged individuals?

5. Do we do an adequate job of teaching our children how to recognize the important human values of integrity, compassion, loyalty, and giving/caring? If not, what can or should be done to address this?

Do you have questions you would like to ask the author? You can reach him at alanmeade@charter.net

Acknowledgments

I've been blessed with the friendship of everyone at Nelson Publishing: Marian's thoughtful guidance and incredible knowledge of the realm of publishing; Ryan, Julayne, and Kathy, dedicated watchdogs and wizards of words; Kim's eagle-eyed diligence; and Shannon's exuberance. Curled atop the back of the couch, delicate paws tucked under wise cat's whiskers, Oreo has also been a steadfast supporter.

About the Author

Alan Meade's varied background shows in the different genres he explores. In his early sixties, this unique storyteller has two master's degrees gathering dust in the drawer and a framed U.S. Patent on the wall. He is a child of Michigan's auto industry, but twenty-five years in the defense industry have instilled in him an intense commitment to our nation's military. In his fifties, a decade of teaching English brought "Mr. M." national recognition from his students. His friends note his humility and booming laugh as defining characteristics, and years spent living below the Mason-Dixon Line have left a subtle twang in his voice. His stories point out an ability to balance human nature with the pretense of life's assumed roles.